Little Green Man

Little Green Man

SIMON ARMITAGE

VIKING
an imprint of
PENGUIN BOOKS

VIKING

Published by the Penguin Group
Penguin Books Ltd, 80 Strand, London WC2R 0RL, England
Penguin Putnam Inc., 375 Hudson Street, New York, New York 10014, USA
Penguin Books Australia Ltd, Ringwood, Victoria, Australia
Penguin Books Canada Ltd, 10 Alcorn Avenue, Toronto, Ontario, Canada M4V 3B2
Penguin Books India (P) Ltd, 11 Community Centre,
Panchsheel Park, New Delhi – 110 017, India
Penguin Books (NZ) Ltd, Cnr Rosedale and Airborne Roads,
Albany, Auckland, New Zealand
Penguin Books (South Africa) (Pty) Ltd, 24 Sturdee Avenue,
Rosebank 2196 South Africa

Penguin Books Ltd, Registered Offices: 80 Strand, London WC2R 0RL, England
www.penguin.com

First published 2001
3

Set in 12/14.75 pt Monotype Dante
Typeset by Rowland Phototypesetting Ltd, Bury St Edmunds, Suffolk
Printed in Great Britain by Clays Ltd, St Ives plc

A CIP catalogue record for this book is available from the British Library

ISBN 0-670-89442-7

I

I know exactly where he is.

I stand at the top of the stairs, the darkest, innermost place in the house, with daylight hidden behind bedroom doors, and sunlight trapped in the bathroom, sieved through the frosting of the window, bouncing off chrome, mirrors and glass. I pull the stepladders down from the loft with the long-handled hook. They slide into my hands, cold to the touch, creaking and rickety as I climb.

The blackness is dazzling, as if I've stuck my head through the roof into outer space. I reach for the light cord, somewhere to the left. A low-energy bulb brightens softly and slowly like an old valve, and the attic falls into place. Thick cobwebs flutter in a breeze that funnels up from the eaves. My breath steams in front of my face.

I haul myself up, treading carefully over the joists, thinking of the time my father's leg came bursting through the ceiling, as if God in heaven had taken the wrong step, exposing a skinny, white limb to the world below. Suitcases are piled on top of wooden crates. I slide between them, past old banana boxes crammed with books and magazines, past bin bags sealed with masking tape or tied with string, then duck beneath the frame of a bike hung from a six-inch nail banged into the main beam. How did we get that in here? Some of the slates have slipped or cracked. It's hard to believe that the outside is just inches away, that these thin sheets of stone tacked on to flimsy, wooden spars can keep out the sky.

I know exactly where he is. In the far corner I click open the two locks of the big trunk and lift its giant lid. My name stares me in the face, neatly stencilled on to the lining, and the long list of my address, beginning with this house and this street, then running all the way into the universe. A smell drifts up from the trunk – the smell of the past. Memory. More books and magazines, a bag of golf balls, a dartboard with stubble sprouting through the wire frame, a pair of goalkeeping gloves, a commemorative wallet for a full set of decimal coins – all prized out of the holder and spent. Rolled-up papers are slotted in a cardboard tube: a cycling-proficiency certificate, exam results, a football programme, second prize in a photography competition, an Airfix catalogue. Loads of pencils bundled together like kindling, tins of pens and crayons like rounds of ammunition. A modelling knife. Scrapbooks and albums full of drawings and doodles, sheets and sheets of loose paper. Paintings, sketches, tracings, prints, all held in the grip of a bulldog clip. A kid's transistor radio in the shape of an electric shaver. A compass. A fob watch with my grandfather's name etched on the cover. I pile them all to one side.

In the bottom-left-hand corner of the trunk, under a plastic bag full of magnets and marbles and polished stones, there's a shoebox, mummified with insulating tape and coils of string. I slit it open with the modelling knife, take out the objects one by one. A deflated football, like a punctured lung. Photographs, documents. And a leather pencil-case. I pull back the zip and bring out a roll of cloth, tied with a length of wool. When I tease out the knot, the bundle unravels towards the floor, and a weight within it begins to shift and fall. I yank the cloth quickly upwards, like a yo-yo, and as it unfurls and flaps open, it throws its possession into the air – spinning, hanging, waiting to drop. I snatch it cleanly with my right hand. When I open my grip, the little green man is snug in my palm, slightly hunched, his long robe flowing around his feet.

He's heavier than I remember, but smaller – no bigger than a pepper pot – and he's cold, like a piece of carved, green ice. I can feel the blood bumping in my head, in my ears, and feel blood flooding the engine in my heart, and blood driving the little turbines in my wrists and thumbs, rising to the stop-tap under my throat.

Lying awake some mornings, I hear a click in the airing cupboard under the stairs – the central heating clocking on – and the boiler, calling for gas, drawing gas from under the North Sea. Then the ignition, when the sleeping genie of the pilot light explodes into life – whap! Then the ticking of the junctions and joints as the pipework rouses itself, stiffens with heat. And an airlock gargles and chokes under the floorboards in the spare room. And the radiators swell up, engorged, and the cistern sounds like it could blast into orbit around the Earth. That's how it feels. It feels like this.

I stand the little green man on the flat of my hand, show him his new freedom, his new life. Shadows fall on his curious face, his blank eyes. Does he approve? I slip him into my pocket, let the lid of the trunk fall, then snap the locks.

Descending the ladders, I re-enter the world of windows and walls, the world of furniture, natural light, and the warmth of the house.

2

There are two types of mates. There are the new friends you make later in life, when you're older. People you've got something in common with. People whose company you enjoy. It's fresh and exciting, you can meet them for a cappuccino, have them over for meals. You like them. And you can really talk to them, about feelings and all that.

And there are the old friends, the ones you were brought up with, who go further back than you remember, who've been there since the beginning. You didn't choose them – they're like family. Like blood. You never see them any more because they've all moved off in different directions, gone their separate ways, but you'd still walk under a bus for them, willingly, if they asked. You don't make friends like that again. It's just that one time – the time before you remember – or it's never at all.

I flicked through the phone book for the numbers, then rang Directory Enquiries for the two I couldn't find, then dialled them up in turn. Lateral thinking: when you're setting out on a plan of action, it's crucial to do everything in the right order.

'Pompus, it's Barney.'
  'Outstanding, I thought you were dead.'

'Hello, Winkie.'
  'Er, Barney, blimey. Er, can I ring you back in a minute, I'm in a staff meeting right now?'

'Would that be a certain Tony Football?'
  'No, actually. Is it Anthony you want? He's not here right

now but you can leave a message if you like. Can I ask who's calling?'

'Stubbs, it's Barney.'
   'Barney who?'
   'How many Barneys do you know?'
   'Barney! Sorry, mate, I didn't recognize your voice. Jesus, how are you?'

There can't be a better reunion for five old mates than a game of five-a-side – it's made to measure. We turned up at the sports centre the following Friday, entered the knockout and got hammered 18–2 in the first round by a team of shelf-stackers from Asda. Afterwards, in the showers, I couldn't help looking. Winkie, with his little dick and the makings of a pot belly; Pompus, with a full-blown beer belly and his gold chains and tattoos, and the turquoise spot on his left cheek where he was shot; Tony Football, going thin on top, with a bottle of shampoo in one hand and a bottle of conditioner under his arm, covered in lather, as if milk were bubbling out of a hole in the top of his head; Stubbs letting the water blast against his face.

In the bar we sat in a half-circle overlooking the baths. Young lads bombed into the deep end from the diving board. A woman in a purple swimming costume flipped water against her tummy before taking the plunge. A middle-aged man in armbands clung to the side as a couple of kids splashed water at him with their feet. From the top of a pair of stepladders at the far side the lifeguard stared into nowhere.

Pompus pulled up a chair and took a long drag on his cigarette. 'That's better. That's better, is that.'
   'We should do this every week,' I said.
   'Bad night for me,' said Winkie, opening a packet of peanuts.
   They were all drinking up, draining their glasses, playing with their car keys, saying how we'd have to keep in touch and all the rest of it, when I said, 'Look, gents, do yourselves a favour and

5

follow me back to my place. There's something I need you to see.'

Tony Football glanced at his watch. Winkie started making his excuses. Stubbs looked at me, waiting for me to say something else.

'Come on, fellers. Trust me. It'll be worth your while.'

'Got any beers in?' asked Pompus. He lifted one cheek of his arse and pulled a face, as if he was about to fart, but nothing came out.

3

For us, football wasn't just a game, it was more of a graduation, a kind of apprenticeship, if you like. Tiddlywink football came first, which was just tiddlywinks played on a cardboard pitch. It was crap. You could press down hard and blast it from one side of the room to the other, so why bother with passing or dribbling or anything like that? Ten quid for a square of green card and a few buttons – whoever came up with that must have been laughing all the way to Bondi Beach. It was crap.

Then it was blow football, which at least had a ball, and a round one at that. You had to blow through a straw, steering the ball around a plastic sheet that looked like something you'd change a nappy on. It got covered in spit, so at half-time it had to be wiped down with a dishcloth, or the ball started to stick. By full-time you could see stars in front of your eyes and had to sit down. Winkie's breath always smelt of pear drops or puke and nobody wanted to play him, so he had to ref. And it was a foul if you touched the ball with the straw, and for sucking you got sent off.

Striker came next. You pressed the top of the player's head and his leg swung forward and booted the ball. It said on the box you could chip it or pass it or swerve it round the wall, but you couldn't. You could hoof it from one penalty spot to the other, and that was it. It was crap. It was as if we had to serve our time with all those stupid and useless games before qualifying for the next stage: Subbuteo.

When my brother left home he gave me a big crate of the stuff, and we pounced on it, the five of us, like orphans attacking the Christmas hamper. The crate was full to the top with smooth green boxes. Inside each pack, the teams were laid out like trays of rings in a jeweller's window, ten miniature men on their shiny pedestals, plus a goalie on the end of a stick. Other boxes had more exotic and complicated contents: a ref and two linesmen with their moulded plastic flags; a dug-out and a bench, complete with the manager in his three-quarters-length sheepskin coat and the coach in his tracksuit; half a dozen spectators, one in a wheelchair and one with a dog; four battery-operated floodlights; advertising boards; a cowshed grandstand; a packet of yellow balls for evening kick-offs and European games. Once everything had been set up and assembled it was too late to play, and anyway it was impossible to reach the pitch because of all the paraphernalia along the touchline and behind the goals. It was the ritual that mattered, not the game. The idea of owning it, getting it all out, arranging it in fine detail, then packing it all neatly away.

In any case, we couldn't do it properly. To move the ball around you were supposed to propel the man forward with one, immaculate flick. But every English kid I knew used a sort of nudging movement with the side of the index finger, a kind of shove-ha'penny, putting action, the footballing equivalent of the push-shot. The failure of the national team to win anything at all since 1966 can probably be put down to a whole generation of youngsters and their ham-fisted Subbuteo technique.

Subbuteo. Or 'Table Football' as it was known, although in the age of Formica playing on an actual table was impossible. The felt pitch slipped on the shiny surface, not helped by our cack-handed method of play. One sliding tackle could drag the whole lot on to the floor – grandstand, corner flags, hot-dog van and all. You needed a flat, quality carpet and plenty of space. And you needed to be out of the way, where adults with their big feet and loudmouth comments couldn't crush the players underfoot or break the spell. You needed a bedroom, a parents' bedroom, with the bed pushed to one side. Then you could make yourself at home amongst the perfumes and slippers and bathrobes of the mothers and fathers of your best friends, and play.

We drew up league tables and knockouts, with fixture lists so long and complicated they would have taken years to complete.

Every now and again, somebody bought a new team, in new colours. Winkie started blubbing when we told him Barcelona had to start at the bottom of Division 2 with an away match at Stoke City. When Pompus slid Brazil out of their box, he stared at them for a couple of seconds, then said, 'There's three coons in this lot. Here, chuck me that Tipp-Ex.'

Me and Stubbs once went to see the Subbuteo world champion playing exhibition matches in the toys-and-games section of Keeble's department store in town. He was a sweaty, red-faced kid from Sicily, too fat to play football for real, too old to be playing Subbuteo, and too big to be wearing shorts. He flicked and kicked his way past four local lads while his dad followed him round the table in a shell suit, telling him what to do in Italian. The ref had the full kit on, except for a pair of Green Flash on his feet. While everyone was watching the game, Stubbs pocketed a couple of super-balls and a fistful of metal jacks, and we went home on the train.

Football. It was a trial, right from the whistle. Even when it came to the real thing it didn't get any easier. First, you needed a ball, which was always flat, and the only way of getting air into it was with a bike pump and a microscopic metal valve, which nobody owned. Second, you needed a field, and there wasn't one, or rather there was but you weren't allowed to play on it. So you needed some other place, which meant the park, or the old bowling green that had gone to seed, or the goods entrance at the paper mill. Third, you needed enough players for two decent and even teams. But there were five of us and Pompus was useless.

One summer Sunday, we were having a kick-about in the school-yard, in the rain, when Stubbs hit a volley from about twenty yards, and the heavy, leather ball smashed one of the cloakroom windows. The ball bounced back, but ten minutes later I tried a curler from up by the dustbins, and stood and watched as the ball disappeared through the same hole. By rights I should have gone in and fetched it myself, but being in possession of the little green man had many advantages. Seconds later, the other four were inside the cloakroom, via the broken window. I remember Pompus, his chubby face looking back out, shouting at me to come and see for myself, for a laugh. Soon we were prowling around the empty junior school, trying the door handles of storerooms and cupboards. The walls were covered in pictures in bright powder-paint colours. Birds and fish, stick-men, a yellow horse under a huge, purple sun, like drawings done by cavemen or Indians. In the classrooms, the chairs were on the desks, upside down.

'I used to hang my pump-bag up on this peg, next to Paul Martindale,' I said. 'I'm taking it home as a souvenir.'

'He carked it, didn't he?' said Winkie.

'Yep,' I said, 'rode his bike under a bus. And Everill had the peg in the corner. So his fleas couldn't jump on to anyone else's clothes.'

Stubbs, Pompus and Tony Football had gone into the main hall. They'd taken their shoes off and were sliding around on the wooden floor, probably because sliding on the wooden floor was absolutely forbidden. Then Stubbs started kicking the football against the ceiling, leaving dark, round dents in the polystyrene panels, like dirty faces looking down. The dare, in fact, wasn't just to go and get the football – it was to see who stayed inside the school the longest. Whether it was two hours or two weeks, the last person out would win, and I'd have to hand over the little green man.

'Don't you think this is a bit daft?' Winkie was saying to me. 'We might get caught.'

'So we get caught.'

He was always the one to crack, always the one to jib out, always the one to say he'd had enough and go home. You could rely on him. You could depend on it. Right from the start he was a weak link. He had a lazy eye. He had glue ear.

'Mind you,' I said. I was jabbing at the wooden bench with Stubbs's flick knife. 'Mind you, you've only had him a couple of times all summer, haven't you? So why don't you stay put for a while, otherwise you won't ever benefit.'

'It's bollocks all that,' he blurted out. He was having a pee in one of the knee-high urinals. I could see him from where I was sitting.

'Well, you for one wouldn't know. The way I see it, having the green man is like having this knife. Know what I mean? Sort of powerful. Lets you call the shots, make powerful decisions.'

'For instance?' he called out, over his shoulder.

'For instance, the powerful decision to carve my name on this bench,' I said.

'That's not power, it's just carving your name on a bench.' He was pulling up his fly as he walked towards me, his cheeks flushed from his little rebellious outburst. 'And for another thing, when they see "Barney" in three-inch letters, it's not going to take Scotland Yard to figure out who did it, is it?'

'Exactly,' I said, 'which is why, as current possessor of the little green man, I took the powerful decision to carve your name instead.'

Winkie stared at the bench, where his name was only one letter from completion, then lunged for the knife. He screamed at me. 'You stupid sod. My mother's a dinner lady here. Give me that thing.'

But I was away through the door and into the hall, sliding the knife across the floor to Stubbs, who twigged what was going on and slid it to Pompus, who threw it to Tony, until Winkie was piggy in the middle, diving after the knife as it skittled past him on the ground or flashed through the air. Eventually he trapped it with his foot and picked it up. For a second I thought he might come at me with it. Most of the time he was a bit of a mardypants, but if he ever saw red it was best to stand well back. He once punched his sister so hard in the mouth that two of her teeth came flying out, just because she wouldn't get off his bike, and would have given her some more if the ice-cream man hadn't jumped out of his van and sat on his back.

But Winkie scurried into the cloakroom to deface his name, and maybe write mine in its place if he had the nerve. I ran with the others down the back stairs towards the art room, and had just got to the bottom when the doors of the fire exit flew open and a policeman rushed in and grabbed Tony. When we turned round there was another copper coming hurtling towards us, so we were nabbed. One of them took out his notebook.

My brother once told me that when the IRA get pulled in for questioning they just stonewall by spouting the names of roads and streets in their part of town. Almost without thinking I'd started doing the same thing, in my head. In fact it's a habit I've never grown out of. But when you're fifteen, you're not that interested in street names and alleyways. You're not really bothered about local history. You choose things a little bit closer to home.

'Haven't I seen you somewhere before?' said the copper.

Caramac, wine gums, aniseed balls . . .

'Last Christmas, wasn't it? That business with the light bulbs?'

Beech Nut, sherbet bon-bons, blackjacks, Parma violets, cherry lips . . .

'Cat got your tongue, has it? I'll deal with you later.'

He turned to Tony. 'What's your name, son?'

I could see a drop of water bubbling up in Tony's right eye, then another in his other eye, which ran down his cheek on to his T-shirt.

'Tony,' he confessed.

'Tony what?'

Another tear dripped off the end of his chin as he looked towards us, and then towards the bottom of the stairwell, where the ball had come to rest.

'Tony Football.'

After he'd said it, I couldn't tell if the noise coming out of his nose was that of a boy about to sob, uncontrollably, or explode with laughter. Stubbs was definitely sniggering – I could see his shoulders jerking up and down inside his jumper – and Pompus actually put his hand over his mouth. We were marched outside to the van. As it swung round in the yard, I saw Winkie's face in the cloakroom, peeping out of the smashed window, smiling and waving. One of those waves the Queen does from the window of her car.

4

They parked outside in the drive, Winkie in his M-reg Mondeo, Tony Football on a new Kawasaki, Stubbs in a black Volvo estate with a couple of kids' seats in the back, Pompus in a breakdown truck with a tow hook swinging from a chain.

'How long have you been back at your mum and dad's place?' asked Tony, as he came into the kitchen, taking off his helmet and smoothing back what was left of his hair. I walked them into the front room, pushed a pile of magazines off the table, and pulled up four dining chairs and the piano stool.

''Bout three years now. They're out in Portugal pretty much all of the time, so I've got the place to myself.'

'Didn't you and Kim live over in Sinsell?'

I drew the curtains and switched on the wall lights, then turned them down with the dimmer. It was chilly in the house, so I struck a match on the hearth and dropped it into the fake coals. When the gas finally seeped through, it lit with a thin blue flame, then burnt yellow as it took hold. I watched the matchstick crozzle into nothing.

'Me and Kim split up,' I said. 'I thought you would have heard.'

'Actually, I had heard. Sorry.'

'Just one of them things,' I said, standing up and looking straight at him.

Pompus had picked up the newspaper and turned to the racing page. Stubbs blew air through his hands, making a train noise or the call of a bird. Winkie sat with his arms folded in front of him, waiting for something to happen.

'These coal-effect fires are crap,' I told them. 'I don't know how many BTUs they're supposed to give out, but they don't. You need radiators as well. They might look good but they're only for show. I wouldn't have one myself.'

Pompus, without looking up from the newspaper, said, 'Weather's all fucked up anyway. What is it, May? Fucking May, and you need the fire on. It's outstanding, is that.'

'It's April,' said Tony Football.

'Same difference.'

I did a round of drinks. Cup of tea for Winkie, coffee for Tony Football, Stubbs wanted an orange juice but I only had the diluted stuff, and a can of lager for Pompus.

'Might as well get two while you're there,' he shouted after me down the cellar steps. I poured them both into a tall schooner with a gold rim around the top.

'Ooh, that's posh.'

'Yeah, too good for you. Anyway, it's strong stuff. Export. You should watch it if you're driving.'

'No point,' he said, 'I'm already banned.'

Everyone laughed. He said he was only joking, then said he couldn't lose his licence, because he'd never had one in the first place. More laughter, which was good.

'Do we need coasters for these drinks?' asked Winkie.

'Don't bother,' I said, but he pulled out the sleeve of his shirt and rested the cup on it between mouthfuls.

'Come on, then,' said Stubbs. 'What is it?'

I went to the bureau and brought out an old biscuit tin, then set it in the middle of the table. Then I sat down on the piano stool with my hands under my thighs and said nothing. Eventually Tony Football reached for the tin, but Pompus snatched it and prized off the lid. He pulled out a bundle of newspaper.

'Outstanding. Fish and chips.'

'Pass the parcel, gents. One layer at a time, clockwise, and no squeezing for clues,' I said.

I got up and turned the dimmer switch down another couple of notches, then went over to the hi-fi and lifted the arm of the turntable on to an LP. After a few seconds of crackles and scratches the music started.

Stubbs looked over and grinned. 'God, I haven't heard this lot for ages. Remember Jerry Dammers – he had his front teeth taken out as a fashion statement, didn't he?'

'I bet he feels a right twerp now, selling insurance or whatever he's doing,' said Winkie.

'"Too Much Too Young",' said Tony Football, nostalgically. 'Chance would have been a fine thing.' He threw a ball of newspaper towards the bin and missed.

'You never could throw anyway,' I said to him, picking up the paper.

'Yeah,' said Pompus. 'You woman.'

The parcel did one more circuit before Pompus ripped open the final layer. The little green man fell from the paper and rolled on the table in front of them. He picked him up and held him between his chubby fingers.

'And?'

'Don't you know?' I said.

Tony Football asked for a look, then passed him to Winkie, who stared as if he'd almost cottoned on but couldn't quite make the final connection. As if he'd recognized someone but couldn't remember their name. He offered it to Stubbs, but Stubbs was looking at me. I couldn't stop a huge, smarmy grin spreading right across my face, like treacle poured from the tin.

Stubbs took the green man in his hand and closed his fist. 'I don't believe you,' he said.

'Don't believe what?' said Tony Football.

'Little green man.'

I could feel my smile getting wider and wider, and had to bite my bottom lip to stop my ears meeting at the top of my head.

'Outstanding!' shouted Pompus. The penny had dropped. 'Give it here for a look,' he yelled, snatching it out of Stubbs's hand. 'Out-fucking-standing!'

'No?' said Winkie. 'Come off it.'

'It bloody is,' said Tony Football, shaking his head. 'It bloody well is.'

Pompus stood up, and held the little green man out in front of him like the FA Cup, and made the sound of an ecstatic crowd with a gurgling noise in his throat. Everyone was laughing and joking. The house was warm now, and by the time I'd come back with another round of drinks, the room was full of talk and stories, full of the old times. How we'd found him in the cinders in the old shunting yard. How we'd said he was a god, sworn an oath on his name, played dares to take possession of him. How it started with Pompus ladling frogspawn down his kecks. Then Stubbs nicking a packet of johnnies from the chemist's. Then Tony Football walking through the graveyard at midnight, in bare feet. And the banger up the cat's arse. Sugar in a petrol tank. Something I'd forgotten involving a bottle of red ink down Stubbs's trunks at the swimming baths. Setting that hen hut on fire. And so on, and so on.

We could have been passing round a drug. Tony Football breathed on the little green man and rubbed him against his sleeve. Winkie held him close to his face, inspecting him, as if he were looking for a hallmark or the maker's name. He gleamed and multiplied in the lenses of his specs. Pompus licked him like a lolly. Stubbs followed him with his eyes, and kept looking back at me, shaking his head and laughing. 'Were you the last person to win it?' he asked me.

'Looks like. But don't ask me how.'

Tony Football said, 'Well, that just kills me. Trust you to keep it. That's a real party piece, that is. I bet the little green feller could tell a few stories, if he could talk. That's priceless, Barney, it really is.'

'Funny you should say that,' I said.

Winkie finished his tea, stood up and put his cup on the mantel-piece. 'That was fun, but I'll have to get off. Maureen will be wondering what's happened to me. I said I'd be home by half-eight.'

'I'd better be going as well,' said Tony Football, getting to his feet and lifting his leather jacket from the back of the chair.

'Hang about. There's one last thing.' I went to the bureau and produced a manila envelope from under the clock. Winkie was over by the door already, with one hand on the handle. I gave the envelope to Stubbs.

'What is it?'

'Open and read,' I said, and sat down.

He yanked it open with his finger and pulled out a slip of paper. Tony Football stood behind him, trying to read over his shoulder.

'Lend us your glasses, Winkie. It's just for close-up stuff when I'm tired. I've left mine in the car.'

Winkie let out a long, exasperated sigh and wandered back to the table. When he took off his glasses he looked completely different, like somebody with no eyes at all, just two empty holes under his eyebrows.

'You blind bastard. Are they double-glazed?' said Stubbs, squinting at the piece of paper.

Winkie pinched the red mark on his face where the glasses had been resting, as if he were trying to stop a nosebleed.

'It's some kind of guarantee,' said Stubbs. 'No, hang about, it's a valuation.' His eyes skimmed the small print.

'Read it out loud then,' said Pompus.

'Late seventeeth-century jadeite Shouxing – if that's how you pronounce it – blah, blah, blah, minimum value for insurance purposes . . . 750 . . .'

His voice trailed off, then his eyes went back to the top of the paper, and he started to read the whole thing again, in silence, squeezing the tip of his tongue between his lips.

'Seven hundred and fifty notes for that scoddy little thing?' said Pompus. 'If this is an auction you can forget it, forget it. That's beer money for a month, is that.'

Stubbs cleared his throat and swallowed. 'Minimum value for insurance purposes . . . 750,000 pounds.'

Pompus grabbed the note from his hand, knocking over his drink and sending a tide of froth across the table. The lager dripped on to the floor. I half-expected Winkie to go running into the kitchen for a cloth, but he didn't move.

Pompus could hardly contain himself. 'Three-quarters of a million, for that. Outstanding. Out-fucking-standing.'

Tony Football drew the paper out of Stubbs's hand and read it to himself, holding it at the top and the bottom, like a proclamation. 'Why so much? That's ridiculous.'

I went back to the bureau for another envelope. 'Apparently there's a gemstone implanted in his head. An emerald. It means he isn't carved from a single piece but joined together somehow, but it's impossible to find the seam. And you can only see the emerald under X-ray. Look.'

They each held the X-ray of the statue up to the light. Within the ghostly outline, a clear geometric shape shone from the centre of his bulbous skull.

'I've been reading up about it. They made thousands, the Chinese, but people have cracked them open, for the gems. Like breaking into the pyramids for the gold. Apparently, there are only six or seven of them still intact. And that crystal ball in his hands – it's actually a peach.'

The lager was still dripping on to the carpet and had formed a shallow lake on the table, with the little green man marooned in the middle. I picked him up and slid him into my pocket. Then I reached for the phone and dropped it into Winkie's hand.

'Call Maureen and tell her you'll be late. Pompus, mop up that mess with a towel. Now, gents, why don't you all sit down while I get another round of drinks. Something a bit stronger this time, eh?'

In the cellar, directly beneath them, I unscrew the cap from a bottle of brandy and take a long swig from the neck. I wipe the sweat from my forehead and my top lip. Up above, I can sense them whispering, pointing, passing round the note and the X-ray. I can hear their feet shuffling on the floor overhead, imagine their toes in their shoes, curled tight with excitement and nerves. I'm thinking, three hours ago they could barely bring themselves to speak to each other. Now look at them. Who said you can't turn back the clock? I glug another mouthful of brandy, screw the top on and head back up the stone steps. When I walk into the room with the bottle and a tot glass swinging from each finger, they stand up, all four of them, to a man.

There's this thing I once heard in a film, and I just come out with it. I say, 'Gentlemen, let's talk turkey.'

5

On the radio, a woman was talking about a hospital test she'd had, called a cerebral angiograph. They injected dye into her brain, then wired her up to a screen. She could see herself thinking. Literally. It was amazing. She said, 'All the time I kept looking at the monitor, seeing my thoughts as swirls of colour and splashes of light. I'd see a thought, then think about seeing that thought, then see myself thinking about seeing that thought . . . and so on. And all the time I was wondering, where is the *me* in this.' I would have liked to listen for longer, but a car pulled out of a parking space on the high street, and I swung in and switched the engine off.

I could see Kim in the corner window of the café as I walked along the street. I turned into one of the supermarket loading bays, then cut through the car park, jumping the chains slung between iron bollards, and came out higher up the street opposite the bank. In the lobby I posted a couple of cheques in the credit slot, drew money from the cashpoint, then walked back towards the café, stopping to look in the art shop on the way.

'You're late,' she said, looking up from a magazine. There was only just enough room to squeeze between the table and the wall, and by the time I'd managed to wriggle my way in I'd knocked over the pepper grinder and spilt most of her tea. I picked up the saucer to pour it back in, but she held her hand over the cup. 'I don't want that now. Just leave it.'

'I don't know why we come here. It's just a trendy rip-off.'

'Where else is there on a Sunday? McDonald's?' she said.

I started playing with the sugar in the bowl, turning it over with a teaspoon, sculpting it into dunes and valleys, but she reached out and moved it to one side.

'Why do we bother doing this? Whose sake is it for anyway? Not for mine and certainly not for his. Does it make you feel better or something?'

'I dunno,' I said. 'Anyway, where is he?'

'Asleep in the car.'

She motioned with her head towards the red Fiesta parked outside. He was fast off in the car seat, with his mouth wide open and his head lolling against the seatbelt. One of his ears was squashed against the window, like one of those boneless sea creatures on the inside of a glass tank.

'How's he doing?'

'Fine, in himself. Some quite good reports from school. Last week he counted up to five, but I don't think he's got any idea what it means.'

'What about getting into junior school next year, you know, mainstream?'

Kim pushed her hair away from her eyes but it fell forward again and covered her face. 'No chance. Not now. I dropped off one of the women from work the other day and popped in for a coffee. She's got a seven-year-old as well. He came up and talked to me about where he was going on holiday, then started playing the recorder, "Three Blind Mice". I could have wept. I did weep. It brought it home to me how far behind he is. How distant.'

'Will he have to go away?' I said.

She leant back in her chair and stared at me coldly. 'He's autistic, Barney, not a bloody convict or a bad dog that's bitten somebody. Why would he have to go away?'

'I don't know. I just meant for some kind of special help. You know, residential type thing.'

'He's staying with me, all right?' she snapped. 'You might have chickened out, but I haven't. I love that boy, and for as long as I can look after him he's staying with me.'

I went to the counter and ordered a coffee and looked through the window at the car. He was still asleep in the same position.

'Sorry,' I said, when I sat down. 'Is he all right in there?'

'I left one of his tapes running – *Jungle Book* – so I've got another five minutes. "King of the Swingers", and then he'll wake up.'

She checked her watch, lit a cigarette. 'I don't smoke when he's with me. I suppose that's one reason for coming out.'

'How's work?' I said.

She knew I was changing the subject but didn't argue. 'It's good, fine. Still enjoying it.'

'Do I owe you any money?'

She shook her head. 'What about you. Are *you* working?'

'I've got a couple of posters on the go, and I'm doing the menus for that new hotel on the ring road. Bit of photography stuff. Bit of odd-jobbing. You know.'

'Well, Barney, you always were very good with your hands,' she said, 'which always comes in useful when you're on your own.' There was a pause, then she said, '*Are* you seeing anyone?'

'No.'

'I know you won't ask. I'm not either. How sad does that make us?'

She looked at her watch again, then crushed the cigarette in the glass ashtray. 'Right, I'm off. Do you want to come and see him before I go?'

'No, I won't wake him, if he's asleep.' It was a useless thing to say, and sounded worse, the way it came out.

'You're pathetic, you do know that, don't you? God help him if he ever gets bright enough to figure out that you're his dad.'

She zipped up her coat, told me to grow up, and left. Outside it had started to rain, and I watched the first few drops racing each other down the café window. She got into the car, started the engine and pulled away along the street. Travis was still fast asleep with his head back. From where I was sitting, it looked as if he was trying to catch the rain in his mouth, taste the rain on his tongue. Kim had left her magazines. Women's stuff, questionnaires about babies and sex. I got another coffee and sat and read them for half an hour, then ran through the weather to the car and drove home.

6

Winkie, Pompus and Tony Football were already in the changing room when I got there, and Stubbs was only a minute or so behind. We lost 11–3 to some lads from the fire service; Stubbs got two and I scored the other, a penalty. Pompus went in goal and got hit in the face with a screamer from point-blank range. By the time we got into the bar half of his face had swollen up and his right eye was almost closed. It looked excruciating, but it didn't seem to bother him.

We sat at the same table as last week, overlooking the pool, a bit closer together this time.

'Go through the rules again, so there's no arguing about it later on,' said Tony.

I leant forward and they all pulled their chairs into a huddle and listened. 'Just like it was back then, except this time it's for real. We draw lots to decide the order, and it keeps going round the same way. We meet every Friday night. Say, for example, Pompus goes first, and he has to dare Stubbs. If Stubbs does the dare, then he's still in, and he dares the next person. If he takes it on and fails, he's out. But he can knock it back instead, which means that Pompus would have to do his own dare.'

'Clever,' said Tony. 'Very clever.'

'Right. Anyhow, if Stubbs does knock it back and Pompus completes his own dare, Stubbs is out. If Pompus fails, he's out. Simple as that.'

Winkie pushed his glasses higher up his nose; they were still covered with mist. 'And then it's Stubbs's turn, if Pompus is out, yes?'

'No. When someone fails, the circle changes direction. That way you never know who you might end up next to. And that's it. Last person gets the little green man. For keeps.'

'Shouldn't we write all this down?' said Winkie.

'No way,' said Tony. 'I don't want to see any of this in print, thank you. We know how it works, let's just leave it at that.'

Everyone was quiet for a minute. Then Pompus got up and examined his face in the glass wall overlooking the baths. 'I look like Fu Man-fucking-chu with this slanty eye.'

'You'll just have to turn the other cheek,' I said to him. 'Oh, and a couple more things. The dare has to be done within the week. And if there's any disagreement about a dare, the three people not involved can adjudicate. Three's a good number – there'll never be a hung jury doing it that way.'

'You really have thought of everything,' said Stubbs, nodding, leaning away on his chair and putting his hands behind his head.

I went over to the counter and drew five drinking straws from the dispenser. I tore them into five different lengths, held them level in my fist and offered them round. 'Shortest goes first.'

Everyone laid their straws down on the table. Winkie's was the smallest – you could have put money on that – followed by Tony Football, followed by Pompus, followed by me, and then Stubbs. I told them I was going for a slash, and that Winkie had to give Tony his dare before we all went home.

The toilets are quiet and empty. I run the cold tap and dip my face in the basin, open my eyes under water for as long as I can, and hold my breath.

Once, when we were kids, we kept heating up the ends of half a dozen metal rods in a bonfire, till they glowed red, then dipped them into a bucket of cold water. We thought the rods might shatter or explode with the change in temperature, but they never did. Then when we'd had enough I stuck my hands in the bucket to wash them, and screamed in agony. The water in the bucket was boiling. I was off school for two weeks, both my hands bandaged to the wrists.

When I come up for air I see Tony Football behind me in the mirror. 'Hot?' he asks.

'Yeah, out of condition. I'll be as stiff as a board tomorrow.'

He drops a paper towel in the waste bin and goes out. I flip over the

nozzle of the hand-dryer and let the warm air pummel my face, then comb
the wet strands of my fringe to one side.

'Well?'

Winkie shuffled in his seat and turned towards him. 'I dare you to nick something.'

'Like what?'

'Whatever you want. Makes no difference to me.'

'Come on, think about it, you skirt,' said Pompus. 'Put a price on it, or he's just going to nick a beer mat or something.'

'Then again, nothing too whopping, in case he knocks it back, and you have to do it yourself,' said Stubbs.

It was superb to see them getting into it, exhilarating to watch them inching their way forward, sizing each other up, working out the next move, calculating the odds. I could see Winkie going red, thinking he might have screwed up on the first go, like someone who'd landed on a twenty-foot python with his first shake of the dice. Stubbs was smirking, and Pompus was laughing all over his huge, swollen head, like a giant pumpkin with a massive, grinning mouth and light flashing from the eyes. 'Come on, you great big skirt, give him a price.'

'All right, then, a tenner,' said Winkie.

'A TENNER!' screamed Pompus. 'A FUCKING TENNER! There's three-quarters of a million sitting on the table, and you dare him a tenner. Outstanding!'

Stubbs covered his face with his hands. Tony Football shook his head, saying, 'You just don't get it, do you, Winkie,' then walked over to the counter and started talking to the woman on the till. He kept pointing at the store cupboard behind her, until eventually she left her seat and went into the back. As soon as she'd gone, he looked over his shoulder, then loaded his pockets with bits and pieces from the display. He even glanced towards us at one point and winked. When he came back he said, 'Funny, that. I could have sworn I'd left my jacket here last week, that one with studs on the shoulders, but nobody's handed it in. Thieving bastards.'

He pulled a Bounty and a mint Aero from his pocket. 'Here Winkie, have a choccy. It's on the house.'

Stubbs and Pompus and me just about convulsed. Even Winkie saw the funny side, although he didn't take the chocolate, didn't even touch it.

'That's not a tenner's worth,' he pointed out.

From his other pocket, TF produced a packet of phonecards, several books of stamps, a fistful of bookmarks, a set of darts in a leather pouch, three squash balls and a pair of swimming goggles. 'I think that should cover it,' he said, scooping them into his holdall and doing up the zip. 'Hand it over then.'

'Hand what over?' I said.

'The little green thing. It's mine till next week.'

'No chance. He stays under lock and key till the end.'

'How do we know we can trust you?' Winkie wanted to know.

It was a fair point, a good question. I'd been expecting it. 'Two reasons. First – you don't have any choice. And second, why would I have got in touch with you in the first place if I was going to keep him for myself? I'd have put him up for auction and you lot wouldn't have been any the wiser. Think about it. I'm the only one you *can* trust.'

'Like I said, he's got it all worked out,' said Stubbs.

'So why didn't you? I mean, just keep it?' said Tony Football. He had a sheepish expression, as if he'd been egged on to ask a stupid question in class, as if he'd said something rude.

'Don't think it didn't cross my mind. Don't think I didn't drool over all that gelt. But we're mates, aren't we? Always were, always will be, as far as I'm concerned. You don't shit on your pals. We got into this together all those years ago and we'll get out of it together. Anyway, it's the spirit of the thing. We're not talking about winning the lottery here. He's a god, a proper bloody god, and we've worshipped him. If I'd have cut you out of the deal, I could have been . . .'

'Could have been what?' said Pompus.

'Cursed,' I said. 'Or something.' I lowered my head and blew my fringe out of my eyes.

26

'Right, I'm away. See you next Friday, daredevils,' said Stubbs.

'Wait a minute. Tony might as well give Pompus his dare, for next week, given that tonight's effort was such a damp squib. Yes?' I looked at them in turn and they nodded their agreement.

'OK,' said Tony Football. 'By next week, I want to have seen you on telly, Pompus. Not the Shopping Channel, or any of that crap. And not home video. BBC, ITV, Channel 4 or 5. By next week. That's the dare.'

'Channel 5? He could make it as a presenter on Channel 5 by next Friday,' said Stubbs.

Pompus swilled the last third of his pint down his neck and burped. His head looked like a Space Hopper now, enormous, just about ready to burst.

'Outstanding,' he said. 'I was once on *Junior Showtime*, y'know. In a choir singing hymns. It was tops.'

7

To be given a nickname is a good thing and a bad thing at the same time. On the one hand, it means you're in, you've made it, you're not on your own any more. On the other hand, it puts you in your place, seals your fortune, tells you to calm down and stop trying to scramble to the top. You've got as far as you're going. Be grateful – at least you're one of the crowd.

I'm not talking about nicknames that are pure insults and nothing else, nicknames like bullet- and stab-wounds that scar for life. Tit-head Thomas with the red nipple on top of his bald head – he was only ten. Wing-nut with his ears stuck out. Flake who was falling to bits with eczema, and Snowstorm in the year below with the same complaint. Bismarck Harris, the girl with the big brown mole on her cheek. She had it removed, but somebody heard that the skin they grafted on was a piece of her arse. Then she was Bum-face instead.

No, I'm talking about something more subtle than that, a nickname supplied to a mate, a name that gives him a leg-up, but also stops him climbing any further, if it works. Of course it's a risky business, a dangerous game to play. I've never broken in a horse, obviously, but I imagine it to be much the same. The first stage is critical, like mounting up. It can be hazardous, violent even, but you've got to keep calling a person his new name over and over, no matter how rough the ride, no matter how much he doesn't want to answer to that word. You have to climb back on every time you come flying off. Someone's got to win, either you or him, and it's got to be you. You've got to keep on saying that name till it sticks, till he's yours. Then you can pat him on the head, give him a sugar lump. Soon he'll be thankful, grateful you took the trouble. He'll carry you to hell and back and a mile further. Now and again you might call him by his other name, the one his parents gave him, just for show. It's a powerful thing to give a person a name, and powerful to take it away as well.

Of course, if you're in charge, that's a different barrel of biscuits altogether. To give the leader a nickname, even just to try – that would be a challenge, a coup. If you're in charge and a nickname comes flying your way, you've got to swat it dead. If a person utters a nickname in your direction, you've got to tell that person where to get off, tell them to walk. Nobody rides on your back. Which doesn't mean you get an easy time of it. Quite the opposite, in fact. You're responsible. You have to do all of the groundwork, all the forward planning, the ringing round and arranging and sorting out. Stubbs and Pompus and Winkie and TF, they would never have made the effort if it wasn't for me. I'd get carted off on holiday for a couple of weeks with my parents; first minute back I'd phone Stubbs. 'Seen everyone else?'

'No.'

'No? What did you do for a fortnight, just sit there wanking?'

'Yeah, mainly.'

Pathetic. Still, once you've given someone a nickname, you can't expect him to suddenly start thinking for himself.

Names. What things are called. It counts for a lot. And numbers as well. Five is good. Odd, prime, whole. Simple enough in itself, but with enough connections and permutations to make it worth the trouble. Like one of those molecular models in the chemistry lab at school, ping-pong balls held on metal springs, the whole thing quivering and tense around one centre of gravity, around one focal point. Four fingers and a thumb. Four dining chairs and a piano stool. Five: it has a ring to it, a special quality, an extra dimension or indivisible charm. I wouldn't be surprised if somewhere along the line that had been mathematically tested and proved.

8

It was Wednesday already and I was having a good week. I'd installed a security light over the backyard of a woman in Rodney Road, then she'd put her brother on to me, who wanted a new washer plumbing in and his old one taking to the tip, which was all easy money and less than a day's work. I don't see myself as a handyman or anything like that, but I've always had the knack of fixing things. The knack of setting things up, making them go. I don't charge much, but then again I don't advertise or pay tax, and it gets me out of the house. It's all word of mouth, one job leading to the next, and it buys me the time to do exactly what I want, which is mainly doodling, sketching and various other bits of arty stuff. I say I don't charge much, but I have to draw the line somewhere. I once spent a week fitting a walk-in wardrobe for a vicar. The day I finished he pressed an envelope into my hand and gave me one of those knowing looks. When I opened it later, it was a ten-quid gift voucher for WH Smith and one of those Easter crosses made from a dead leaf. Cheeky get.

I've got inner strength, I reckon. Hidden depths. Something to fall back on. If I didn't, I'd be working in a booth in the covered market by now, cutting keys, gluing fake-leather soles on to plastic shoes, engraving pewter tankards. The only profession I ever thought seriously about was masonry. Monumental masonry. Headstones, statuary, that kind of thing. Imagine writing that in your passport. Occupation: monumental mason. It's a long, slow apprenticeship, a day-release job under the sharp eye of some bloodless and tight-fisted undertaker. I had the talent, but not the get-up-and-go. In the end, I decided five years sitting in a pile of stone chippings wasn't really for me, not to mention the blisters and broken nails. Even so, I rate sculpture as the most important of all the arts, mainly because it's 3D, not just laid flat on a sheet of photographic paper or across the level plane of a canvas. You can get round a sculpture, be amongst it.

It was about four in the afternoon when the phone went. It was Kim.

'I need you to look after Trav, pick him up from school, take him back to mine and give him his tea. I'll be home later on. OK?'

'Yes, I suppose.'

'No need to sound so bloody thrilled about it. Something's come up at work, it'll be about ten o'clock – all right?'

'OK.'

'You've still got a key, haven't you?'

'Yes.'

'Ten or eleven. Don't forget his diet. Thanks.'

He was waiting in the cloakroom with one of the teachers and six or seven other pupils of different ages. A tall girl in wellies was wearing her anorak the wrong way round, with the hood pulled over her face. A boy in National Health glasses was spinning on one heel, making circular scuff marks on the lino. 'Don't do that, Patrick,' said the teacher, and reached over to stop him. But the boy squealed, ducked under her arm and carried on pirouetting. Travis was standing by the staffroom door, the smallest child in the group, his gabardine coat fastened at the belt and his hands lost inside the long sleeves.

'I'm collecting Travis. I'm his father.'

I don't think the teacher recognized me, but she didn't ask any questions. She looked exasperated, exhausted, and huffed at me, as if what I'd said were ridiculous. Take your pick. Who in their right mind would want to steal one of these?

As soon as I got near him he began whimpering, and when I held out my hand towards him he screamed, and started to twist and squirm, turning his feet inwards and his face to the ceiling.

'His mother usually picks him up,' I said, as if that explained everything.

In the car, he fretted all the way back to the house, and was sobbing heavily by the time we got inside. I poured him a drink of orange, which quietened him down as he slurped from it and bit at the plastic beaker. Then he shuffled into the living room and I heard the television going on.

Not much has changed. There's a new rug in the hall and a couple of interior doors have been stripped back to the original wood. Plants and seashells are set out along the skirting board in the bathroom, but the cold tap is still dripping and the handle on the loo needs to be cranked a couple of times to flush it, like the clutch of an old car. In the bedroom, the cat's asleep on the star-spangled duvet cover some distant relative gave us as a wedding present. The wicker chair in the corner is piled high with knickers and socks. I stand here, waiting to feel it, but nothing happens. Three years. The place should be a memory bank. Peering into the wardrobe or sliding open this drawer or turning the key of the ebony jewellery box ought to trigger the past. The pillow should breathe back into my face, the sheet should crackle or spark.

'Veejo, veejo!' Travis was shouting.

'No, Travis, we're not having a video. Let's play a game instead.'

'Veejo, veejo!'

His bottom lip was quivering again, but before the floodgates opened I produced the box I'd brought from the attic at home.

'Lego,' I said. 'Daddy show Travis how to make things. Come on, Trav, come and build something with daddy.'

I poured the red and yellow bricks from the box, and he watched, turning his head to see them cascading horizontally along his line of sight. I knelt and picked up some of the building blocks, trying to press one into his hand.

'Come on, Travis, sit with daddy.'

For a second I thought I'd caught his attention. He seemed to be surveying the scattered bricks on the carpet, taking it all in, seeing where each piece had landed, noticing how they made a shape, a constellation, a pattern. Then, 'Veejo,' he mumbled, almost absent-mindedly, then louder as he heard himself saying the word, then louder still, until he was shouting.

'VEEJO. VEEJO. VEEJO, VEEJO, VEEJO, VEEJO . . .'

'All right,' I snarled.

I opened the cabinet under the telly and pulled out one of the videos. The case was battered and bitten around the edge.

'Tok Hap. Tok Hap.'

'Please.'

'Pweese Tok Hap.'

'OK, *Top Cat*.'

I rammed it into the slot and set it playing. Travis dragged a seat cushion from the armchair and positioned it about a foot away from the screen, then lay on his back with his legs out in front of him and his feet on the control panel. I got up and pulled the cushion away from the telly.

'Don't sit so close and don't use your feet,' I told him, but by the time I sat down again he was back where he wanted to be.

I said to myself that it would be different this time, that he would have forgotten, that he couldn't possibly still be interested in the same uninteresting thing. But as soon as Officer Dibble tripped over the baseball bat and went flying through the air, Travis hit the rewind switch with the big toe of his right foot, and the cartoon ran backwards for four or five seconds. Then he hit the play button with his left foot, and the video clunked into forward gear, and Officer Dibble tripped and flew, and Travis stuck out his right foot. Rewind, whirr, clunk, play, clunk, rewind, whirr, clunk, play. Each time, Travis turned his head, watching from sideways on, letting out a little yelp of delight and pedalling his legs in the air before reaching out for the button again with his toe. Clunk, rewind, whirr, clunk, play.

In the kitchen I went through the cupboards, looking for something without sugar, without flavouring, additives, gluten, without everything he wasn't allowed this week. As if a miracle diet might be the answer. I went back and stood in front of the telly.

'Travis tell daddy where mummy keeps food. Show daddy where food is.'

'Pweese Tok Hap.'

It was a stupid thing to do, leave him on his own, but I could only think about what Kim would say if I didn't feed him. How annoyed she'd be. How she could have guessed, might have known. It probably took fifteen minutes all told to drive to the garage, to read the labels on the cans of soup and the bags of crisps and the packets of bread. Then the woman in front wanted to pay for a pint of milk with a credit card, and the manager had to be called. I raced back in the car, unlocked the door and ran into the room. Clunk, rewind, whirr, clunk, play . . .

I went into the kitchen and opened the tin of soup.

About an hour after he'd eaten he fell asleep. I dragged the cushion he was lying on away from the telly, closer to the fire, and he brought his knees under his chin and buried his hands in his chest. I covered him with his coat. Then I flicked the telly over to the football and brought the volume up slowly so as not to wake him.

Putting my feet up, I remembered the time the three-piece suite was delivered, how the two chairs came in all right, but the settee wouldn't fit through the door, no matter which way it was turned or how hard we pushed. Waiting there in the drive it looked small and manageable, but wedged in the doorway it seemed to expand, swell up, until it wouldn't budge either way. I've read about horses like that. When you're saddling up they breathe in, filling their bodies with air. Then when you mount they breathe out, stubborn beasts, so the strap comes loose and the saddle slips and the rider gets dumped on his arse. The settee stayed outside all night in the yard, and it rained. Next morning, Kim measured up and said we should take the glass out of the picture window in the front room. I said no. She said yes. It was still raining. I said absolutely not, it's too much hassle, let's take it back and get a smaller one. She said,

'You know your problem, don't you, Barney?' Then she fetched the ball-headed hammer from the toolbox and threw it underarm into the middle of the window. Months later we were still hoovering the glass out of the carpet, thinking we'd found every last sliver, until the sun swept across the room in the afternoon and lit up yet another splinter, another shard waiting to spike Kim as she padded through the house in bare feet, or needle Travis as he crawled around on all fours. The sofa was always damp, and had a smell that reminded me of a school trip to the Blue John Mines. And it was uncomfortable and the colours had run, but it was going nowhere. You can't break the same window twice. Or maybe you can, but a stunt like that needs an audience as well as some poor sap to pick up the pieces, and I was gone, out through the front door. Whatever my problem was, that settee wasn't it.

There'd been another domestic when Kim wanted satellite TV and I didn't.

'It's a waste of money.'

'It's not a waste of money. Travis can watch the cartoons, and you can watch all those nature films you like.'

I pointed out there was a world of difference between the occasional natural-history programme and meerkats peering out of their burrows twenty-four hours a day. But she looked at the telly the same way she'd looked at the window that day. Two weeks later, there was a man in blue overalls threading cable through the ceiling and bolting a big white dish to the chimney stack.

The football droned on, a relegation battle on a soggy night in the Midlands. I only had one eye on it, really. Then midway through the second half, just as the keeper was about to take a goal kick, someone from the crowd bundled past him, galloped up to the ball and hoofed it as hard as he could, falling on his backside in the mud. Stewards ran on to the pitch from all directions, but the big fat spectator set off towards the middle, looking up at the camera position and pointing at his face with both hands. The commentator was blabbing about something else and pretending not to notice, the same way they ignore streakers these days. But suddenly there was a close-up of the fat man's face, grinning like a loony as two coppers frogmarched him into the tunnel.

'Pompus,' I said out loud, 'you absolute star.'

9

'*Junior Showtime* and *Match of the Day*. How about that for a fuckin'
brace? Outstanding.'

'All right, stop crowing about it,' said Tony Football.

Pompus was finishing rolling a joint, licking his tongue along the
loose hem of a Rizla, having sprinkled what looked like dried lawn
cuttings on to a furrow full of Old Holborn.

'Don't do that in here, for Christ's sake,' said Winkie, looking
around anxiously as Pompus blew a long breath of sweet-smelling
smoke into the air, followed by a smoke ring that wobbled and
expanded above the table. 'This is a sports centre, for Christ's sake.
You're not even in the smoking section.'

Pompus didn't hear him, or pretended not to. 'I've got it on
video if you want a copy. The coppers just gave me a bit of a
slapping round the back of the terrace, then told me to get lost. It's
the paperwork, you see. They can't be bothered nicking anyone,
it's too much like hard work. I was going to do it in the buff, but
for one thing it was chuffing freezing, and for another they wouldn't
have filmed it. You couldn't have my great donger swinging about
on national telly. Now that's what I call using your noddle. Hey,
did you see the goalie flinch when I went barrelling past him?
Thought I was going to cuff him or something, soft tatie.'

'What was the score?' Stubbs asked him.

'What?'

'What was the score, at the end of the match?'

'I don't know. Pompus one, Tony Football nil. Hey, did you see
that bit when the stewards brought me down? Took four of 'em.
Give someone an orange diddy-jacket and he thinks he's cock of
the shop, but it took four of 'em to pull down old Pompus. What
do you think about that, Widow Twankey?'

He blew a long stream of smoke towards Winkie, who turned his head and closed his eyes, trying not to breathe.

We were twelve or thirteen when Stubbs finally convinced us we should be smoking. 'But my supply's dried up, so we'll need another source.'

My father had an ornate wooden dispenser he kept on top of the piano. If you pulled out the sliding drawer at the bottom, it produced a single, slightly stale Senior Service. We lit the first one in the rhododendrons behind the bus shelter and passed it round, sucking at it and holding in the smoke. It didn't matter that it felt like waking up in a house fire, or that by the time it came round again the tab was soggy and warm. We were smoking, and it was about time, too. Then one day I pulled out the little wooden drawer and the slot was empty. There would be questions asked, probably at Christmas, when my father got tipsy and decided to 'flash the ash', as he put it. I'd have to let my brother take the blame – he'd left home, he wouldn't mind. But for now we had to find another source, which turned out to be Carol McCannon in the fourth year, a famous smoker at the time, who charged us for a pack of twenty and came back the next day with ten Consulate and no change. 'Call the police,' she shouted over her shoulder as she flounced off down the tuck-shop corridor. The cigarettes weren't bad, compared with Senior Service, that is. Not exactly like smoking a waterfall, as the adverts promised. More like chewing gum, or one of those menthol jobs you stick up your nose to clear your tubes. Later that year we tried smoking dried leaves and wood shavings in a pipe, with limited success. Eventually it was too much of a faff. God knows what kind of dedication you need to get really hooked. Pompus got the hang of it, but Winkie and Tony Football and me had quit before we'd even started.

Which was a pity for Stubbs. He'd just invested in a fancy cigarette lighter, one of those with a woman on the side in a blue bikini. When you turned the lighter upside down her clothes peeled away. She was totally nude apart from thick red lipstick and an ankle chain that gave out a glint of light. It was an interesting piece, though from my point of view it had two design faults. Firstly, you had to practically stand on your head to fully appreciate it, and who can appreciate anything with all that blood sloshing about behind the eyeballs. Secondly, there was something cheap and off-putting about the way she stood there, showing everything she'd got. If I'd designed that lighter, she would have moved her limbs as well, folded her arms in front of her chest and crossed her legs. That would have been more natural, more life-like in my opinion, and altogether less vulgar. That kind of thing might have been funny in the trenches, but not any more. Subtlety is the key – my father had said so on many an occasion.

Stubbs carried his flick knife with him at all times. He'd smuggled it back on a school trip to Paris, wedged inside a baguette. With his hand hidden up his cuff he was always clicking the catch and shooting out the blade. Like it was part of his body. As if it sprang from a secret groove in his wrist.

If we were ever bored, there was always the knife. Carving things, slashing things, throwing it at each other's feet. Like the time it landed in Winkie's trainer, right between his toes. We watched as he drew it out of his shoe, expecting a spurt of blood or the leather to turn slowly red. It didn't, but he fainted anyway.

One day I threw a dart in my brother's head. I was throwing to win. He was looking at the board, ready to add up the score, but the dart went straight into the crown of his head and stuck there. It must have lodged in a part of the skull where there aren't any nerves. He turned round and said, 'Come on, chuck it.' The dart was sticking straight up, the plastic flight like a tap or a key. When he looked back at the board I took a couple of strides towards him, reached up and plucked it out of his scalp. He would have killed me, if he'd known. My hand was shaking, and I missed the board completely with my next throw. Then Troy threw double-top to finish the game.

'Good arrows,' he said, congratulating himself. 'You should have finished me off while you had the chance, but you choked.'

So I'm a big believer in the idea that pain is all in the mind, and that you can feel pain even when there's no hurt, if you're expecting it. Like the trick with the fork. It was my idea – I'd read about it in a book. Winkie was on holiday, so it had to be Tony Football. Pompus was the more obvious candidate, but even if he was a dunce, he was too big for physical punishment. We pinned TF on his belly, then Stubbs got a fork and held it in the gas fire. It glowed orange, and threads of black smoked streamed from the prongs. He had to wrap his hanky around the handle as the heat travelled through the metal. Pompus held Tony's head, making him look at the fire. Then I pulled up his jumper, and Stubbs went behind him with the red-hot fork. 'Right there,' said Pompus, jabbing at a point between Tony's shoulder blades. 'Go on, right there.' Tony was screaming and thrashing about and we couldn't hold him much longer. Then Stubbs pushed the fork flat against Tony Football's skin, pressing it into the flesh. He let out an ear-splitting cry and lifted about ten feet into the air. Then he curled up in a ball and cried.

It was a joke. The fork was actually a cold one Stubbs had put in the freezer half an hour before. Tony saw the funny side of it. Eventually. But the next day, he pulled off his T-shirt to show us a mark on his skin. Four vertical stripes, angry and blistered and giving off heat. No doubt about it. It was a burn.

All this was going through my brain as I soaked in the bath, scooping water on to the sore, watching tiny red scabs bobbing around on the surface, thinking about the ink in my blood, green ink flowing through my heart and my veins. I patted the sore dry with toilet paper, then pointed the hairdryer at it to draw out the moisture. The hot, fierce air made it throb and sting.

I wore a loose shirt and slung my jacket over the other shoulder. They say they're addictive, tattoos. Have one and you'll want another, then another, till you run out of skin. Like sticking a needle in your veins. Even junkies who manage to clean up their act still spike themselves with an empty syringe every now and again. That's what I've heard.

*

The four of them were sitting in the bar when I arrived. I could feel the heat radiating from my shoulder, as if it were burning its way through my shirt.

'Well,' said Pompus. 'Did you get one, or did you chicken out?'

'What do *you* think?' I said.

'He got one all right,' said Stubbs. 'I can tell from the big grin on his mush. Come on, let's see it.'

I unfastened the top three buttons of my shirt and slipped it carefully off my shoulder, then turned slowly, showing them one at a time.

'What the fucking hellfire is that?' said Pompus. He came towards it with his cigarette and I jumped backwards, shielding it with my hand. Stubbs stood up, then they all crowded round, wanting to see. It looked like I was keeping a mouse in my hand or a small bird. I opened my fingers and they peered at the tattoo, which was moist again and hot. Small, rust-coloured specks stippled the surface, as if I were sweating blood. I dabbed at it with a serviette.

'It's the little green man. I designed it myself.'

'What else?' said Stubbs, lifting his drink to his mouth. 'Well, I think we can safely say that Barney's through to the next round, surprise, surprise.'

'It might be one of those stick-on ones,' said Winkie.

I looked at the bloody mess on my shoulder and then back at him.

'OK, maybe not.'

Tony Football came closer to inspect it. 'Are you sure you didn't just fall asleep on a frog?'

I sat down, leaving my shoulder bare, letting the heat escape and the blood dry. Minute by minute the tattoo was starting to heal, as if it had been embarrassment or anxiety that had caused it to swell and bleed. After half an hour it had calmed down, relaxed, no longer just a smear of green ink but a precise outline of form and shape, kind of perfect. When I flexed a muscle in my arm, it moved.

The conversation had gone quiet. I buttoned my shirt, screwed up the manky napkin and lobbed it in the ashtray.

'Being as how we're not playing football any more, why don't you all come to my place next Friday instead? How about eight o'clock?'

'What about my dare, aren't you going to give it me now?' asked Stubbs.

'Nah,' I said. 'It's one of those things you can do on the night. And I wouldn't want you chewing it over all week.'

I threw my jacket over my shoulder, walked through the automatic doors without breaking stride, and strolled into the cool of the evening.

10

Winkie went straight upstairs to the bathroom and came back down in his full football kit – shorts, replica shirt, even a pair of shin pads under his socks.

'All right, don't say it. Maureen thinks we're still five-a-siding and she's going to get suspicious if this stuff hasn't been worn. So just don't say it, all right.'

His shorts had been ironed. They had that sheen on them, and neat creases between the fancy trim on the sides.

'Won't she think it odd that you're not all sweaty and wet?' I said.

'Well, last week I splashed around a bit in the fish pond in the garden before I went in, and she didn't say anything. We've got three koi carp.'

'She's going to say something if you keep going home smelling of fish,' said Pompus, from behind the newspaper. 'Anyhow, what about the fact that you're not getting any fitter? She's only letting you play so you last a bit longer on the job – that's how women's minds work. If that belly of yours is still slapping around on top of her in a few months' time, there'll be questions. Outstanding questions.'

Winkie didn't rise to the bait. He sat on the edge of the settee with his hands on his knees, like a schoolboy in the changing rooms waiting to be told which team he was on. Tony Football and Stubbs arrived together, Tony carrying a four-pack of Kaliber in one hand and an umbrella in the other. Stubbs slapped Winkie on the thigh as he sat down next to him. I left them all yapping while I went downstairs to the cellar for glasses and drinks.

I once sent off for one of those 'improve your memory' things out of the newspaper. That Fifties-looking clean-cut chap in the advert with the sensible haircut and homespun smile. He'd been beaming from the bottom-right-hand corner of the front page for ever and ever but I'd never taken any notice. Then one day I thought, why the hell not, it's not like I've got anything better to do. Anyway, memory is genius. And, basically, you pay your twenty quid and they tell you it's all to do with numbers. For instance, when we were kids we played the tea-tray game. There's a dozen objects on a tea tray, covered by a towel. The towel gets whipped away for a minute, and the game is to remember as many items on the tray as possible. I was always poor at it. I'd remember the rubber duck and the pot dog, and maybe the ship-in-a-bottle if I was prompted, but after that – blank. The good-looking bloke in the advert suggested making a list, and imagining each item combined with an actual physical number. The rubber duck with the figure 1 impaled in its throat, like a fishing hook. And then the dog trying to mount the figure 2 from behind, then the ship with the 3 as an anchor, and so on. It was a strain at first, but I got quicker and better at it, and now I do it almost without thinking. When you tell a lot of stories, you need a good memory. What I mean is, you don't want to bore anyone by telling the same story twice.

I think it all forward in my head, play it out, run through the numbers, one to five. The exact wording of each question. Tone of voice. Possible answers. What I'd say if I were him. I put my hand inside my shirt and feel the little green man on my shoulder, comfortable now and at home. As if I'd be born with him. As if we were twins.

We sat around the table. It was like a board meeting, or a seance.

'I'm going to ask five questions and you've got to answer them truthfully and correctly, Stubbs. That's the dare,' I said.

'Sure,' he said, and crossed his arms and sat back in the chair.

'You don't want to knock it back, ask me five questions instead?'

'Fire away,' he said.

TF and Pompus and Winkie listened and watched, Pompus sticking his tongue into the neck of his beer bottle like an anteater,

Winkie in his football kit with goose bumps all the way along his arms, and Tony Football with his head cradled in his hand and his long, thin middle finger across his lips.

'What's your earliest memory?' I said.

Stubbs looked at me without any particular expression, then breathed in through his nose, filling his chest with air.

'A hot-air balloon coming low over the garden one afternoon,' he replied.

'Are you sure?'

'Yes, Barney. Unless, of course, you know better about my first memory, in which case I'm out of the game.'

'Just warming you up,' I said.

'Sure. Anyway, it was a blue one, in case you're interested.'

'Question number two. Three football teams that begin and end with the same letter.'

This time he bit the end of his tongue, and his eyes narrowed. 'English, or Scottish?'

'Whatever.'

'York City, Charlton Athletic, Dundee United.'

'Correct.'

'Celtic.'

'Yes, OK.'

'Northampton Town, Aston Villa.'

'Well, *you're* on the money tonight, aren't you, Stubbs?' I said.

'I am,' he answered, smartly. 'And that's your third question.'

I could have kicked myself – I'd walked straight into it. I had to rethink, quickly. Reformulate. Luckily, Pompus was laughing to himself. He'd pulled a dictionary out of the bookcase and was gazing into it like a dog looking down a rabbit hole.

'Listen to this. Merkin: a pubic wig, also known as St Peter's beard.' He laughed with his head back. I could see every filling in his mouth. 'Imagine that, a cunt-rug. Eh, Tone, you could use one of them on your head, mate, keep the cold out.'

Tony was very cool. 'I don't think I'd suit a centre parting,' he said.

It's the best way to deal with an insult, I reckon, to try it on like a big stupid dress, make a pantomime of the whole thing. I made a mental note of it, and laughed along until I'd gathered my thoughts.

'OK, question four. Have you ever been unfaithful to your wife? By which I mean sexual intercourse with another woman since you've been married.'

This time he was rattled. He cleared his throat and tugged on the elasticated neck of his sweatshirt, and I noticed a purple blotch at the base of his throat, like a rash, in the shape of South America. His Adam's apple moved mechanically under his skin.

'Is that the full extent of the question?' he inquired.

'It is.'

'Then the answer is "yes".'

Yes. I let the word dangle in the air.

'Who with?'

Stubbs pushed away the chair with the back of his knees and went into the kitchen. I could hear the sound of a glass being taken out of the cupboard and the tap running. Then he came to the doorway drinking the water, sipping at it first, then draining it in one long gulp. He was leaning on the door jamb, looking into the bottom of the glass.

'With Kim,' he said. Then he went back into the kitchen.

I could see the number 5 in my mind's eye, the actual number, like one of the letters in the Hollywood sign up on that dusty hillside. A big, solid number 5, with Kim sat on top, sitting on its crossbar, swinging her legs and waving.

I don't remember them leaving, but Pompus, Tony Football and Winkie had disappeared. In the kitchen, Stubbs was standing by the sink with his hands in his pockets and his eyes aimed at somewhere in the middle of the floor.

'I'm sorry. It was after you'd split up. I'm sorry.'

'Don't worry,' I said.

'It was only the once. It wasn't anything, really.'

'I know. Don't worry about it.'

He looked up at me now. 'How do you mean, you know?'

'She told me.'

'You knew all along?'

I nodded. He shifted his weight from one foot to the other, and made himself taller. Now he had something to come back at me with. Now he didn't have to look so damned sorry. 'You're sick, using that to try and catch me out. I thought we were friends, or supposed to be.'

The moral high ground was sliding around all over the place. Like playing chess in an earthquake.

'We *are* friends. That's why I brought it up, can't you see? I didn't want it hanging over us like a cloud. I didn't want it to come between us, and this was the only way I could think of to get it out of the way. It's just my way of saying there's no hard feelings.'

'Really?' he said, after a while.

'Really.'

I stuck out my right arm, and we shook hands. It was one of those moments. He wanted to talk some more, about Kim, but I closed my eyes and shook my head. The matter was closed.

I went to the door to see him out. After turning his car round in the drive, he wound his window down.

'You should have asked me the one about the three types of fish beginning with "k".'

'Go on,' I said.

'Killer shark. Kwik Save deep-fried haddock. And Kilmarnock.'

'Kilmarnock?'

'It's a place. Plaice – geddit?'

'Yes, very good.'

'I thought you'd remember. It was you that told me. See ya next week.'

He pomped his horn, then shot off along the road. I stood there for a while until the security light went out, leaving half a dozen moths flapping around in the dark, wondering what to do next.

II

There's always a decommissioned rocket launcher in the window, and somewhere inside a man at a desk reading a book, or playing solitaire on the computer. Nearly every town's got one. They're always the same.

A bell rang when I opened the door and the man looked up and nodded hello. I flipped through some of the magazines on the shelves, like I'd just walked into Lunn Poly or Argos. Glossy photographs of tanks churning up Salisbury Plain. Lads with acne troughing bacon and beans straight from the can.

'Can I help you, son? Why don't you take a seat?'

I plonked myself in the chair in front of the desk. He was drinking milky coffee from a yellow smiley mug, and a skin had started to form on the surface.

'I've been thinking of joining up,' I said.

'Excellent.'

Without standing, he spun round on his swivel chair and glided over to the water heater on the wall to switch it on. Then he glided back to the desk, taking a pen from behind his ear and pulling out a printed form from one of the drawers.

'If I could just take some details: name, address, date of birth.'

It took a long time because I had to spell everything. Also, he was wearing leather elbow-patches on his jumper, stopping his arm from sliding freely across the desk as he wrote.

'That's N-o-v-e-m-b-e-r.'

'Yes, thank you. And what makes you want to become a soldier?' he said.

'I don't know. I haven't really thought about it.'

He took a sip of his coffee, then had to lick the sticky membrane of milk out of his moustache. 'What qualifications do you have?'

'I didn't know you needed any.'

'Any TA experience?'

'No. I didn't even have an Action Man.'

He clicked the top of his pen three or four times. 'Have you come here to waste my time?'

The Singing Ringing Tree, Crystal Tipps and Alistair, The Tomorrow People, Barbapapa, Button Moon, Rentaghost, Vision On ('I'm sorry, we cannot return any of your pictures . . .'), Mr Benn ('Then, as if by magic, a man appeared.'), Bod . . .

'No. Sir.'

'Well then.' He leant towards me. 'If you want to sit in a muddy ditch for the rest of your life, taking orders from a big hairy sergeant, wiping your arse on dock leaves and eating toadstools, then I can probably sign you up right now in the warm-and-breathing category. But if it's something more rewarding you're after, something more ambitious, then you're talking about skill, years of training, and dedicated professionalism. Are those the kinds of qualities you think you have?'

Battlin' Tops ('It's all in the wrist action.'), Coppit, Etch A Sketch, Operation ('Sorry, Lawrence!'), Connect 5, Haunted House . . .

He was Scottish, especially now he was annoyed.

'Five O levels. Is that enough?'

'What subjects?'

'English, maths, art . . .'

'Art, eh? Well, if we ever need someone to camouflage the tanks we'll give you a ring. In the meantime, why don't you think about a job in a shoe shop or something, just until you're more sure about yourself. Know what I mean?'

The water heater had started to sing on the back wall, like one of those pedal organs in a country church.

'I wouldn't mind killing someone. I think I could do it.'

The anger in his face seemed to clear a little, and a calmer look came over him, sympathetic even. 'Look, son, if it was as simple as that, the army would be full to bursting, and I'd be out of a job. Why don't you take some of these brochures home and read them?

Take your time. We need people with cool heads, you know, and you seem to be in a bit of a mood.'

A couple of months later, I walked past the recruiting office again, but it had closed down. In the whitewash on the window someone had scratched that joke about joining up, travelling to foreign countries, meeting new and interesting people, and shooting them. I could see in through one of the letters. The rocket launcher had gone, and the desk and the shelves. There were just a few dozen magazines scattered on the floor, two big boxes sealed with brown tape, and the yellow smiley mug tipped on its side on the carpet, furry with mould. It didn't make sense. The army was still doing its stuff in half a dozen trouble spots across the world. It wasn't as if they didn't need anyone to die, all of a sudden.

I shivered a little bit, wondering why I'd gone there in the first place, wondering what the hell I was playing at. I was only nineteen at the time. You're not always accountable for your actions when you're nineteen, but it's no excuse. Lucky for me I'm not lying in a hole in a jungle, or dodging bullets in some nowhere town on the other side of the sea. Or wearing leather elbow-patches on a chunky-knit khaki jumper. Lucky I came round to seeing sense.

12

I was driving over the moor when they announced on the radio that Subbuteo was finished. About to be discontinued. There'd be a big fuss about it, pressure groups, petitions, protests by enthusiasts all over the country, and the picketing of the factory at Tunbridge Wells, of course. But these days if it doesn't come with batteries or computer graphics, the kids don't want to know. From now on, Subbuteo would join the likes of train sets and model buses as collectors' items or cult toys, gathering dust in the attics of over-grown schoolboys and immature dads. That's what they said. When I got home, I went straight into the loft and hauled the crate down the stepladders into the living room. It had that musty smell, like a shower curtain or water from a vase. The cardboard was ever so slightly damp. Pulling off the lid, I expected a big mess of mildew and mould.

Cleaning the house one day, mum rolled back the carpet and saw that three or four floorboards were crumbling away. They were shrunken and flaky, like polystyrene, and as we prodded and poked, a great cloud of rust-red dust billowed up from the floor. It got into all the kitchen units and under the sink and even into the oven. My father put on his reading glasses and sat with his head in the spiral-bound pages of the *Reader's Digest DIY Companion*, and had no hesitation in diagnosing dry rot. It was a classic case, and it was serious. There were frantic phone calls to the insurance and several heated exchanges. Finally, a team of builders arrived early one morning wearing breathing equipment and carrying pump-action spraying devices loaded with powerful fungicide. 'It's a cancer,' one of them mumbled from behind his mask. They cut out the rotten wood and removed it to a fire in the garden. They were looking for something called a 'fruiting body', which was clamped to the underside of one of the joists, a terrible fungus like an octopus, with brown and white tentacles and a big orange sac, pumping out its red seeds. It was taken away in a sealed plastic bag. But by this time the dust was everywhere. It didn't seem to bother the workmen that we were eating our dinner from plates covered in poison, or that the air we were breathing was heavy with the evil, microscopic spores. For years I had bad dreams about fruiting bodies.

So when I lifted the lid from the crate of Subbuteo I expected to find one, its roots and suckers clinging to goalposts and floodlights, strangling the little plastic men. I expected a huge waft of red seeds to mushroom into the air. But everything was perfectly preserved. A bit dusty perhaps, but everything stacked in order, neat and tidy, exactly as it had been left all those years ago. The crate itself was a heavy-duty Cape-apple box, Golden Delicious – 'deciduous produce of South Africa'. Inside, the Subbuteo boxes were still waxy and shiny, almost evergreen. It was all there: the grandstand, the terraces, the yellow balls. Then a load of stuff I'd completely forgotten about, such as the scoreboard, the spring-loaded throw-in figures 'for live-action realism', the Goliath-sized corner kickers, the 'continental-type' TV tower, like a gas platform, complete with a camera and cameraman, a monitor, and a highly muffled commentator seated on a packing case. A selection of advertising hoardings including 'Esso for happy motoring' and 'Mars are marvellous'. Two pitches: a well-worn thing gone ragged at the corners, and a brand-new one, still in its original packaging. From a two-ounce tin of St Bruno Ready Rubbed I tipped out the ref and his linesmen, flagging or whistling in their plum-coloured outfits, along with half a dozen balls of assorted colours and sizes, a manager wearing a brown trilby, a stick of tailor's chalk for re-marking the penalty spot, and, bizarrely, five miniature plastic deckchairs, possibly for fixtures at Brighton or Torquay. There were eight English teams: Villa, Man City, Ipswich, Spurs, Sunderland, Stoke, Newcastle,

QPR, and a ninth team I couldn't recognize, wearing all-white with red cuffs, red stocking tops and a single red stripe down the front of their shirts. Ajax? All in their 1:100 scale. All lovingly kept, with not a snapped neck or a bent arm or a dab of Copydex or blob of Blu-Tack anywhere to be seen. To the outsider it might have looked as if the set had never been played with, never used in anger. But a large folder backed with Anaglypta told a different story. I flipped through dozens of Silvine notebooks and jotters, yearbooks from many seasons of Subbuteo, crammed with results and fixture lists, hundreds of games, thousands of hours. The books were written in best joined-up writing, with illustrations of team colours in crayon and felt tip. In the back of one was a list of the various trophies up for grabs that year, including a silver christening cup (League Championship), a pewter bud vase (FA Cup), a German beer stein (European Cup), a car pennant in the shape of a plastic boot (leading goalscorer), and the World Cup itself, Subbuteo product C.119, the Jules Rimet trophy. Like a golden plastic angel in an evening dress holding a bird bath above her outstretched wings.

It was irresistible. I pushed back the settee and shook out the big, green cloth. It took an hour at least to put everything in place, but it seemed daft not to set the whole thing up, once I'd started. I stepped back when I'd finished. A crowd of eight men and a collie dog braced themselves for the televised clash between a serious- and starched-looking Spurs and the pyjama-suited, claret-and-blue men of Villa Park. As a final master stroke, I rigged up the flood-lights, yanked the curtains across and turned out the living-room light. It was beautiful, like a candlelit supper all laid out. The playing surface looked rich and lush under the tiny yellow bulbs. Beneath the brim of his hat the manager was deep in thought, and every player stood ready for the whistle, each one casting four crisp shadows in the shape of an X. Fantastic. I went to the kitchen for the camera, but while I was ferreting about in the drawer looking for a slow film, the phone rang. It was Kim. On her mobile. Some problem at work, blah, blah, blah, no other option, et cetera, et cetera, the long and the short of it being that she was on her way to the house right now and would I mind having Travis for a couple of hours? He'd already eaten but could I just entertain him until she picked him up later? About eight. Nine at the latest.

I didn't mind, did I?

'Course not. How could I?

The minute she dropped him off, all hell broke loose. He squatted on the kitchen floor, crouching with his elbows between his knees and his fingers interlocked above his head, covering his ears with his wrists. The only other people I've seen in this position are starving Ethiopians, hundreds of them, usually sitting beside a crusty river bed or an army tent, their huge eyes looking straight down the camera and out through the *Ten O'Clock News*. But they're silent and patient. Travis, in this mood, is frantic and noisy, and rolls his eyes upward, looking for a fly buzzing around in the top of his skull. Kim says he's scared, terrified even, which might be true. But to my way of thinking he's a boy as well, and boys are bad, sometimes. How do we know he isn't being a pain in the arse because he can't watch his favourite video, or goof around for five hours at a time with Thomas the Tank Engine and friends? You have to draw the line somewhere, right? So after half an hour of trying to calm him down, I decided to draw the line with a Milky Way choc ice, diet or no diet. Two minutes later he was sitting quietly in the corner with half of it around his mouth and the other half on the carpet. Poor little sod. I scratched my head for a while, wondering what to do with him once the sugar kicked in, thinking about his list of favourite things. Number one, videos. Number two, more videos. Equal third, chocolate and trains. Number four, water – either playing in the bath with a rubber duck and a plastic beaker, or throwing stones in the sea. I decided to kill two birds with one stone, fished out a pair of my old wellies from the back of the broom cupboard and slotted them on his feet while he was still up to his ears in ice cream. They were about two sizes too big, but everything was two sizes too big for Travis. He never looked dressed, more like he was dressing up. He had the knack of giving everything he wore the style and shape of hand-me-downs from an older brother. Coats were a particular problem. Like he'd been weighed for them rather than measured.

On the lane down to the woods he whimpered all the way, walking behind me and dragging his feet, until the farmer's scabby sheep dog came tearing out of its kennel, growling and spitting. After that he wanted to hold hands and stay as close as possible. His bottom lip trembled silently, and he kept looking back under my arm to check the dog hadn't got any further than the end of its chain. I lifted him over the style at the bottom of the field and he ran straight to the edge of the stream. I carried him across and plonked him down next to the high banking of shale and loose stones. He knew what to do. In the lap of his anorak he piled as many pebbles and rocks as he could manage, then waded into the water and began lobbing the stones into the heart of a shallow pool. The ripples slapped against his wellies. Stone after stone after stone, then back to the shore for more ammo, then back to the water. I scrambled up to the top of the banking and sat overlooking the stream, keeping one eye on him and gazing further off into the trees. I've seen badgers and foxes in there, and know of at least three places where owls are nesting. As kids, we sometimes went over to the next valley, to the secret stream. There was no path along the side, just overhanging birch trees and pussy willow. There was a car in one of the pools, a Cortina that had been rusting away for donkey's years. God knows how it got there because there are no roads, not even a cart track. But the roof of the thing made a good crossing point if you wanted to go up the other side of the valley and come out on the top road. Twenty years ago the woods were full of dens, tree houses, rope swings and the charred remains of campfires. These days, boys just sit at home and sulk. Still, all the easier for me to go roaming about the place without being pelted by stones or shot at with air rifles. And anyway you can't go around whinging about what children are like today. It makes you sound like an old man.

When I was eight, I came to the woods with my big brother, Troy. It was Christmas. We'd been sent by mum to gather holly. 'Get enough for a wreath for the door and some for the hearth.' She dropped a pair of secateurs into Troy's hands, and pushed us out of the house. I followed him down the path and into the trees, watching him slash at plants and bushes with a stick he'd found. He walked straight through the stream in his shoes, and turned round once or twice and told me to hurry up. Otherwise, I didn't exist.

There was one enormous holly tree at the top of the wood, absolutely on fire with bright-red berries. Troy flicked the safety catch on the clippers and began hacking at the tree, throwing sprigs for me to collect. Suddenly, a man came over the brow of the hill with a golden retriever jumping about at his feet. He was heading towards us, and looked pretty annoyed.

'What the hell do you think you're doing?'

He was wearing a waxed walking jacket and a flat cap. The dog bounded up to me and knocked me over, leaving dirty big paw prints on my new winter coat.

'Is there a problem?' said Troy, casually.

'I'll say there is. You can't just come and cut down the trees in this wood – it's vandalism. This is a nature reserve and these trees are protected. Don't you understand?'

The dog growled at Troy, but he stood his ground, squeezing the handles of the secateurs in his hand.

'But this is our tree,' he said.

'What on earth are you talking about, *your tree?*'

Troy looked at the ground. 'We had a little sister and she died.' He took off his bobble hat. 'Our parents planted this tree, in her memory. Every Christmas we collect a few cuttings. To remember.' He seemed to have finished talking. Then he said, 'I'm sorry.'

The dog sat down on its hind legs. It looked like one of those plastic Labradors with big eyes and a slot in its head for money.

'No, *I'm* sorry,' said the man, in a low voice. 'I'm so, so sorry. Please forget everything I said.'

He turned and clicked his tongue and the dog followed him until they were deep in the woods, out of sight. Troy lifted the clippers, like a revolver, and fired a pretend shot in his direction.

'Tosser,' he said, under his breath.

Following Troy back home, I ran alongside him with my arms full of prickly leaves and twigs.

'How did she die?' I asked him, looking up at his face.

'Who?'

'The baby girl.'

'Which baby girl is this, then?'

'You know. Our . . . sister.'

He roared with laughter. 'You mean *Holly*?' Then he roared again and pulled my hood over my head. 'Don't be an idiot. Next thing you'll be telling me you believe in Father Christmas.'

It was one of those days when everybody hates each other. Cutting back across the top of the dam, a man with a fishing rod started shouting at us from the far side. 'Don't you know this is private property? Can't you read?'

I thought Troy was going to answer him back. Instead, he unzipped his fly and pissed in the water. The urine steamed in the winter air. I threw down the holly and ran.

Travis was up to his knees in the stream by now, with water exploding from his welly tops every time he sloshed back to the bank. It took umpteen million years for those rocks to form, for the clay to flatten and dry and crumble under the weight of time. Argillaceous, fissile, felspathic; that's what they said about shale at school in physical geography – I can still see Mr Spackman in front of the pull-down world map, bending his tongue around the words. Argillaceous, fissile, felspathic; a squillion years to form that deposit on the bank, and less than an hour for one seven-year-old autistic boy to send it on its way downstream. I picked him up by his waist and slung him over my shoulder. The dog didn't bother us this time, which was just as well because I had to go back to look for one of Travis's boots, and found it floating in the pool, sole-up. At home I ran the bath, stripped him off and dropped him in. I threw in the duck and the beaker, and sat on the toilet seat for ten minutes or so, watching him fill the beaker with water and pour it slowly over the duck's head, making it bob up and down, diving and surfacing through the bubbles. Every time, Travis let out a little shriek of happiness, mumbled something to himself that I couldn't decode, then filled the beaker again. He could do it for hours, long after the water had gone cold, and didn't even try to drink the shampoo any more. I went downstairs to throw his clothes in the spin-dryer and the phone rang.

'Hello, son.'

'Hello.'

'What are you up to?'

'Actually, I'm looking after Travis for the evening.'

'Ah, that's good, that's nice.'

I think I miss my parents. On some level. But a couple of minutes into every conversation I find myself making excuses or resenting having to hold the receiver next to my ear for a second longer. Maybe the talk is always the same, maybe that's the problem. Same questions, same responses. My father going on about how 'sweet' the weather is over there, and showing an unhealthy interest in how many times it's rained in England. I bump up the meteorological damage, just to get him excited.

'Two inches in three hours last week. Biggest downpour since records began, they reckon.'

'Really, really.'

'Yeah, that pub in York by the side of the Ouse, the river was coming out through the chimney.'

'No! Nancy, just listen to this.'

Then mum comes on the phone, spends ten minutes talking about how clear the line is, how she could be 'just next door'. Followed by her famous, 'Any news?', meaning are you and Kim back together, has Travis made some miracle recovery, and has anyone died.

'No, no news.'

She prattled on for a while. I was half-listening and opening the post at the same time: the electricity bill; a catalogue from a DIY centre; a letter from the Community College – 'I hope we will see you again. Here are a list of courses you might be interested in. Very best wishes, Leonard Ainsley, Co-ordinator.' Then my father came back on and told me a story about a missing golf ball and a wild dog, and then we got cut off. I made a cuppa, and was just going back to the bathroom when I saw the trail of small, wet footprints leading from the bottom of the stairs to the living room. I burst in, expecting the worst. Expecting damage on a large scale. Imagining a kind of Subbuteo holocaust with Travis at the centre, pulling the head from the last man, jumping up and down on a pile of broken plastic limbs. Already I was wondering how to act, who to blame.

In the living room, the soft-yellow bulbs of the floodlights still shone from the four corners of the pitch. But the little footballers of Tottenham Hotspur and Aston Villa were no longer spread out across the field waiting for the kick-off. Instead, they formed one orderly procession from one penalty area to the other. And not only those two teams but the other seven as well, all facing the same way, all queuing in a perfectly straight line, with goal-keepers, spectators, officials, photographers and the manager taking their place in the pilgrimage. At the far end, Travis had stacked the grandstand on top of two blocks of terracing, making a sort of Arc de Triomphe. His face peered through the archway, sideways on, looking back down the column of miniature figures processing towards him, like people in the Bible being summoned to the palace of a great king. I believe I could have cried. The World Cup glowed on top of the grandstand, like the eternal flame.

I thought he was engrossed, far away in his thoughts and oblivi-ous. But he was asleep. I pulled the brand-new pitch out of its wrapping, folded the velvety, green oblong in two and draped it over his puny, naked frame. Then I went back to the kitchen to look for that film for the camera.

13

There was a scuffling noise outside, and the sound of the back door flying open. I jumped out of my chair, wondering what the hell was going on. Only Stubbs was calm and collected.

'That'll be Winkie,' he announced.

'How do you know?'

'Just a hunch,' he said. 'You see, I phoned him in the week to give him the dare. I thought he'd chicken out, but by the sound of things he's going for it.'

'What did you tell him to do?' asked Pompus.

'Kill something,' said Stubbs, flatly.

'Oh, what, like a fly or a spider? Good one, Stubbs.'

'Actually, Pompus, I did think of that, thank you.'

'So what does he have to kill?'

'Anything he wants, as long as it weighs more than two stone.'

'Oh, Jesus.' Tony Football's face started to curdle.

There was more banging and scuffling in the hall, then I heard the cellar door opening and the sound of something descending the steps at great speed. Pompus rushed into the hall, then stuck his head back into the living room.

'It's a sheep. He's got a fucking sheep. Oh my God.'

We listened to the noises under the floor. Squealing and bleating, then the sound of big, rusty tools spilling from the old chest of drawers, then wrestling sounds and the clattering of hooves on the stone floor. Then a couple of sharp thwacks, followed by several dull thuds. Then nothing. Pompus had been trying to give a running commentary by peering down the steps, but couldn't really see.

'Here he comes,' he shouted, and ran back into the living room and dived into a chair.

In his football kit and carrying a monkey wrench in his hand, Winkie emerged in the doorway, his glasses steamed over, sweat dripping from his chin.

'You underestimate me,' he said.

He threw the monkey wrench at Stubbs's feet, and where it bounced on the carpet I noticed a dab of dark, jammy liquid – blood. And there were fibres of blood-soaked wool stuck to the spanner end of the tool.

'I hope you're going to get rid of it,' I shouted at him as he turned to go.

'No one dared me to clean up afterwards, so FUCK RIGHT OFF.'

I heard the back door slam, and the sound of his car in the drive. Pompus went down into the cellar. He let out a wolf whistle that echoed against the walls and the steps, then came back up.

'That's one dead sheep down there all right. Credit where it's due. I wouldn't have thought he had it in him, but it just goes to show. Outstanding.'

'Is there a lot of blood?' I asked him.

'Lots of blood, lots of shit.'

'Look, I'm sorry, but I think I'm going to puke,' said Tony, holding his stomach. He followed Pompus towards the door, and before I could say anything Stubbs was out of his seat as well, and all three of them were leaving the house.

'Come on, fellers. For God's sake, give me a hand, even if it's just carting it back up the steps?'

Stubbs winked. 'Bad form, Barney, asking your guests to do the washing-up. See you next week.'

I kicked the door shut and sat in the kitchen for five minutes, wondering where to begin. I'm not squeamish by nature, but who wouldn't baulk at the thought of a dead sheep in the cellar with its brains stoved in and God-knows-what-else plastered all over the show? I got cleaning fluids and a bucket from under the sink and a couple of bin bags. First, I scrubbed the carpet in the front room and disinfected the monkey wrench, then smeared a dab of vapour rub on to a hanky and tied it around my face, covering my nose and mouth. Smell is the most disgusting of the senses; everything else is on the outside, but smell has a direct tunnel through the nostrils into the head or the lungs. That's the reason we're all losing our sense of smell – not because we don't use it, but because it's disgusting. I pulled on a pair of rubber gloves, and as a precaution dropped the latch on the back door. I didn't want anyone to come in and find me in this rig-out – Mrs Mop meets the Lone Ranger – and a dead sheep in the house. I'm pretty confident when it comes to telling stories or making excuses, but this would have been a tough call.

I backed my way into the cellar, cleaning one step at a time, sweeping the pellets of shit into a dustpan and wiping down with Jeyes fluid and hot water. When I got to the bottom, I took a big breath of air and turned round. I don't know what I was expecting to see – something white and fluffy with a bleeding head, I suppose. But this was a shock. For one thing, it was black. A black sheep. It was lying on its side, facing the wall. There was a small puddle of bilberry-coloured blood under its ear, and other spills and splashes on the floor and walls. And for another thing, it was real. Not a cartoon, not a soft toy, not a sheep on a hillside seen from a car. This was close-up, existent, an actual beast of flesh and bone with a curly black fleece. Right here in the house. It was warm. I could smell the warmth.

It could have been worse. That's what I had to tell myself. He could have killed it with the hedge clippers or even the chainsaw. I gritted my teeth, literally. Butchers have to deal with this kind of thing every day, for a job, including giblets and tripe and all kinds of innards, so why didn't I just pull myself together and get on with it. I swept the floor and mopped up. I put a newspaper under its head to soak up the blood, lifted it by the short stub of its horn, and jumped when its tongue lolled from one side of its mouth to the other. Its teeth were horrific, like fossils. I did everything I could not to look in its eyes and toyed for a minute with the idea of getting it into one of the bin bags. But the thought of its fours legs

63

poking through the black plastic was too ridiculous. Instead, I slipped one over its head and pulled the drawstring tight, which served the dual purpose of stopping it leaking, so to speak, and saving me from its stare. When it came to picking it up, it was hard work. A real lump. Dead weight, in the true sense. I would have tried the fireman's lift, but couldn't stand the idea of it on my shoulder, next to my face. Anyway, aren't these things riddled with ticks and lice? So I dragged it upstairs, its head knocking on every step, and laid it down in the hall for a moment while I thought about the next move.

It was a clear, summery night. I opened the back of the car. When I turned round, Mrs Szlachcic was standing by the gate with a shopping bag.

'Hallo, Barney, hhow arr you?'

There were hundreds of Poles in the town. Most of them had come over in the war and hadn't gone back. The north of England made them feel at home. They'd learnt just enough English to make it clear they weren't German, then called it a day. They had great-sounding names – Wawiocho, Węgrzyn, Szostak, Szydełko – but they'd given their kids English names like Carol or Gary or Dean, which I always thought was a bit lame. Dennis Zawacki – what does that mean?

I'd taken off the hanky face mask, thankfully, but was still wearing the rubber gloves. 'Hi. Just fettling out the car. You know.'

It seemed a perfectly reasonable thing to be doing. If she could be standing there with a shopping bag at half-nine on a Friday night, why couldn't I be cleaning the car? Free country, and all that.

'Zay hallo from yooz parentz to me in Zpain.'

'Portugal. Yes, I will. Goodnight.'

Back in the house, I turned out the security light, put on an old coat, then checked the road both ways before dragging the sheep into the drive and hauling it into the boot. I drove up to the edge of the moor and parked in one of the passing-places at the side of a deep gully. I'd seen dozens of dead sheep over the years, hit by cars in the fog, or taken out by lorry drivers for the hell of it. Everyone knows not to drink the hill-water around here, there's always a dead sheep a couple of miles upstream, not to mention car batteries and asbestos and a whole range of illegally dumped rubbish, all washed down with lashings of acid rain. One more old lonk wouldn't harm.

I hauled the animal out of the car on to the verge, but something wasn't right. It wasn't dead. The plastic bag on its head was moving in and out, like a lung, and both of its back legs were jerking and flinching. It was alive.

Occasions like these are a test. It would have been the easiest thing in the world just to roll it down into the ditch, leave it bleeding to death. But sometimes a person has to look into himself, see if he's got what it takes to go the whole way. Every problem is a challenge, every obstacle an opportunity – that's what they say. Of course, technically speaking, it meant that Winkie was out of the game. But what could I do? Drive over to his place before it really croaked? Get Maureen out of bed in her curlers and dressing gown? I'd need to show the others as well, by which time the creature could be a pool of dead, festering goop in the back of my motor. I thought about twisting its neck – I'd heard stories about finishing off a sheep by twisting its neck. Or was that chickens? But it wasn't the time or the place to be sumo-wrestling with a dying sheep. I made a positive move. I went to the car, came back with the tyre lever, and cracked the thing three times on the skull. One, two, and three. Done. I pulled off the bag, shot a glance at its cold, motionless eye, and kicked it into the shale gully. Argillaceous, fissile, whatever. Who says I wasn't cut out for the army?

It still isn't ten o'clock and I don't feel like going back to the house. I want some time, some air. I lock the car and set off walking on the other side of the road, over the top of the old quarry and up to the summit of the hill. There's no breeze at all. I sit in my T-shirt at the highest point, looking down on the lights of the town, and the masts on the other hills with their cherry-red warning lights, and the headlights travelling across moorland roads in the dark. Cars circling the ring road, the motorway disappearing to the east, strange-coloured smoke pouring out of the chimneys of the dye-works and the chemical plant. I sit here for an hour. It's peaceful, and anyway there's nothing else in the entire rest of the world I'd rather be doing.

14

It was June. Flaming June, although that phrase must have been coined before the weather started going stupid. It's just one long season now as far as I can tell, a bit colder at Christmas and a bit warmer in the holidays, and wet most of the time. Maybe if I had a proper job with regular hours I'd notice the nights drawing in or blossom on the trees or the street lamps coming on earlier or the clocks going forward and all the rest. But it blends together when you've got nothing to measure it against. It's all one.

Kim was very big on saying when it was summer and when it wasn't. I don't mean she wrote to *The Times* in March if she heard the first cuckoo. For her, it was all about clothes. She was the only person I'd ever met who had two completely separate sets of clothes. As soon as the thermometer got over the sixty mark, all the big coats and woolly jumpers went into a chest of drawers and wardrobe in the spare room, and out came boxes of shorts and skimpy tops. It didn't matter if we had an inch of frost the next night; from that point on it was summer, and that was that. Of course she never *wore* any of those clothes, some of them being *at least* five months out of fashion. They were just a prompt, to remind her to go straight to Leeds or Manchester, and kit herself out in the latest gear. The principle, as far as I could tell, was to spend the most amount of money on items containing the least amount of fabric. I didn't mind. I'm not a skinflint, and anyway she'd put on a little fashion show when she came home, getting changed in the kitchen, then strutting through the front room, showing off her legs and her breasts, swishing her hair from one shoulder to the other.

Kim had a great body. Even after she'd had Travis. She was

always tanned and always slim – took after her mother. If you're thinking of asking someone to marry you, a good piece of advice is to look at the mother. That's what they say, and I reckon it's true. I'm not sure if it works the other way, if the woman is supposed to look at her boyfriend's father before she walks down the aisle. She couldn't have looked at mine.

It was flaming June, without the flames. Everything was shaping up nicely. Every Friday we met at my place, eight o'clock prompt, and got on with the business in hand. It was a regular event, a fixture. Almost a tradition. The second round of dares was pretty tame by comparison. Maybe everyone needed a breather after the dead sheep, or they were scared of things getting totally out of control. Or maybe they were just enjoying themselves for a change, and didn't want it to end.

Winkie dared Tony Football to break the law. He zoomed off on his bike and came back an hour later waving a speeding ticket in his big, leather gauntlets. Tony Football dared Pompus to get a job, and by the following Thursday he was digging graves at the Parish Church, a pile of dirt on one side and a four-pack on the other. By Saturday he'd resigned. 'Three pound an hour? Didn't even pay for the ale, and it's thirsty work, shovelling. I told his holiness he could bury his own stiffs for that price and stick his three measly quid where the sun don't shine. I'm going to be cremated, me, when I go.'

'That's a relief,' said Winkie. 'They'd need a hole like Gaping Gill to drop you in.'

Pompus shook up his can of Stella and exploded it in Winkie's ear. 'Tell your Maureen you went out drinking with the lads. She'll cream you.'

When it came to my turn, Pompus dared me to do something so crafty and underhand, I couldn't believe he'd thought of it himself. There was a girl from school called Patricia Cramm, or 'Cramm the Man' as she was known, on account of her hairy arms and hairy legs and moustache. Everything about her was masculine, even the way she walked, striding around the school in her size elevens, like a sergeant. Rumour had it she'd had 'the op'. Or she was German. Either way, she became more of a man with every term. By the end of the fifth year, her name was 'Bloke'. Nothing more or less. Just Bloke. Bloke by nature, Bloke by name. They say children are cruel and honest, but they never say how razor sharp they are, not blunted by age and ideas. Or maybe they do, and I just wasn't listening.

'Anyhow,' said Pompus, 'Turns out she's started work in the library, with my mother, stacking books and what have you. So I want you to cop off with her this week. Simple as that.'

'Brilliant, Pompus. And you thought of that all by yourself, did you?'

He said he did, but out of the corner of my eye I could see Stubbs keeping quiet, sitting still.

'What does copping off involve, precisely?'

'Do you want me to draw a picture?'

'Are you saying I've got to sleep with her?'

'Sexual intercourse, that's what he's saying,' said Stubbs. 'You've got to get her to *stamp your card*, Barney, let her *check you out*.' He slammed the side off his fist on the arm of the chair, and made a clicking noise with his tongue.

I was trying to process it all, run it as a sequence, the way astronomers predict the end of the universe with models and numbers, put the whole lot into a computer programme and press the button. At that moment, all I could see was a big black hole with me and Bloke in the middle of it. I could knock the dare back to Pompus, but it wasn't hard to imagine him sauntering into the library and asking her out, especially with his mother working there. Could he really get her into bed, though? In a week?

'Whose dare is this, anyway?' I said to Stubbs, playing for time.

He folded his hands over his head and leant back in the chair. 'Well, pardon me for speaking. Sorry for breathing.'

I smiled at Pompus. 'Fine, fine. But are you sure you know what you're saying, Pompus? Because if I bounce this back to you you're going to have to sleep with that thing, or you're out of the loop. Do you understand? You're going to have to put it where most people wouldn't put a walking stick, or you can kiss goodbye to three-quarters of a million pounds. And let's face it, Pompus, no offence, but you're not exactly pin-up material yourself, and as ugly as she most certainly is, there's just an outside possibility that she might not fancy you. Do you understand, my friend? I just want you to make sure you know what you're saying before I make my mind up, because I'm not sure you've really thought this through. In your own head. Do you read me, friend?'

It was quite a speech. It's amazing what comes out when it needs to. Like in the war.

'Well, er, I'm not saying that you've got to completely fuck her and all that.'

Stubbs was out of his seat now. 'Oh come on, blockhead, don't let him off the hook. Stick it to him while you've got the chance.'

I saw a chink of light, light at the end of the tunnel, sunlight at the far side of the black hole.

'Blockhead, eh? Well, Pompus, are you going to rise to the bait, or have you worked it out? Because it seems to me it's *your* funeral that clever Mr Stubbs is plotting. Not only that, he's getting you to make the coffin as well.'

'I know what I'm doing,' he blurted. 'It's my dare, and if I say he doesn't have to fuck her, he doesn't have to fuck her, all right? A snog and a feel, and a bit of stinky pinky, OK? That's all I meant.'

Stubbs turned away and let out a huge sigh. Defeat, masquerading as disgust.

'What's stinky pinky?' said Tony Football, who'd been quiet up to then.

'Smelly finger,' said Winkie. 'Isn't it?'

I didn't even have a library card, which turned out to be lucky in the end. I read a lot, non-fiction mainly, or magazines. I think of it as reference work, so I keep all the stuff in case I want to look things up. That's the major problem with libraries, as far as I can see, having to take books back. It's like handing over your memory.

Pompus's mum was at the returns desk when I went in. She pointed me towards the inquiries hatch, and after I'd rung the bell a couple of times, a tall woman with black hair and a grey woolly jumper popped up from under the counter.

'Sorry, I was just changing the floppy.'

She was a couple of inches taller than me – big for a woman. Her voice was deep and an unmistakable baritone, although, when I looked closely at her, she had none of the facial hair I remembered from school, and her features had softened. Maybe she was wearing heavy make-up, or she'd had electrolysis or some kind of hormone treatment. Maybe she shaved.

Before she retired, mum had worked for years as a receptionist in a surgery, answering the phone, making appointments, and filling in forms. She was sworn to secrecy, but every now and again couldn't help telling us about some of the weirdoes whose case notes fell open on her desk. There was one poor chap who couldn't stop his hands sweating. Even if he just stood there doing nothing, sweat would drip from the ends of his fingers, and if he turned his hands upwards, a pool of perspiration gathered in each palm. It wasn't funny. He couldn't read a book without it disintegrating in front of his eyes. Holding hands with his girlfriend was out of the question. It was a social handicap. Eventually he had an operation, a trans-thoracic sympathectomy. They injected poison into his armpits, and bingo, he was cured overnight. My father was always very scathing about mum's stories, possibly as a way of telling her off for leaking professional secrets.

'This "sympathectomy", did he have it on April first, by any chance?'

Another of mum's indiscretions involved a woman suffering from fish-smelling syndrome. An actual condition, apparently. 'And she sits there in reception, and after five minutes the whole place smells of haddock, poor love. She's a good-looking girl as well.'

Something genetic in the glands, apparently. Mum went on to

say how there was no cure for fish-smelling syndrome, and how the woman was condemned to a lifetime of strong perfume and several baths a day.

'She could always go and live in Grimsby,' was my father's concluding comment on the subject.

'Donald! And you a medical man as well.'

It was a ticking off but also a compliment, and whenever she passed that comment he visibly swelled with pride. Because, in truth, he was only a dentist.

Bloke told me I'd have to bring in some proof of address and ID if I wanted a new computerized card.

'Don't you recognize me from school?' I said, smiling, trying to open up the conversation. She grunted at me and her face dropped. I'd taken a wrong turn.

'You're Patricia, aren't you?'

She looked surprised and nodded. I smiled again, and this time she smiled back.

I'm not proud of myself, doing what I did that week. Sarnies in the park that lunchtime, a sticky bun at the Tudor Rooms on Tuesday teatime, a drink after work on Wednesday, a curry on Thursday, and a film on Friday, followed by a drink, followed by, 'Do you fancy coming back to my place for coffee?' I felt like Solomon Grundy on speed. Bloke must have known there was something dodgy going on. She was pretty smart, and let's face it, I'm no Prince Charming. But I sensed a kind of resignation, a what-the-hell attitude. It's a small town and nothing much happens. So when a feller turns up on Monday lunchtime and asks you out and you're thirty-six and a junior librarian, where's the sense in saying no? You could wash the colour right out of your hair staying in every night in a town like this.

So I'm not proud. True, I get a kick out of fun and games, but this felt seedy. Like I was a conman, like one of those bogus social workers who turns up on the doorsteps of the poor and ignorant and waltzes off with their kids. If it had been up to me, the dares wouldn't have gone any further than the five of us. But someone else had been dragged in now, and it was a shame. It was Stubbs's fault. Some people don't know where to stop.

We sat in the kitchen for a couple of minutes staring into our cups. I'd avoided talking about school all week and now I'd run out of things to say. She had nothing to say to me, either. It was just a question of going through with it, having got this far. For both of us. We could have been two strangers waiting for a bus in the rain. I leant over, pushed back her hair and kissed her on the cheek. She rested her face against mine and I put my arms around her shoulders. They were big shoulders. Now we were two brothers after a funeral, saying how sorry we were. I kept thinking of Kim, not because she was the last person I'd been with or even kissed, but to block out the image of the woman in front of me, in her baggy school jumper and clod-hopper shoes, marching from one lesson to another, barking out the hymns in assembly. I took her hand and led her up the stairs. There was an atmosphere of despair now, even dislike, but no reason to stop, not for me, and apparently not for her either. On the bed, I put my hand inside her shirt.

'You've got an autistic son, haven't you?' she said.

'Yes.'

'What's his name?'

'Trav – Travis.'

'You probably think this is my first time, don't you?'

'No. No, I don't.'

Mousetrap, Frustration, Cluedo, Risk . . .

She knelt up on the bed, pulled the bottom of her shirt out of her jeans and over her head, clipping the lampshade, bringing down dust and fluff that drifted between us, past our eyes. I kept on looking at her face. Then it was my turn. I kicked off my shoes, took off my T-shirt. I didn't know what she was staring at until she put her hand against the tattoo and traced the outline with her finger.

'What is it, blue?'

'Green.'

'It's good.'

Her hands disappeared behind her back as she undid her bra, and I pulled her towards me, to look beyond her, over her shoulder. I could feel the goose bumps on her skin as I moved my hands along her arms.

Ludo, Spirograph, Battleships, butterscotch, aniseed twists, pear drops, liquorice laces, Camberwick Green, The Flintstones, Reginald Mole-husband – 'the safest parker in town'. 'And Charlie got something he liked, too . . .'

I felt her tugging at my trousers, picking off the metal buttons one by one.

'I've got . . . contraceptives,' I said, like an idiot.

She nodded. I rolled over to the far side, and with one hand on the floor lifted up the trailing duvet cover and peered under the bed. It was dark, but not dark enough to hide their stupid mugs, their four upside-down faces: Winkie, Tony Football, Pompus and Stubbs, like pigs in a butcher's window, with their tongues hanging out and their eyes bulging. I glared at them.

'Ring it,' I hissed.

Stubbs shook his head and pressed a packet into my hand.

Bloke was lying on her back with her arms at her side. My eyes strayed from her face, but carefully, vertically, down her throat and her breastbone, and further, to a line of hairs that ran from her belly button to the top of her jeans. I took my time opening the orange-and-white packet, fumbling on purpose. Tasty Ticklers: peaches-and-cream flavour. When I tore the foil, a smell like tinned fruit-cocktail escaped into the room. Tinned fruit, and Carnation. Sunday tea at my grandmother's. The condom itself smelt worse, like children's medicine mixed with powdered milk. I fiddled with it, pretending I couldn't find the end, holding it up to the light to see if it was inside out. I was shocked, truly shocked, when she took it from me and put it to one side. Then she leant forward, and kissed my tattoo, and my chest, making her way down my body towards my half-open fly. With her fingers, she parted her hair in front of her face and pushed it behind her ears. I could see the white of her scalp on the crown of her head. I watched her thumbs curl through my belt hoops, one at either side. Dust hung like plankton under the glare of the bulb. The smell of rubberized fruit was thick and gooey in the air. I closed my eyes and held my breath. One more second and it was plan B, and there wasn't a plan B. It was now or never. A photo finish. The nick of time. Right down to the wire.

Although . . . nobody's life was at stake, exactly. That has to be said. *I watch the curve of her spine, arching away between her shoulder blades to the small of her back.* It wasn't as if I was tied to the track with the Flying Scotsman bearing down at full steam. *And the vertebrae, like drumlins, like the swell of the sea. And her skin, the flesh of another, close enough to touch and feel.* Not as if I was lashed to a stake with flames biting my heels. There was no firing squad taking aim, no ten-ton weight hanging by a thread. So what if the cavalry didn't come piling over the hill? It wasn't the Alamo, for God's sake. It wasn't Dunkirk. It wasn't Custer's Last Stand.

'What the hell's that,' she said, sitting up, banging my chin with the top of her head.

There was a high-pitched wailing noise, a sort of muffled screaming coming from my groin. I stuck my hand into my trouser pocket, pulled out the bleeper, and turned it towards the light.

'You're not going to believe this,' I said.

'What is it?'

'A call-out. Shit, I'm sorry, I've got to go.'

'What sort of call-out? You're not in the fire brigade, are you?'

'No, it's plumbing, 24-hour service. Must be a burst pipe.'

She covered herself, bringing her knees up in front of her chest and folding her arms across her legs.

'In summer?'

'Yes. They dry out.'

How crap did that sound? I was ready for a big scene, expecting to get my face slapped, or punched in the mouth with those big fists. But she swung her feet to the floor, pushed her bra into her bag and did up the buttons of her shirt. I followed her downstairs into the kitchen, where she poured herself a glass of water from the tap, took two or three sips, then emptied it down the sink and walked out of the house. I stood at the door pretending to be putting my boots on and getting into my coat. She was very dignified, I thought. Very noble, a good loser.

'Shall I call you?' I said.

She looked up at me from under her fringe, just for a moment, then closed her car door and started the engine. It was in gear and lurched forward and stalled. But she didn't panic, just dropped it into neutral, fired it up again, eased back with the clutch and moved off smoothly into the road. In her diddy Nissan Micra she looked bigger than ever, like Noddy driving into town. I felt like a pig. But that was on the inside. On the outside I was jubilant. Victorious.

The four of them were rolling around on the bed, just about puking with laughter.

'I thought you were never going to set that bleeper off, you bastards.'

'You seemed to be enjoying it so much, we didn't want to spoil the moment, didn't want to spoil your tea!' said Stubbs, producing the condom packet, shaking it at me.

'Did she have a hairy chest?' said Pompus.

'She had hairs where no woman should have hairs,' I said.

'Where's that, then?'

'On her balls.'

Like all the old jokes, it was the best. 'On her balls,' somebody would say when everything had gone quiet, and the laughing would start again. Mad, funny-farm laughing. I was laughing too, but I couldn't stop thinking. I was thinking about Bloke. About her mother. About her father as well.

The following week, I dared Stubbs to swim across the mill dam, and he walked it. He's a strong swimmer, very powerful in the upper body. The dam's full of all sorts of rubbish, the kind of place where people go to drown puppies. I wouldn't have fancied it, myself. But this was a gift, a gimme.

*

He emerges on the other bank, weed round his neck, hair slicked back over his head. He shivers and smiles. I pass him the towel and say, 'Well done', put my hand on his shoulder.

I knew he could do it, he knew I knew he could do it, I knew he knew I knew he could do it, and so on, but sometimes you've got to make sacrifices. We were coming up to the holidays, and the dares were going to be put on hold for a few weeks. Conceding a goal just before half-time can be a big psychological blow, and I didn't want to spoil anything, not when we were laughing like drains.

15

Same window, same café. Travis was in the car, head back, snoring.
There is such a thing as a time loop, but you don't need to travel
through space to fall into one. I ordered the usual coffee from the
counter and sat in the same chair. I was late, ten minutes, the usual.
Kim filled me in about Travis at school, various reports and tests. I
was watching the waitress making the cappuccinos, wondering
how she didn't burn her hands with all that super-hot steam blasting
out all over the place. If there are European laws about the correct
size of a pint, or how yellow a banana can be before it becomes a
hazard to the naked eye, how come nothing's been done about
scalding jets of vapour exploding left, right and centre in public
eating houses?

Kim had lit up. She used to hold her cigarettes as far away as she
could, as a courtesy, but the smoke always came curling back over
her shoulder towards me, circling my head like clouds round a
mountain. Like now.

'How's your love life, Barney?'

'All quiet on the Western Front,' I said.

'That's not what I've heard.'

I stirred my coffee and tasted a teaspoon of froth from the top.
'Go on.'

'Patricia, is it? Someone you knew from school?'

Monopoly, Totopoly, Scrabble . . .

'Christ Almighty, can't a person do anything around here? Who
told you that?'

'Just a rumour I heard. You know, idle gossip.'

'Not just idle, bone-bloody-lazy, if you ask me.'

'Well, it's certainly rattled your cage,' she said.

I thought about storming off to the toilet in a huff, but just in

78

time remembered a line of my father's, about protesting too much. Shakespeare, I think.

I laughed. 'Patricia Man, if you must know. She was collecting for Christian Aid. It was raining. She came in for a coffee and left twenty minutes later with ten bob in a small red envelope. Why, do you know her?'

'No. She went to your school, not mine.'

'Well, if you did, you wouldn't be accusing me of whatever you're accusing me of. She's the missing link. I only asked her in because I felt sorry for her, poor cow.'

'OK, I'm sorry . . .'

'And so you should be. The woman does voluntary work for starving Africans and suddenly all the tongues in town are wagging. It's a disgrace, it really is.'

There was no answer to that. As an argument it had everything, even God. Kim looked suitably embarrassed.

'I'm sorry, OK?'

'Forget it.'

'What did you say her name was?'

'Patricia Cramm.'

'You called her Man.'

'When?'

'Just now.'

'Did I? Well, if you'd seen her, you'd know why. Christ, give me some credit. I'm not that desperate.'

Kim went for another drink, then brought Travis in from the car. He lolled around on her knee, mumbling and singing, and staring at the big oriental fans on the ceiling.

'He's had his medicine, then?'

She nodded. 'I feel bad sometimes, like it takes all the sparkle out of him, but I can't cope otherwise. At least this way I get my own life as well. I can't think straight when he's hyper – he's like a whirlwind.'

'It's speed, isn't it?'

'Ritalin. It's an amphetamine.'

'So how come it slows him down?'

'It makes him concentrate.'

'I read in a magazine that loads of kids in America just take it as a matter of course, to help them with their exams. You know, just normal kids.'

She looked daggers at me. 'Normal kids? Not a freak like ours?'

I stuck around for a few more minutes, then drained my cup and made an excuse to leave. I'd just slipped my arm through the sleeve of my jacket when she said, 'Barney, what would you say if I told you I was pregnant?'

I sat down again. She was looking at me from behind Travis, kissing the back of his head, peering around the side of his ear – a human shield.

'I don't know what I'd say. What do you think I should say?'

'I don't know. You're still my husband, aren't you, technically? I thought you'd want to know.'

'Well, I suppose it's your business, isn't it?'

'Yes.'

In life, there are times when you just can't help yourself. Chemicals and electricity react in your body, telling you how to feel. You put a piece of foul-tasting cheese in your mouth and straightaway you want to heave. Someone cuts in front of you on the ring road, and you feel like hitting the horn with both hands and screaming words that would make a soldier blush. You listen to a sad song, and tears start queuing up behind your eyes, or someone cracks a joke, and a great big laugh begins to stir in your belly, like an oil well ready to blow. It's instinctive, a kind of animal response from way down in the guts, right in the pit of the stomach, where all the threads are tied. Not the heart, though, that's just a muscle for pumping blood. I don't believe in the heart as the centre of emotion, not since mum drew me a diagram on the back of an envelope. It took the magic away. Some chap at the surgery went in for a heart transplant, and donated his old one to a medical museum. Imagine that, seeing your own heart in a glass cage. The week after, she showed me a picture of it, covered in fat like a battered meatball,

all yellow and horrible. There was even a wire sticking out from a pacemaker that hadn't worked. Don't tell me a lump of gristle like that is the thing you love somebody with. Or, if it is, maybe that explains everything.

Chemicals and electricity react, telling you how to feel. But you've got to bite your lip, swallow your tongue, grit your teeth. You've got to keep both hands on the wheel.

'Whose is it?'

'I don't know.'

'I see.'

'No, you don't. Because it's not mine either.'

She put Travis down on his feet, and he wandered into another part of the café to fiddle with the dials on an old radio set. It was a theme café. The theme was the past.

I must have looked like I'd just fallen off a Christmas tree. I'm pretty good at getting the drift, as a rule, but, to be perfectly honest, I hadn't a clue what she was talking about. Not the foggiest.

'Look, Barney, I've thought this through, so let me explain it to you. I want to be pregnant again and I don't suppose I've got that much time left. Being pregnant – it's wonderful, special, like being famous. When I was pregnant with Trav I used to talk to him and touch him. Even when I was on my own I was never lonely. Well, I want that again, but I don't want another child. I couldn't cope, for one thing, and I never want to compare Travis with somebody else. And, if I'm completely honest, I'm scared to death of having another one the same, another autistic son or daughter. That would kill me, thinking it was all my fault. Do you hear what I'm saying?'

I could hear what she was saying all right, but it didn't stack up. What was all this about it not being hers? I was flummoxed.

'You're not that old,' I said.

'Don't kid yourself. We're older than you think. A lot older, Barney.'

She always put my name at the end of the sentence when things were serious or when she was being sincere. She'd learnt it on a marketing course.

'There are people out there who can't have babies, who need help. Science, it's changed everything.'

'So whose baby is it, then?'

'I don't know. Somebody's egg and somebody's sperm, mixed together in a test tube.'

She went round the corner to collect Travis, who was making a nuisance of himself with some other customers. The waitress smiled at us, pretending she wasn't annoyed.

'So you didn't have to *go* with anyone?'

'No. Look, I've brought you all the literature and some articles. Why don't you take them away and read them?'

'I don't think so. Like I said, it's your business.'

I zipped up my jacket, ready to go.

'It's your business as well. You're Travis's father.'

'How does that come into it? Tell me if I've got this right. You're having a baby, but it's nothing to do with you. So it's nothing to do with Travis, either. So it sure as shit isn't anything to do with me. You're just keeping it warm for nine months, right? Well, if you really want to know what I think, I think it's bloody weird. I think you're bloody weird. It's just about the stupidest thing I've ever heard. What if you want to keep it?'

'Why would I want to? It isn't mine. Anyway, I've signed a contract.'

'For money?'

'Yes, there is some money involved, and let's face it, I could use it, and so could he.'

Travis was standing by the door, tugging at the handle. The tears had started.

'Mimmy's car, mimmy's car.'

Kim lifted him up and he hid his face in her shoulder. 'All right, sweetheart, we'll go to mummy's car in a minute. Look, he's upset now. He thinks we're arguing.'

'WE ARE ARGUING.'

Kerr-plunk, Twister, Buckaroo . . .

I walked around the town centre for an hour or so to cool down, looked through the windows of the second-hand shops, saw poor people trying on jackets and shoes. Watching poor people doing sad things is always a good idea if you're upset or annoyed. It takes the heat out of it, brings things into perspective. I also made a couple of promises to myself. One: never to go back to that stupid café as long as I live, with its great hot bursts of steam and useless fans on the ceiling. And two: never be surprised by what people do. People are strange. It takes a long time to work that out, but, once you've got it into your thick skull that people are pretty damned peculiar, you'll never be shocked when they tell you they're running away to join the circus, or they're made out of flaky pastry, or thinking of having their brain pierced. That way you'll be ready for it. That way you won't get hit.

Yeah, Buckaroo. If there was ever such a thing as a one-trick pony, I said to myself, that was it.

16

There were five of us. Me, Pompus, Winkie, Tony Football, and Stubbs. Did everything together, went everywhere. All lived in the same part of town, all went to the same school. All the same age just about, except for me being a year older. Did everything together, went everywhere.

I was fifteen. It was the holidays, so it rained. Two months of no school stretching out in front of us, and already we were bored. We were playing cricket on the old shunts, where the railway sidings used to be, and as I hacked the toe of the bat into the cinders to make a crease, something dirty and green worked loose and showed itself. I picked it up, spat on it and rubbed it clean on my jumper. There he was, the little green man, some fancy kind of stone carved in the shape of an old bloke in a long robe with a ball in his hands.

Pompus and Winkie and Tony Football and Stubbs huddled around, and straightaway we said he was good luck, said he was a god, and it was bad luck to mess him about, to go against him. If you lost him you'd probably die.

'He can get in your head, tell what you're thinking,' I said.

'All swear on the little green man,' said Stubbs.

And Pompus said we should do it properly, with blood. So we sliced our thumbs with the knife and made one big fist with our hands, with the little green man in the middle, his shiny head poking out above the bloody knot of knuckles and flesh.

And the way it went, to take possession of him and keep him, you had to do a dare. It started with Pompus and the frogspawn, then Stubbs nicking the johnnies, then Tony Football walking the graveyard at midnight under a full moon. Then it went mad. Hoax calls to the fire brigade and the plod. 'FUCK OFF' in green spray-paint on the church door. Pompus trying to pierce his ear with no anaesthetic except an ice cube, stabbing the lobe again and again with a compass and not even flinching. The hen hut we burnt at the side of the moor – hens coming flying out with their feathers on fire. Tony Football pouring a pound bag of sugar into the petrol tank of a car – his dad's. It's unbelievable what some people will do when they have to, when they've got something to prove. Then it went pop. Somebody blabbed. Winkie got whisked off to Butlin's with his family, Stubbs got an arseholing from his stepdad. And me and Pompus and TF all got an eight-o'clock curfew and no buts. And that was that, which was just as well, because it had all gone mad.

Twenty years ago, that was, give or take a month. So he's mine. Belongs to me. Mine by right. Probably. Finders-keepers, as they say. Possession being nine-tenths of the law. He was mine at the end, just as he was mine at the beginning, when he came to light out of the earth. Suddenly there he was, green, solid, miraculous, as if from nowhere. He's amazing. And almost unscathed, considering. But when you've been in existence for several hundred years, a summer of being passed from one set of grubby paws to the next is pretty insignificant, I suppose.

I look closely at him, see things I've never noticed before. The folds of his gown. The thick, wedge-shaped shoes poking out underneath, like plat-forms or big clogs. His delicate, thin-fingered hands clasping the peach, witches' fingers with long, pointy nails. With one hand he offers the giant fruit on the palm of his hand, with the other he guards it, holds it back. Here's something else, the way he seems to be on the move, taking a confident step forward, into the future perhaps. And his head, with its massive skull, like one of the Teflon men. The skull, and then the huge frontal lobe. From thinking too hard. And his face – blind, the way all sculptures are blind, but staring, seeing everything. There are bags under his eyes from living for ever, but he smiles – patient, rather than happy or smug. The straggly beard. The droopy moustache that hangs from the corners of his thin mouth. It seems to have woven its way into the neck of his cloak.

Someone made this man. Imagine the effort, the work. Someone's whole being went into the little green man, all the purpose and energy and power of their own existence came out through their fingers and into this stone. They traded a life of flesh and blood for a life of hundreds and hundreds of years in the shape of this jade. And now I hold him in my hand. I put him down gently on the windowsill, next to the solid-silver photograph frame. Troy's face is daubed with polish and mud. In full battledress, he carries his gun across his shoulders, like a yoke, with one hand at the end of the barrel and one on the butt. He wears ammo around his neck. It's a good likeness, the classic pose. Troy, looking the part, from the leaves and twigs that sprout from his helmet, down to the polished toes of his boots, where sunlight detonates and explodes.

Of course, back then, I'd no idea he was worth so much. If I had, there's no way I would have let that lot get their filthy mitts on him. In fact, if I hadn't been browsing through *The Magic of Jade* in a second-hand bookshop a few months ago, I might not have remembered him at all, lying there in the attic in his makeshift tomb. My English teacher, Mr Shanks, had a theory about books dropping into your lap, falling open at a particular page. He said books were angels, winged creatures full of incredible secrets and knowledge. When the Bible spoke of angels, it meant books. Books full of thoughts and judgements and ideas. Tiny marks in black and white, silent speech, communication without the need for talk. A miracle, in fact. When Percival Midland-White put his hand up and pointed out that the printing press wasn't in fact invented until 1476, thereby post-dating the death of Christ by some 1,476 years, Mr Shanks simply smiled and said, 'So, none the less miraculous for that.'

Obviously, I don't believe in angels, or miracles, but the fact that *The Magic of Jade* was poking from the shelf, and the way it flopped open on a full-colour page of little green men are two things I can't account for in the normal scheme of things.

Books, though, only go so far, and it isn't far enough. Books are like maps – simplified versions of the real thing, and no substitute for getting off your arse, pulling up your bootstraps and seeing for yourself. I'd only been to London twice before. Once to the Pompeii exhibition in 1976 on a school trip, and once to Heathrow, which doesn't count. Two weeks after the day in the bookshop, I was wandering through the capital with an A–Z in my hand, like Dick Whittington, looking for Sprake & Co.

I buzzed, and the woman behind the desk let me in through the glass door. It was all very posh, more like the lobby of a swanky hotel.

'Is it possible to see Mr Kerslake, please?'

'Mr Kerslake?'

'Yes, Mr Richard Kerslake.'

She was a temp. She flipped open a folder, and ran her gold-painted fingernail up and down the list of numbers and names.

'We don't appear to have anyone here by that name,' she said.

'Oh. Could you check again?'

There was a bald man behind her in a dark-blue suit, feeding a sheet of paper into a fax machine. When he spoke, he sounded like a radio newsreader from the Fifties, or a butler in one of those films.

'Perhaps I could be of some assistance, sir?'

'I was looking for Mr Richard Kerslake. I want to talk to him about a piece of jade.'

'Have you been in contact with Mr Kerslake, sir?'

'No. But I've read his book. He wrote a book called *The Magic of Jade*.'

'In fact he was the editor. But I'm afraid Mr Kerslake doesn't work here any more. He left some time ago.'

I'd screwed up. Thirty quid for a train ticket. Money down the pan. I should have phoned to check, but I'm not much good on the phone. There would have been a security guard with a twenty-inch neck waiting for me when I arrived. They say surprise is the best form of attack, but this attack had backfired. You can't walk in off the street in your trainers and Harrington jacket and ask to speak to the top man. It just doesn't work like that – not where precious stones are concerned. It's big business. There are rules to obey, procedures to follow. A suit and tie wouldn't have gone amiss either.

'Is there anyone else I could see? Maybe the person who took over from him?'

'Who happens to be me, as a matter of fact,' said the man. 'You'll need to make an appointment. Tamsin here will give you a card. Thank you, sir.'

He raised his open hand in the direction of the door. Most times, I would have turned and walked. Normally, I don't need telling twice. But there was something in the air that day, and 200 miles is 200 miles, and thirty quid is thirty quid where I come from, and anyway I was just an ordinary bloke with an honest inquiry. What was he going to do – slap me with his umbrella? Frogmarch into the street with the tip of his fountain pen to my head? I put my hand in my pocket and pulled out a woollen football sock. The woman with the gold nails thought I was going to cosh her, and ducked under the desk.

'No, it's just this,' I said, and squeezed the little green man out of the sock, and set him down on the counter. The man in the blue suit had picked up the phone, but took one look at the carving, all shiny and brilliant on the limewood table under the halogen lights, and replaced the receiver.

'Is this the piece?'

I nodded.

'May I?'

I nodded again, and stuffed the empty sock in my pocket. He lifted the little green man in his left hand, and tapped and rubbed at him gently with his right.

'I'm sorry, sir, I didn't catch your name?'

'It's Barney.'

'Tamsin, could you make Mr Barney and myself a cup of coffee, and bring it through to the orangery? Or perhaps you would prefer tea, sir?'

We sat either side of a leather-topped table in a large room with a glass roof. Every wall was floor-to-ceiling with shelves, and every shelf was crammed with carvings and sculptures and pots, mainly jade, but ceramics and bronzes, too, and the odd piece of wood. Ivory as well. Most of the carvings were in the shape of animals, some of them real, some of them mythical, like dragons and lions with wings. It was like the inside of the Ark.

'How rude of me. My name is Mr Hanley. Here is my card.'

I took the card and we shook hands. He had a firm grip, but not one of those knuckle-crushers that cause the testicles to lift into the bladder. His hand was dry and cold.

'Could I ask how you came to be in possession of this piece?'

I said, 'Somebody died.'

'Very enigmatic, but better than the one about the Summer Palace or the Beijing gambling den.'

'What do you mean?'

'People can be very . . . shy. They tell us their grandfather was one of the looters who ransacked the Summer Palace, or won a bet with a deposed emperor after the fall of the last dynasty. It's a kind of code. Like saying something fell off the back of a lorry. It means you have no paperwork, no documents, correct?'

I nodded.

'And what do you know about the piece?'

'It's not ancient. Eighteenth century?'

'Yes, or possibly seventeenth. But age isn't the issue with this kind of work. It's all in the craftsmanship. Anything else?'

'It's jade. Chinese, I guess.'

'It is jadeite, yes. Imperial jadeite, we might say, sourced in Burma, very probably. And the style is classic Qing, Chinese design and subject, Chinese workmanship. Which makes it very interesting.'

'In what way?'

He put the little green man down on the table and folded his hands in front of his chest, resting his elbows on the arms of the chair. 'I've catalogued similar pieces, but always in white, nephrite jade, sourced in China.'

'Chicken bone and mutton fat,' I said.

'Yes, they're trade names for white jade. I see you've learnt from Mr Kerslake's book. But your piece is true emerald-green. It makes it something of a rarity, even if it is impaired.'

'What do you mean "impaired"?'

He lifted an anglepoise lamp from behind him and switched it on, positioning it so the little green man stood in a pool of hot, yellow light. I'd never seen him looking so magnificent and so magical, so alive. Mr Hanley took what looked like a rubber pencil from his pocket, and tapped the little green man on his head.

'This is a Shouxing. A star god of old age. A very wise person – look at the size of his head and this bulging cranium. Full of wisdom.'

'Is that why he's carrying a crystal ball?' I said.

'Look at the detail,' he said, pointing at the round object in the god's hands, tracing a narrow cleft in the ball. 'This is a peach. See the contour of the fruit, and a sprig of leaves underneath.'

'It's big for a peach.'

'It was an important symbol for the Chinese at the time. A symbol of longevity, and marriage, and springtime. It was a very pleasing thing. But look here, and here. What do you think these marks are?'

He pointed at two lighter patches of green, one on the left shoulder, the other on the robe, lower down on the right-hand side of the figure.

'I just thought they were different colours in the stone.'

'I might have thought so myself, had I not seen the complete grouping elsewhere. But no. These are not just tendencies within the original rock. They are polishings. Other figures were attached on either side, here and here. They must have broken off, or were removed, possibly, to be sold separately. Whoever repaired the piece did a very good job. A very good job indeed. Feel the smoothness. Only the colour gives it away.'

'Could you say what the other things were, the things that were broken off?'

'I can do better than that,' he said, and bent to a cupboard under the desk, and ran his finger along the spines of several dozen magazines.

Tamsin came in with the coffee on a silver tray. 'Milk?' she asked. 'Just a splash.'

She poured the drinks, set them out on matching saucers and left. I cupped my hand to the warmth of the coffee and lifted it to my lips. It was cold in the room. The only heat seemed to be from the lamp.

'Yes, I thought so. Here we are.' Mr Hanley blew dust off the catalogue and thumbed through to the right page. It was a photograph of another Shouxing, but white, not green, with a smaller man or boy to his left, and an animal to his right. 'This piece went through our sale rooms about ten years ago. The animal is a deer, believed to be the only creature capable of finding the *lingzhi* – the sacred fungus of immortality. And the boy holding a spray of *lingzhi* is his young attendant. A fine grouping. You can see now on your own piece where the boy and the deer were once attached.'

Mr Hanley put two lumps of brown sugar into his coffee, stirred it and tapped the spoon on the rim of the cup. Then he sipped at the black coffee, holding the saucer in his other hand. I stared at the photograph of the carving, the colour of it, not white exactly, more like the flesh of a pear, slightly yellow with just a hint of green. And the chunky deer. And the boy, holding what looked to me like a giant celery stick.

'Why would they have been broken off?'

'Oh, it's impossible to say. Perhaps someone thought that three pieces of jade would be more valuable than one. Or perhaps it was a question of ease of passage.'

'How do you mean?'

He smiled. 'Well, let's just say that slipping three smaller pieces of stone through international customs would be easier than trying to conceal one rather bulky piece. They could be anywhere now. Locked in a glass case in New York. Lying at the bottom of the sea. Anywhere.'

The deer nuzzled at the elbow of the god, and the boy sheltered under his shoulder, proud to be stood at his side and protected by the long, flowing robe. I picked up my own, green statue, which was warm from the light, and ran my thumb over the two light patches, and curled my fingers around his back until I held him in my fist. A peach. Amazing, I would never have guessed.

I said, 'Is it cheeky to ask for a price?'

Mr Hanley took another sip of his coffee, and licked his lips. 'Let's call it a value, shall we?'

'Yes, a value.'

'Well, of course, it all comes down to taste in the end. Let's see . . .' From the inside pocket of his jacket he pulled out a pen and a small notebook in a leather case. 'Bearing in mind everything I've said, the detached figures on the one hand, and the rarity value on the other, not to mention the quality of the stone and the exquisite detail, plus the fashion for this kind of piece at the moment, and the vibrant market . . .'

It was as if he were adding up a grocery bill.

'. . . minus the lack of authentic provenance . . .' he said, raising his eyes, briefly, in my direction. 'Well, let's imagine a number something like this.' He wrote a figure on the paper, tore the page from the notebook, folded it in half and pushed it at me across the table using the tip of his finger.

I peeped inside. 'Really?'

'Give or take,' he said.

'That's . . . brilliant.'

'Well, as I said, give or take. It isn't an exact science, you understand. But if you want a full valuation, you'd have to leave it with me for a while. With your permission I'd like to scrutinize it more closely. The most intriguing aspect of any stone is what lies beneath the surface, on the inside.'

'How long would it take?'

'Three hours. Four, at the most.'

'Great. Yes. I mean, thank you.'

He switched off the lamp, and rolled the little green man in a square of cloth from a another drawer in the desk.

'I should say, Mr Barney, that a charge is usually incurred for such a service. But, on this occasion, I think we might overlook a fee. Instinct is everything in this business, and my instinct today tells me not to charge.'

'Thank you,' I said. I meant it. I was grateful.

'Would you like to wait here, or do you have somewhere to go?'

'How far is Islington from here?'

He drew me a map of tube stations and streets in his little notebook, and tore out the sheet. Of course I'd got an *A–Z* in my pocket, but I didn't want to spoil his day. There was something in the air – he felt it too. I could read his face like a book, and he was having the biggest thrill he'd had for years.

17

'You're just copying what Barney did to you,' said Winkie. 'Can't you come up with anything yourself?'

'Think of this as the refined version. Now, if you're sitting comfortably?'

Stubbs had put the armchair in the middle of the room with the standard lamp next to it, and turned out the other lights. Winkie sat there in his football kit with his hands in his lap. In his specs were two identical reflections of the four of us facing him. We looked like Queen, in the 'Bohemian Rhapsody' video.

'There will be four questions only. You need to answer them all correctly. Do you understand?'

Winkie nodded.

'Oh, yes, and you can phone a friend.'

'If you've got any,' sniped Pompus.

'Question one. In a third-year chemistry lesson you were once given a bollocking by Thunderbird Underwood for messing around with a gas tap and a box of matches. Standing in front of the rest of the class, did you respond by: a, telling Thunderbird to get back in his spaceship; b, taking it on the chin like a man; c, crying like a baby; or d, some other response? You have twenty seconds.'

'Answer d,' said Winkie, without waiting.

'Correct. In fact, you pissed your pants if my sources are correct, and stood there in a little puddle of urine. It was very touching. I wasn't there at the time, being in a higher set, but Tony Football gave a full account of it to everyone in assembly next day.'

'Get on with it.'

'Question two. I went round to your house today and left something in your fish pond. But what?'

'How did you get my address? We're ex-directory.'

'A little bird told me. So what's the answer, Winkie? If you don't mind me making a suggestion, you could always phone Maureen and ask her to go and have a look.'

'Oh, I get it,' said Winkie. 'You think I daren't phone my wife and tell her what's going on. Is that it?'

Stubbs tossed him the cordless phone. 'Yes, I'd say that comes into it. Go on, Winkie. Phone a friend.'

Winkie pushed his glasses up to the bridge of his nose. 'You're pathetic,' he said, and punched in the number. 'Mo? Hello, love, it's me. Yes, well, the football was cancelled, so I've given one of the lads a lift back to his house. Anyway, there's something I want to ask you . . .'

Stubbs grinned and looked at the rest of us. In fact, he was smirking.

'I just wondered if you fancied any chips? I could pick them up on the way. OK. Fine. See you soon.' He pressed the red button at the bottom of the phone and threw it back to Stubbs.

There was a pause.

'Well?' said Stubbs.

'No, she doesn't want chips, but she'll have a fish tea-cake. And I'll probably have a pie.'

Stubbs leant forward in the chair and looked hard into Winkie's face. 'Listen, Winkie, your supper arrangements might be very important to you, but I asked you a question, and I still haven't had an answer. Do I take it you're retiring from the competition?'

'Could you repeat the question?' said Winkie.

Stubbs shook his head in despair. 'I left something in your fish pond today. What was it?'

'Was it a turd?' shouted Pompus. He'd been lying on the settee looking at a magazine, but suddenly was very excited. 'Was it a turd, man? Did you lay one in his fish pond, Stubbs? Oh, that would have been a corker, if you'd left a floater in there with the koi carp, and his Maureen plodding off down the garden with a torch to find it. Outstanding.'

Stubbs ignored him. 'Well, Winkie? Maybe you should have asked the little lady, instead of thinking about food.'

'I didn't need to ask her,' said Winkie, defiantly, 'because I know what it is. In fact, I've brought it with me.'

He pushed his right hand inside his shorts, and after a moment or so of rummaging and rootling between his legs, pulled the loose, cloth pocket out over the waistband, and drew out a brown-and-yellow Tasty Ticklers packet. He flicked it towards Stubbs's face. 'You see, Stubbs, I had a call from Maureen today to say she'd seen some creepy-looking guy in the garden, sniffing around the fish pond. She thought he was after the fish, and took his registration number, but when she said he'd driven off in a big black Volvo, I told her not to worry. And when I got home, I found a chocolate-and-banana flavoured johnny floating on the surface, and figured it was something to do with tonight.'

'Hey, nice work, Sherlock,' said Tony Football, clapping his hands together.

Winkie smiled. A big, toothy smile. Even his glasses seemed to be smiling.

Stubbs smiled back, robotically. 'Question three. For as long as anyone can remember, you've been known not by your proper title but by the nickname Winkie, a reference to your exceedingly small penis, hence "Wee Willie Winkie". But who gave you that nickname, Winkie? Was it: a, Pompus; b, Barney; c, Tony Football; or answer d, yours truly?'

'It just happened. It was just one of them things,' said Winkie.

'No, I'm afraid that isn't the correct answer. I'm going to have to press you on this.'

Winkie looked at each of us in turn, focussing on us one at a time. 'Give me a clue,' he said.

It was a pitiful request. I thought Stubbs would tell him to take a running jump. Let him sink without trace. Instead, he threw him a lifebelt. I was stunned.

'Let's say it's a kind of theme, shall we. A sort of running gag. Your specialist subject.'

Winkie shrugged his shoulders and swallowed hard.

'Same person that gave me your address,' said Stubbs, rolling the condom packet between his finger and thumb.

Winkie looked at each of us again. I looked back at him, right into his brain. Stubbs checked his watch. Pompus smiled and burped. But Tony . . . Tony Football looked at the carpet, tried to small down in his chair, tried to look like the invisible man.

'So it was you, was it, big gob?'

There was no reply.

'Is that your final answer? Tony Football?' inquired Stubbs.

'Look at him. Of course it's my answer.'

'Nnnnnnnnn . . . yes. Correct, it was indeed answer c, your old mate, Tony Football. He was the only one in your PE lesson, wasn't he? I thought you might have been able to work it out for yourself.'

'You blabbermouth,' said Winkie, shaking his head in disgust.

'Oh, come on, we were just kids. I only happened to mention what everyone was singing in the showers, and the next thing it was your nickname. I never thought it would stick.'

If somebody had lifted Winkie's glims from his face at that moment, two laser beams would have shot out of his head and fried TF in his seat, blasted him into the middle of next week. I could imagine his eyes glowing red with fury behind those lenses. He sat there, staring blindly, steaming up. I thought again about the time he clobbered his sister for nothing, and wondered who he'd go for first if he boiled over. It was really exciting.

'Your last question, then, little star, to stay in the money. Are you ready?'

His head moved up and down, just fractionally.

'Question four. In 1992, you married Maureen Wince and lived happily ever after. Loving couple that you are, though, you're still childless after several years of marriage. What's the reason, I wonder? Is it: a, you don't want kids anyway? Is it answer b, your Maureen is actually a man? Answer c, none of my business? Or answer d, some other reason? Take your time.'

Winkie could have been made out of wax, his face had that look, someone about to melt on the spot with embarrassment and fear. 'It's none of your business.'

'Well, in a perfect world that would certainly be true. But on this occasion I'm afraid it most definitely is my business, to the tune of 750,000 pounds. So I can't accept that as a correct answer, but, in case there's any dispute, I'm going to give you another chance. What's the answer?'

From behind his glasses a tear appeared, making its way down the side of his nose towards his mouth. Then another, following the same channel.

'You're not going to piss on Barney's lovely carpet, are you, Winkie?'

With a slow, almost imperceptible movement, Winkie moved his head from side to side, which launched another tear, this time from the other eye. 'How do you know?' he whispered.

'Answer first,' said Stubbs. He'd been reading the questions from an index card, which he now folded and tucked into his shirt pocket.

'Some other reason,' said Winkie, without moving his lips.

'Correct! Let's have a big hand for the winner.' Stubbs applauded loudly, on his own, then stood up and pushed his hand out towards Winkie. 'Congratulations, young man, you're through to the next round.'

Winkie didn't move. 'Who told you?' he croaked.

'Well, it's that recurring theme again. Mr Tony Football here might be a bit of a photography anorak on the side, but it's a long time since he worked behind the film-processing counter at Boots, eh, Tone? He's a proper scientist now in a laboratory, shaking test tubes, peering into microscopes and taking pictures of itsy-bitsy organisms, like sperm, for instance. It's very rewarding work.'

An ice-cream van went past outside, playing its silly tune.

''Course, there's usually millions of the little critters zipping around, but in your case, Winkie, they took a bit of finding. Seems like you're not even into double figures on that front. More life in a dollop of mayonnaise. Isn't that right, Tony?'

That was the moment. Blast off. Winkie came out of his seat like the plastic James Bond who rocketed through the sunroof of the toy Aston Martin when you flicked the catch. He sailed past Stubbs. As he landed, he grabbed Tony Football by his ears and screamed at him. I tried to pull him off by his legs but he was kicking out like a madman – he could have broken my jaw, or something worse. And before I could get hold of him, he snooked up all the snot in his nose and throat and spat the biggest lump of gob into Tony's face. Strands of phlegm connected Tony Football's eyes and nose to Winkie's lips, as if they'd just been prized apart, like Siamese twins joined at the face. They fell on the floor and bounced around between the furniture, locked in the same position, until Tony let out an almighty scream and Pompus waded in to sort it out.

'Come on, girls, pack it in.'

He deposited Winkie on the settee and put his giant hand on the top of his head to keep him from getting up. His mouth was smeared with blood – I thought he'd lost a tooth or split his lip, until I looked back at Tony, and saw the gash on the bridge of his nose.

'He fucking bit me. Jesus, he's bitten my fucking nose off.'

He flung open the door and pounded upstairs to the bathroom.

After the red mist had cleared, Winkie sat in the middle of the settee, sniffing and snivelling, pulling himself together.

Pompus went into the cellar and came back with a tray of drinks, 'to calm everyone down a bit'.

Stubbs picked up the chair and carried the standard lamp back into the corner.

Tony Football finally emerged, spitting feathers and announcing he'd lost a contact lens in the fracas. His face looked as if he'd been cleaning it with a scrubbing brush, and there were still pearls of water in his eyebrows from running his head under the tap. When he took his hand away from his nose I could see the bite mark in his flesh – only a nick, really, but still bleeding and dripping on to his lip.

'I only told Stubbs. I thought he'd be worried about you, same as I was. I didn't think he'd do this.'

Tony took a step towards Stubbs and raised his arm, but Stubbs grabbed his fist and crushed his fingers until Tony backed off. It was crazy, like tag-wrestling. Winkie going for Tony Football, Pompus throwing his weight about, now Tony having a pop at Stubbs. It was a miracle nothing got damaged that night. Not one drop of beer spilt. Not a single ornament broken.

'Don't you think you two should kiss and make up?' I said, playing the peacemaker.

'Excuse me, but he just tried to bite my nose off, if you didn't notice, not to mention showering me with gob. I'm sorry I told Stubbs, OK, but it wasn't out of malice. And anyway, if he can't take it, he shouldn't be in the game. I'd rather eat my own shit than kiss that little runt. I'm off.' He pushed past Pompus and slammed out of the house, making the front window rattle in its frame.

Stubbs took a drink from the tray. 'Sorry, Wink, but don't say you wouldn't shaft me given half a chance. You want that money as much as anyone. But for what it's worth, I'm sorry, OK? This isn't a normal situation.'

'Too right I'd shaft you. Talk about the kettle calling the frying-pan black-arse.'

'What's that supposed to mean?'

'I'm not the only one with a stupid name. Where do you think yours came from?'

'I know where mine came from,' said Stubbs.

'Oh, really? You think it was because you smoked when you were ten, don't you, like it made you some kind of hard man. But it wasn't. It was because of what your stepdad did to you with his cigarettes, why they kept sending him away, why you ended up living with your auntie Connie. So don't think I'm the only one with a dumb name, STUBBS.'

'Who told you all that?' In one seamless movement he lunged forward and grabbed Winkie by the throat and lifted him against the wall. 'WHO TOLD YOU THAT?'

Winkie's glasses went spinning from his head to the floor, and his face turned purple. He had to force his words up through the vice of Stubbs's fist and out through his mouth. 'Who do you think, STUBBS?' he coughed. Then, like one of those nodding dogs, his eyes opened wide and his head turned, slowly, in my direction.

Lying awake in the small hours, I think it all through. Every word. Every move. It's been a good night. Stubbs on top form, pushing Winkie right to the brink, and marking Tony Football's card, dropping him in the brown and sticky stuff. Next week's will be a real cracker, and no mistake. Pity about the business with the cigarette burns, though. I could have done without that. Mustn't end up on the wrong side of Stubbs. Mustn't wander into the line of fire.

One puzzle, though. Why give Winkie a clue? What was all that about? I can hear Stubbs's voice, see him swaggering, laughing it off. 'Why spoil it when we're having such a hoot?' But that's not the reason. I know the reason. It's called a soft spot. It's called a bleeding heart.

Weakness. Metal fatigue. Stress fractures. Hairline cracks. Faults like that have to be closely watched. If I had a pen in my hand I'd write that down. But it's three in the morning. Not long till it's light. I roll over and sleep.

18

I once read a story, in a magazine, about a man who went crazy and walked off into the woods in Canada in the middle of winter. Or Alaska. He lived in a clapped-out caravan that had been airlifted into the forest for hikers and hunters who'd lost their way or shot themselves in the foot or whatever. This particular chap was 'in search of himself', and he stayed in the caravan for a long time, living off nuts and berries and maybe the odd squirrel that fell into his cooking pot, until the day came when he felt he could face the world again. So he set off through the trees, making his way back to the road. It was a true story, so I guess he's pretty smelly and wearing a big beard by this time and hair down to his collar, like a grizzly bear, and suffering from all sorts of fungal infections like jock itch and trench foot. All that time without toothpaste and bog roll has taken its toll. It's springtime by now, and he finds himself on the banks of a wide, fast-flowing river, which of course was frozen when he crossed it all those months ago. Now there isn't a hope in hell of him getting across without drowning, which he doesn't want to do, because today he's all centred and calm and happy with the world. So he's trapped, and there's nothing for it except to yomp back to the caravan and stay there until winter, until the river freezes again. And we know all this because he's keeping a diary, a little notebook of everything going on in his head, all his strange and lonely thoughts jotted down in shaky handwriting. Not long afterwards, he goes down with something – poisoning maybe from eating the wrong mushroom – and he gets sick, really sick, and weaker and weaker. It's coming cold by now, really cold, and there's no way he's going to make it back to that river, let alone the road, so he holes up in the caravan, just him and his notebook, and beds down in his sleeping bag in the corner, and dies. If I remember rightly, some hikers or hunters find his body the next summer, and the notebook as well, and the last entry just says 'Great jeopardy'.

How about that? 'Great jeopardy.'

And this man was real, so he has friends and relatives that can't get him out of their head, who can't stop thinking about him in his caravan out in the woods with ice in his beard. All those pitch-black nights with animals snuffling around in the undergrowth or scratching on the roof, the stars hammered into the sky, hard as nails. Great jeopardy.

Well, I suppose we'd crossed that river and couldn't go back. Not now. Not yet. We'd burnt the bridges and eaten the horses. We could only go forward. Three-quarters of a million quid. And when you think about it, it's nothing. You couldn't live on the interest, could you, not even if you stuffed the lot of it into some long-term bond? And who could keep that kind of money in their pocket without wanting to splash out? You pay off the mortgage, you fly to Barbados, you put a jukebox in the front room, you buy that people-carrier you've had your eye on, you go to some flash restaurant in London and point at the signed photographs of ex-soap stars and retired disk jockeys. Next thing you know, you're scratting around for a few pence to pay the milkman. And that's not even mentioning all your so-called friends tapping you for a few quid here and a few quid there, and the scroungers and spongers that crawl out of the woodwork. You can't keep money quiet, not with that new van sat outside on the drive. Not with that winter tan.

We'd crossed the river. Punches had been thrown, blood spilt, secrets told. Nobody had come this far just to go home with a bust lip and a cauliflower ear. There were scores to settle. Now we were cooking with gas.

It was as if we hadn't moved from last week, except this time Tony Football was in the chair, and it was Winkie asking the questions. 'Why don't you tell everyone who you're sleeping with at the moment, Tony *Fuckball*?'

'Is that the dare?'

'Nope.'

'Well, then, it's none of your business, is it?'

'Oh sorry, did I tread on a pet corn, Tony *Suckball*?'

'Look, Winkie, if you've got something to say, why don't you just say it?'

Winkie ran his finger around the top of a glass, making it sing. Tony was sitting forward in the seat, ready for anything. The cut at the top of his nose had dried into two neat little scabs, as if he'd been tweaked with a pair of pliers or punched with a staple gun.

'You're queer, aren't you, Tony?'

'And what if I am?'

If Winkie had planned an ambush with this bit of news, he'd failed. If that was Winkie's bouncer, Tony had let it go sailing past his head, then walked casually back up the wicket to tamp down a pockmark in the track. Maybe he'd been expecting it. To be honest, it wasn't exactly a revelation. There was something about Tony Football. It wasn't a shock, more of an expected surprise, if such a thing exists. It didn't matter to me.

'You? Shopping around the corner? That's outstanding is that. Hey, lads, no more five-a-side if he's playing at the back, know worra mean? Tony Football, a shit-stabber all those years. Not that it bothers me, like. Outstanding.'

'Thank you for your charity, Pompus,' said Tony.

'Not a problem, mate. Queer as a coot – it's no skin off my nose. Hey, no skin off my nose, geddit, lads? I should be on the stage, me?'

'Yeah, you're a natural,' said Stubbs, who'd been keeping quiet in the corner.

'Oh, cheers, Stubbs. Is he outstanding or what?'

'Come on, give him the dare, Winkie.'

Winkie hadn't finished. He was wearing an inane grin on his face that said it all, how this was his big moment, how he'd been waiting for this all week. It said it all, how smart he was, how angry, and how scared.

'Well, Tony *Puffball*, it was something you said last week. Strange kind of comment really, about how you'd sooner eat shit than do something else. Maybe that's what put me on to you. Maybe only a woofter would come out with that kind of talk. Anyway, it's time to put your money where your mouth is. You'd rather eat shit, would you? Well, go on, then. That's the dare. Eat shit. Human shit. Right up your street that, eh?'

Pompus leapt out of his seat and punched the air. I'd never seen him move so fast, didn't know he could. 'Unbelievable. Unbe-fuckinglievable. This is *It's a Knockout* on drugs, this is. Eating shit. Oh, Winkie, you dirty little get, that's a bloody Brahma.'

'Don't do it, Tony. Make him do it. He won't,' said Stubbs.

But Winkie still had the look on his face. That painful grin. 'Oh, won't I now? Well, maybe I'm prepared. Maybe I'm a bit more careful about what goes into my arse from the top end than he is about what goes in from the bottom. Anyway, Tony Football, it's up to you, mate.'

Tony walked over to the window and looked out into the garden. It was drizzling lightly, one of those gentle, damp summer evenings, less like rain and more like the world sweating with the effort of just existing. Pompus was still jumping around with excitement, clapping Winkie on the cheeks, telling him what a little star he was, what a Jack Russell, what a Brahma.

Tony Football turned away from the window and looked at us. 'I'm thirty-four. I've got a good job, I've got a nice motorbike, read books, look after myself. I'm an adult. I belong to a wine club. I don't eat shit.'

'Well there's three-quarters of a million quids-worth of green jade locked in that bureau says you do, pal. But obviously it's a matter for your own personal taste,' said Winkie.

Tony looked through the window again for a good five minutes, longer, leaning against it, so that when he turned back towards us eventually he left a large, pear-shaped blob of condensation on the glass where his face had been, bigger than his head. 'Whose shit did you have in mind?' he said, calmly. 'Because, if it's all the same with you, I'd like to go with my own.'

Rules were discussed and agreed. One mid-sized turd to be eaten there and then, with sauce or relish as required. Pompus, who could hardly contain himself by this time, hared into the kitchen and came back with a soup dish, a fork and a bottle of ketchup. Winkie sat on the piano stool with his hands tucked under his armpits. He'd done his bit. He'd got away with it. Stubbs looked on from his chair, not saying much, but obviously gripped. Tony Football wasn't really going to eat a turd, was he? Somebody couldn't really sneck their own shit in this house tonight, could they?

Tony had fetched a half-bottle of vodka from the cellar and was drinking huge gulps of the stuff straight from the neck. 'You underestimate me,' he blurted out, screwing his eyes up to mimic Winkie, then took another swig.

Pompus stood behind him, holding out the dish and the sauce. TF emptied the bottle, exchanged it for the dish, then headed for the hall. He was laughing as he disappeared upstairs.

'And I hope all your doughnuts turn out like Fanny's,' he shouted, then howled again as he closed the bathroom door.

'You're disgusting,' said Stubbs to Winkie. 'Pure filth.'

'It's the company I'm keeping,' he snorted.

'Yeah, leave him alone,' said Pompus. 'You're just mardy because you didn't think of it first. Eating shit – it's a Brahma, a total, total Brahma. Hey, Wink, you should write in to Channel 4, you could get this on telly. I'd watch it, no worries.'

He'd turned the lights right down on the dimmer, put a tablemat and the fork on the dining table, then folded the tea towel over his arm, and was standing like a waiter at the Ritz. 'Put some music on. Some of that "dinner jazz" stuff.'

Ten minutes later Tony Football came back into the living room holding the dish out in front of him. He was rocking somewhat as he flashed the contents to the four of us – I only half-looked – and pushed it right under Winkie's nose as he swayed past him, then dropped into the dining chair. Pompus offered him the ketchup, and he squeezed the whole bottle into the dish. Pompus then tried to tuck the towel into his shirt collar, like a napkin, but Tony pushed him away. He took a deep breath, and picked up the fork. None of us could watch, except for Pompus, hovering over him, saying, 'Wouldn't sir be better off with a spoon, perhaps?' The sound of the metal fork scratching the bottom of the dish was about as much as I could take.

Quarter of an hour after Tony had gone back upstairs I went into the bathroom – the door wasn't locked. Tony looked up from the floor, heaved again and put his head back in the toilet. I turned on the shower and left him a cup of coffee on the weighing scales. There was toothpaste all over the sink and the carpet.

'Have they all gone?' he shouted after me.

'Yes.'

'Bastards,' he mumbled.

It was about half-ten when I pulled up outside his flat, but he was almost comatose by then, and I had to drag him along the alleyway by the scruff of his neck as he mumbled and blubbered to himself. There was a light on in the upstairs kitchen, so I rang the bell, dropped him on the doorstep and scarpered. When it comes to talking my way out of a scrape, I'd back myself nine times out of ten. On the other hand, the impulse to jump in the car, turn the key and push the pedal all the way to the floor is sometimes overpowering, and never to be completely ignored.

I took the long way home, over the top of the hill, instead of the main road along the valley bottom. Just after the golf course, I saw a white van parked diagonally in a lay-by on the right-hand side. Suddenly a man in a bomber jacket, fingerless mittens and a bobble hat walked into the road and waved his arms in the air. I slowed up, and hit the central-locking button. Then I wound down the window. He leant into the car. He had a stubbly black beard and a London accent.

'Cheers, mate. One of my dogs has done a runner. Can you pull off the road a minute and shine your headlights into those fields? Cheers.'

Then he leapt over the drystone wall and walked off into the darkness.

'What kind of dog is it?' I called after him.

'Border terrier,' he shouted back.

I turned the wheel and eased the car off the road, parked at forty-five degrees to the white van, then flicked the headlights on to full beam. They reached out into the rainy night, all silvery, like searchlights in an air raid. With the lights from the van, the whole of the field was illuminated. It could have been a scene from some arty Russian film. Or a Guinness advert.

I put the radio on and flipped through the stations. Dance music, like someone hammering their way out of a metal dustbin. Or country and western, a dead mother and a drunken father and a dog. Or the interval of an opera, a posh woman explaining what had happened already and what was going to happen next. Or the shipping forecast. Or a phone-in show, a man saying that cricket was dead in this country, and so was tennis come to that, and he blamed the government.

Every now and again the man in the bobble hat appeared in the light, shouting and whistling with his fingers in his mouth. Then he'd disappear behind a bush or down a ditch, then emerge again on top of a wall, staring into the blackness beyond. In his van, two other terriers were standing on the seat with their front legs on the dashboard, following his movements through the windscreen. On the skyline, the silhouettes of dead elm trees could have been the antlers of half a dozen giant stags.

When I was thirteen, my parents sent me on an adventure holiday in the Lakes. It was OK. Canoeing, lighting fires, potholing. It rained most of the time, but it was fun sleeping in hammocks and eating sausages grilled on a stick over an open fire. One morning, we were given compasses and maps and driven to the Grisedale Forest for a day's orienteering. There were sculptures in the middle of the woods, and it was our job to track some of them down, using grid references and landmarks. Each party of five boys had also been given a Polaroid camera, to take a snap of the sculptures, to prove we'd found them. It was a great idea, even if it was raining. It would have been even better if Stubbs and the rest of the gang had been there, but for once I was on my own. Of course, it wouldn't be allowed these days, because of all the kiddie-fiddlers waiting to jump out from behind the trees, and the cost of insuring every child against getting a pine needle stuck in his thumb.

I was put in a group with four Boy Scouts from Wigan and St Helens, who had badges for showing old ladies across the road, and wore shoes that made animal tracks in the mud. They ran on ahead, which was stupid of them, because I had the camera, so I veered off on my own into the woods, which was stupid of me, because they had the map. I walked for a few miles, sheltering under trees every time the rain came on strong. I didn't mind being lost so much, but didn't like walking through the woods with my hood over my head. It covered my ears. Someone or something could come at me from behind and I wouldn't hear until it was too late. So I let the rain pour on to my hair and my face, and felt it trickling down inside my anorak and my T-shirt. I didn't know which was rain and which was sweat. I felt like an animal, hot and excited and wet.

I pushed through tall green bracken, taller than a man, then stumbled on to a path, and followed it down a hillside towards a stream. There was a pile of stones to one side in the shape of a seat. I sat down to rest, tore open a bar of chocolate. When I looked up, I saw the creature. It was *The Deer Hunter* – a tree, maybe dead, maybe alive, still rooted in the ground, but trimmed and cut to the shape of a stag stood up on its hind legs. The upper branches were the antlers. It leant forward slightly, stalking, hunting, on the scent, and slung across its shoulder was another branch in the shape of a rifle. Spooky. Shocking. I'd seen its name on the list of sculptures we had to locate – *The Deer Hunter* – but pictured it in my mind's eye as a carving of a man in a lumberjack shirt with a hip-flask swinging from his belt. I could hear shouts from far off in the forest, the other boys calling my name. I pulled the camera out of my pocket, wiped the steam from the lens, and took the picture. Then I ran.

When my parents arrived to take me home, I wittered on about *The Deer Hunter*, how it wasn't a hunter at all, but a deer with a gun.

'Ah,' said my father, from the driving seat. 'A play on words.'

I've still got the photograph pinned to my bedroom wall. The deer, silhouetted against a grey sky, tracking his prey, presumably a man.

Years later, when I first met Kim, we'd drive up to a lay-by on the road to Barnsley, walk along the river bank for a couple of miles, hop over the fence and the padlocked gate at the end of the path, and enter the sculpture park. By day it was full of tourists or students, dribbling their ice cream on the Barbara Hepworths or sat cross-legged in front of the Henry Moores with their sketchbooks open and pencils behind their ears. By day it was theme park, but at night it was quiet and still. It was private. We'd sit in the palm of one of the huge bronzes, loving the coolness and smoothness of the metal, tapping at its emptiness, half-expecting it to close up around us like a hand or shell, expecting something in its depth to answer back.

I turned the radio off. Why was a man in a black hat walking his dogs at eleven o'clock on a Friday night? Rabbiting? No, foxes more like. No, badgers. There were badgers in those woods. Some people pay good money to see a badger dragged from its set by dogs like these. I've read newspaper reports about badger-baiting going on in out-of-the-way farms, men betting thousands of pounds, badgers tied by their back legs to a metal peg while Border terriers worry and taunt them, then rip them to shreds.

It's not my idea of a good night out.

I revved the engine and reversed on to the road, spinning the wheels in the gravel verge. I needed to be miles away, before the police arrived and found me here with a van and two dogs, pointing at some non-existent cockney out there in the darkness. As the headlights arced across the field, they picked out the man in the hat about a hundred yards away, his face suddenly alight as he turned to watch me go.

Badger-baiting. Jesus, that's a nasty business. An ugly thought.

At home I locked the door and put the chain on, then went into the living room and sat down in the dark. A few minutes went by. Then, outside, the clouds suddenly broke, and through a gap in the curtains a bar of hard, colourless moonlight fell across the dining table, picking out the empty bottle of sauce, and the ketchup-smeared dish, and the fork.

19

I might not be the hardest chocolate in the box, but I'm not the strawberry cream either, or the fudge centre. In any event, being tough isn't about muscles or size or anything physical at all. It's about what you're willing to do, how far you'll go. If people know you're prepared to go all the way and a little bit further if necessary, they back off, leave you alone. There was a kid at school called Everill, a real scarecrow. In the first year he turned up in a second-hand blazer that was five sizes too big, and he was still wearing it four years later, with the cuffs up by his elbows and the hem halfway to his neck. His dad was a rag-and-bone man, used to ride a horse and cart up and down the main road, looking for scrap. Everill couldn't have weighed more than about six stone, wet through. In the good old days he would have been a chimney sweep, or a powder monkey, or drowned at birth. He was an urchin, a piece of trash. Maybe his dad had found him thrown on a skip. But one day in assembly I bumped into him, accidentally, and he came at me like a wild cat trapped in a garden shed.

'All right, Steptoe, calm down,' I said.

Then suddenly he was on my back, punching me on the side of the head, and the next minute we were rolling around on the floor, him trying to kill me and me trying to pin him down until he stopped. One of the PE teachers pulled us apart, but he was still throwing punches as the teacher held him in mid-air, and still spitting and snarling as he was packed off in the opposite direction. Crazy. I could have murdered him, pound for pound.

So later that same day I get a visit from one of his cronies, some muscle-brain in the retard group, who tells me that Steptoe wants to sort this out once and for all with a scrap – just name the time and place. I got out my diary, but the knucklehead tore it in half, and told to me to be at the delivery entrance at the end of school on Monday.

'It's half-term next week,' I pointed out.

'OK, smart-arse, the Monday after. And don't be late, because we're running a book on it. And we've got you down to lose.'

He cuffed me over the head, leaving me to figure it out for myself. Was I really second favourite to that little melt? Or did I have to let Everill kick my head in because he was their buddy? Or was it all about dosh? And now it was serious, because the people who lurked behind the school weren't to be messed with. They were just killing time until they were legally old enough to go to prison. They had two heads or three eyes or some other deformity, and at dinnertime they ate everything in front of them, even the boiled turnip. They taxed people at the gates for their money and sometimes their trainers as well. Most of us spent our whole school career avoiding them.

I thought long and hard about the fight over half-term. Practised my hard look in the bathroom mirror, did some shadow-boxing around the bedroom and aimed a few kicks at the beanbag in the living room. I even went for a run. By Friday night, though, I realized the whole thing was hopeless. That the odds were a thousand to one. That even if I did squash that little stick insect, his mates would probably put the boot in afterwards, shine up the toe end of their ox-blood Docs on my head. Maybe that's what the jogging was all about – thinking I'd need to leg it afterwards.

So I picked up the phone and called a meeting. Stubbs, Winkie, Tony Football and Pompus. We weren't the softest chocolates in the box, but we weren't the Brazil nuts either. We had to put our brains together and think.

On Monday dinnertime I was looking out of the form room when a police car pulled in through the school gates and parked in the bus bay. The two coppers put on their helmets as they walked towards reception, then took them off again as they went in through the main entrance. Ten minutes later, there was a commotion as the doors flew open, and the coppers struggled through, one holding

Everill by his arms, the other holding his feet. Everill was shouting and squirming, and somehow broke free, and set off across the muddy grass towards the long-jump pits and the cricket field. Suddenly it seemed like the whole school was watching, lining the banking above the sports fields or leaning out of classroom windows, cheering for Everill as he side-stepped one tackle after another, jeering when one of the coppers downed him with a shoulder charge, then cheering again as he scrambled to his feet and ran. They upended him eventually and carted him off to the car, all three of them slarted with mud. As they pulled off, I could see Everill thrashing about on the back seat, and one of the coppers using his fists, really laying in. Apparently, he'd been reported for making threats of a very violent nature. He was wild and disturbed, capable of anything – you only had to look at him to realize that. There'd been an anonymous telephone call to the headmaster. When they'd searched his bag, they'd pulled out various weapons including – would you believe it – a flick knife. And that's when he did his nut. And that's when the fuzz had to be called.

My point is this: here was a kid who didn't know where to stop. Who gave as good as he got, even to Her Majesty's Constabulary. I could never have won that fight. I could have knocked him over a million times and he would have come straight back at me. He was hard, because there wasn't anything he wouldn't have done to finish me off.

On the other hand, there was only one winner that day. I've heard it said if you carry a knife you should be prepared to use it, but that doesn't mean you've got to stick it in somebody's ribs. At the end of school that day, I opened a window in the hall above the delivery bay, and looked down at his dunderhead mates, all smoking and swearing and spitting and sticking their hand up Carol McCannon's skirt.

'Where is he, then?' I shouted.

'He's not here, is he,' said one of them, looking up to see where my voice was coming from.

'Pity,' I said. 'Kid's no trooper.'

If they'd known how funny that last remark was, they'd still be laughing about it today. But that's tough guys for you. They just don't get it. And I might not be the hardest rock on the planet, but I'm not the squidgiest, either. They measure gemstones on a scale of one to ten. The Mohs scale. Ten is diamond. One is talc. Jade comes in at between six and seven, which is a good place to be, I reckon. Solid, but not impenetrably thick. In the middle band, but slightly ahead of the pack. Forgeries of jade in calcite or serpentine wouldn't stand the hardness test – you could scratch those stones with a wooden toothpick or even your fingernails. But forgeries in quartz, bowenite, zoisite, idocrase and maybe glass – you'd need some other gemological test. Refractive index readings, X-ray diffraction, specific-gravity determinations, spectroscopic analysis, and so on. You'd need to use the soft part of your head – your brain. You couldn't just smash your fist against them and see if they cracked.

It's nice when things work out. A gun would have been better than a knife, just to be on the safe side, but apart from the pistol in my father's bedside cabinet, the only guns I've ever seen were the shotguns up on the moor. Every August, fat businessmen paid hundreds of pounds for the privilege of tramping across the moors on the Glorious Twelfth, taking pot-shots at non-existent grouse, and the five of us went along as beaters. Ten pounds a day was a fortune at that time, but it was hard work. We'd meet at six in the morning at the bottom of the hill, and climb into an open-top Land Rover or a horse-box. The businessmen stood around with their shotguns broken over their arms, with green wellies up to their armpits, with waxed jackets, little quilted waistcoats and feathers in their hats, passing hip flasks between them, breathing brandy fumes into the clean, morning air.

They looked perfect, but they hadn't a clue. And behind their backs we were sneering, pocketing their money and watching them stumble over the moors half-cut for eight or nine hours, loosing off cartridges at larks and crows and the odd stray seagull. As beaters, our job was to walk on in front making as much din as possible, to spring the grouse from their nests. We carried sticks and something to hit, usually a dustbin lid or a hubcap, except for Winkie, who brought a little tin drum that he wore on his waist. Personally, I think the farmers and squires had been across the moors on August eleventh and bagged all the birds for themselves. For two years we didn't see a single grouse. Not a feather. But the summer after that, just when I'd started to wonder if the red grouse was actually an extinct species, they were everywhere.

The moors are beautiful in the sunshine. That sounds sissy, but there's no other word for it. It only happens five or six times a year. The rain stops and the wind dies to nothing and the sun burns down on to the hump grass and cotton grass and heather, and the peat dries into a hard, black crust, and it's beautiful. And there's nothing to see except the next few miles of moorland, then the next, then the next, and you feel as if you're the highest person in the world, as if you're right on top of the globe, pushing the earth around under your feet, spinning the planet at your own pace. Totally silent, too, away from the crowds and the cars. Silent, that is, until five boys appear on the horizon, banging their sticks like the ghosts of some lost and tatty band, still marching through time.

On this particular day, grouse were everywhere. Maybe they'd been imported. Every couple of hundred yards a grouse burst upwards from under our feet, like a clockwork toy wound to the top. Each bird climbed frantically into the air, then veered horizontally across the skyline, the feathered legs and white underwings sharp and unmistakable, only to be downed in the next second by the thudding shotguns, and tumble and fall, all shapeless and gawky towards the earth.

'Good shot, sir, well done,' you'd hear from the farmers across the moor, though in truth, they'd brought down the birds themselves. The punters couldn't hit a bull's arse with a brass banjo, which is why us beaters tended to hit the deck whenever a grouse broke cover. If two or three birds lifted at the same time, which happened over and over again that day, all hell broke loose, with guns blasting in every direction, and birds falling out of the sky, and smoke and the wonderful smell of gunpowder hanging motionless over the empty moor, and five hysterical beaters huddled together in a ditch, waiting for the ceasefire. It was carnage. By evening, dead grouse were everywhere, poking from pockets, dangling in the mouths of the dogs, hanging from sticks and belts, spilling out of knapsacks and bags. As we hopped out of the pick-up at the bottom of the road, the farmer paid us from a thick roll of tenners, then went back in the truck and brought out five birds.

'Get them in the oven with blackcurrant jam. Lovely.'

In the mysterious world of grouse-shooting with its many strange rituals, this was probably a highly generous and symbolic gesture. But what did *we* want with five, stinking dead grouse, especially the one male, with the rubbery red wattle around its eyes? 'This one's got twat-lips on its head,' said Pompus, holding it by its neck. We'd got our money and we were off to the chippy. First, Stubbs put his bird down the back of Tony Football's shirt. Then Pompus floored Winkie and smeared blood on his face. And for the next half an hour we chased across the shunting yards and along the towpath, hurling the birds or coshing each other with the things. Until they were just tatty rags. Until their feathers were everywhere. Until there were many more than just five pieces of red grouse. Afterwards, we kicked the remains into the canal, leaving the feathers drifting on the surface, weightless and water-resistant. Then at the mill dam we stripped down to our nothings and plunged feet first into the cold water, cleansing ourselves and cooling off at the same time.

What we did with the birds was disgusting, but was it any worse than peppering them with buckshot as they came flapping into the afternoon sky, all blameless and terrified? People have funny ideas about animals. A physics teacher once told me he'd worked for an aerospace company, testing the effects of bird strikes. All day long he threw dead chickens into spinning, metal propellers, then examined the damage. And he was a vegetarian. They kept the birds in a big, walk-in freezer. On the day he left, he lobbed a frozen turkey into a jet engine to see what would happen. Everything went bang.

Anyway, we were kids. I've eaten grouse once or twice since then, and to be truthful, can't really see what all the fuss is about, although I have to admit I wouldn't mind squeezing the trigger of one of those shotguns, even just once. The recoil can knock a man flat on his backside, or put his shoulder out of joint.

I see Everill's father, Steptoe senior, every now and again. Drives an old Dormobile instead of the horse and cart, but still ferrets through wheelie bins at the side of the road or plunders the tip for old beds and toilet seats. Everill died. Cancer of the throat. Unusual in such a young man, they said, but then again it was rare to see him without a fag in his gob. And when you've got the body of a stick insect and less brain cells than a dead battery, something's going to snap, eventually. Maybe it's a blessing, because he was a maniac, that kid. If he'd still been alive today, he would have killed somebody.

Firepower. Cap guns, pop guns, spud guns, water pistols, laser pens, air rifles. The turquoise mark, like a borstal spot, on Pompus's cheek where Stubbs shot him in the face. An accident. The pellet's still in there and he's got an X-ray to prove it. The army pistol in my father's bedside cabinet, wrapped in a square of cloth, and the carton of bullets.

20

I was having a good week. On Monday I'd painted some bloke's summer house in Lepley and creosoted his shed roof. Ten-o'clock start, four-o'clock finish, fifty pounds cash and no questions asked. He kind of hinted that he wouldn't mind me washing his windows as well, but I don't really see myself at the top of a ladder with a bucket of water in one hand and a chamois in the other. That's not what I'm about.

The hotel on the ring road liked the menus I'd done for them and wanted some more, and also a notice for every room, asking guests not to use all the towels unless they're having a baby, and not to flush the toilet fully unless they're getting rid of illegal substances before the drug squad arrive. Or something like that. For the environment, in fact. Anyway, I drove up there on Tuesday lunchtime with a few samples, and got a free meal in the bar while the owner gave my handiwork the once-over. He was chuffed, and I finished the job the same afternoon. I didn't drop them off until Wednesday evening, though, in case he thought the 120 I'd charged was too much for four hours' work. They offered me a three-course meal in the carvery that night, but the restaurant was full of slimy reps with their M&S ties dangling in the chicken noodle soup. Not really my scene.

Thursday I was supposed to pick Travis up from school while Kim went to a new aerobics class at the town hall.

In her condition.

He was dosed up when I got there, all dreamy and soft, swishing his head slowly from one side to the other and singing his version of one of the Disney tunes.

' "When you wiss upon a thtar." '

There was an envelope stuffed in his top pocket with my name on it, a note from Kim asking me to take a few photographs and get them framed. It was a year since he'd had a proper portrait done, and she didn't want the school photographer to do them again. He made all the children at that school look like inmates at an asylum, or case studies in one of those pictorial-diagnosis manuals they sell in medical bookshops.

I set up the backcloth and ran off a couple of films, close-ups mainly, from the shoulders upwards, and three or four in profile. Without the Ritalin it would have been impossible, like trying to photograph a Tasmanian Devil on heat. The drug made him slow and obliging. He sat for almost an hour as I adjusted the lights and tinkered with the camera and snapped away. He stared into the middle distance, lost in one of his thoughts. Every time the flash went off he screwed up his little face and shut his eyes tightly, as if he were keeping the light inside his head for as long as he could, trapping it behind his eyelids. Then he'd blink over and over again, looking at something I couldn't see, holding out his hand to try and catch or touch it, grabbing at thin air. I was daydreaming myself, imagining a paranormal moment in the darkroom, lifting the negatives out of the tray and seeing the magic myself. Some ball of light or silver angel caught on camera for the first time, hovering there in front of Travis's face, at his fingertips. Evidence of his own little world at long last, a sign, something that proved him right.

I studied his features, noticed the smallness of his mouth and his dry, bloodless lips. And the strain across his forehead, and the tiredness under his eyes, and a tension in each eye, enclosing or guarding a darkness, there, in the pit of the eye, that could only be fear. He was peeping out of his own head. Not looking with his eyes, but looking out from somewhere behind. That blackness, when I found it in the lens, made me jump. As if I'd lifted a stone. Such a contrast as well with his face, not flesh-coloured at all but white in the proper sense of the word, without colour or shade. I pulled back, and finished the roll with a couple of full-length shots of Travis stood on his head – his one and only trick – then ran him a bath.

'Butteo. Butteo.'

'No Subbuteo tonight,' I said.

I thought the tears might start, but the Ritalin was still doing its stuff, and after I'd dried him off and dressed him ready for bed, I sat him down behind a huge plate of biscuits and stuck a Tommy Tippy cup full of warm milk in his hands.

'Film time, Travis. Want to watch daddy on film?'

'Veejo, veejo.'

'Kind of. Travis eat his supper.'

I hadn't watched the old cine films for ages, but with the white cloth draped across the wall of the living room, now was as good a time as any. I fished one of the reels out of the box and threaded it across the lens and around the second spool, then set it going and dipped the lights. The projector purred. Black and white numbers flashed against the screen in descending order, and the show started.

We were twelve, thirteen maybe, when we scrambled along one of the overflow ducts at the side of the reservoir, and came out through a manhole cover behind the pump house. I remember the stink, and the rats scuttling about up ahead, their red eyes flashing in the beam of the torch.

'Look, Travis, there's daddy.' I pointed a huge, shadowy finger at myself.

Four of us lowered ourselves into the hole. Then the action cut to the manhole as we hauled ourselves out, Stubbs, Winkie, me and Tony Football, covered in weeds and mud. I think we'd been watching *The Great Escape* and fancied ourselves as English prisoners of war tunnelling our way to freedom. In the next scene, we jumped on our bikes, and the camera followed us down the terraces of the reservoir bank and off along the side of the river.

I hooked up another reel, a birthday party this time, starting with my brother blowing out the candles on his cake, and Pompus jamming a whole bun in his mouth in one go, then grabbing for a second. The third film was older still, my father drooling over his brand new Ford Corsair. Lots of footage of chrome bumpers and polished hubcaps, and ten minutes of indeterminate landscape shaking past the car window, presumably shot by mum, cut with shots of my father at the wheel, upright in his seat, hands at ten to two, the model driver.

I'd forgotten about the last film in the box. I'd been going out with Kim a couple of years when we set off for a weekend in North Yorkshire. We'd stuck a tent in the back of the car but it was raining, as per, and we were feeling pretty flush for some reason, so we stopped at the tourist information office in York and picked up leaflets for B&Bs in the Dales. Kim liked the sound of a place called Lighthouse Farm, so we pulled up at a phone box off the A1, and booked. We had a good day, despite the weather. Took in a couple of country houses and their walled gardens, wandered the length of the lawned terrace above Rievaulx – like a fairway on God's private golf course – then started out for Lighthouse Farm, following the farmer's very basic directions.

'He said we'd know it when we saw it,' said Kim.

Sure enough, after bouncing along a cart track for a couple of miles, stopping every two or three hundred yards to open and close a gate, we came over the top of a steep hill, and immediately on the left was a smallish stone-built farmhouse, dwarfed by an actual lighthouse. It must have stood at least a hundred feet high. Two sheepdogs came out and barked at the car, followed by the 'farmer', wearing a fishing smock, a pair of deck shoes and a sailor's hat. He was an American, and straightaway launched into his story. How he'd skippered a cargo ship up and down the Great Lakes until the company he worked for went bust. With his English wife they'd come to Yorkshire about fifteen years ago, bought the farm with his redundancy money, and gone into the guest-house game. Then his wife had died, so there was just him and the dogs. All this information came out of his mouth like a recorded announcement, a tired and uninspired speech he'd given a thousand times to tired and uninspired travellers. But as his hand swept upwards to indicate the huge wooden structure towering above us, his tone changed and his face began to glow.

'Which brings us to this.'

He was a fanatic. The more he talked, the more I wondered if he wasn't a nutcase as well. The building was a precise scale model of a lighthouse somewhere on the western seaboard of the States. It had taken nine years to build, single-handedly, not to mention about 20,000 pounds and two heart attacks. It was made of the finest materials available and could withstand wind speeds of over 200 miles per hour. The lamp itself was pukka lighthouse tackle imported from Sweden, and the many documents framed in the glass panels of the door were all types of operating licences, one of them granted by the Civil Aviation Authority.

'Low-flying planes, ya see. Might think I was an airport. Wouldn't want a jumbo landing in the kitchen.'

He explained, without a glimmer of irony, that this was the only inland lighthouse in the county, then embarked on a monologue of lighthouse trivia, including the tallest, the stoutest, the oldest, the loneliest, and so on. His party piece was a roll-call of all the lighthouses safeguarding the shores of Lake Superior, in the correct, clockwise order, followed by a lament for the ancient trade of lighthouse-keeping, followed by some seething comments on the age of automation.

His wife had obviously killed herself or run away to Leeds.

We followed him up the narrowing corkscrew of wooden stairs, my face level with the heels of his pumps, then emerged through a trapdoor next to the lamp itself, and went outside on to the observation deck. The view, it has to be said, was amazing. Even in the fading light I could see out across the Vale of York and the North York Moors, and further.

'I bet you can see the sea from up here, on a clear day,' I said.

'No,' he said. 'Not the sea.'

Over dinner he tortured us with more facts and figures about lighthouses. The smallest, the worst disaster, the first woman lighthouse-keeper.

Kim said, 'I've never been to America but I'd like to go to Florida. What's Florida like?'

He rubbed his Captain Birds Eye beard between his fingers. 'Oh, sure, they've got a lot of lighthouses in Florida.'

We took a bottle of wine to our room and locked the door. We got drunk, had sex, fell asleep on top of the bed. At three o'clock in the morning I woke up dreaming about shipwrecks and black-box flight recorders. I imagined a full moon outside in the sky filling the room with a cold, silvery glow, and clouds passing across it as the room darkened, then the moon again. It was only when I stumbled into the bathroom for a pee and looked out of the little window that I saw the great beam of light arcing across the night sky, reaching over acres of moorland and fields. I ducked under the windowsill as it swept past, blasting the loo with a flash of harsh, mercury-coloured light, and as I peered after it, I definitely caught a glimpse of the captain himself on the observation deck, looking out across the land, watching for vessels in distress. It was a hot night. I lay awake on the bed for another hour at least, with the light from the lighthouse threshing through the room every thirty seconds until dawn.

Kim swears that Travis was conceived at Lighthouse Farm. It's part of our history, a given fact. I've no idea how she can say for definite that the drunken fuck on top of those nylon sheets underneath the huge, useless lighthouse was the one that did the trick, but she seems to know about these things.

Clearly, she knows quite a lot about this type of thing.

In my opinion, the cine camera has something to do with it. The past is full of holes. Something like a film or a photograph feels certain and fixed. Maybe we'd done it a dozen times or more that month, but we'd never forget the night at Lighthouse Farm, and the film was a kind of evidence that made it real and true. So that was the one.

'Look, Travis, look at mummy and daddy on the film.'

Travis stood up and wandered into the stream of light. Psychedelic colours played on his shirt, swam on his shoulders and the back of his head. His shadow filled the screen, massive and blurred at first, then smaller and more defined, solid and black and sharp as he moved towards his own, empty likeness with his arms outstretched. Then he turned towards the beam, and our features –

Kim's and mine – flashed across his blank face, and he stared and blinked, and reached out once more to touch that impossible, invisible thing only he could see.

On Friday I picked him up again, this time with instructions to take him for a haircut. I drove down to the barber's only to find a notice Blu-Tacked to the door saying the barber was off on holiday and wouldn't be back for a fortnight. Half a dozen lank-haired brats were milling around outside the shop, with their mothers banging on the window. Can't people read? Most of the kids were better off hidden behind their greasy mops, in my view, being ugly as sin, and just at the age when having to look more than an inch in front of your nose is too much trouble in the first place.

Not to be defeated, I sat Travis down on one of the dining chairs at home, slung a tablecloth around his neck and started to give him a quick trim. Unfortunately, he was in one of his more active moods, and kept jolting his head from side to side and giggling every time a lock of hair fell in front of his face. I had visions of perforating his eardrum or impaling his eyeball with the scissors, or committing some other inexplicable act of child cruelty. It was a case of a snip here and a snip there, darting in and out whenever I saw a chance. When I stood back, the poor lad's head was a total disaster area, with some strands still hanging down over his ear-lugs and other patches that were cropped to the bone. I tried to tidy things up, but another twenty minutes of cutting and trimming only made it worse. It looked as if I'd set about him with a knife and fork. Time was running out. Pretty soon Kim would be knocking at the door. In one last desperate measure, I got the old dog-clippers that were hanging on a hook behind the cellar door, gave them a quick slush under the tap, and in four or five strokes from his forehead to the nape of his neck, sheared off every hair on his head to a length of not more than a quarter of an inch.

In front of the mirror he pawed at himself, rubbed the palms of his hands against the stubble, felt all over his head for the missing hair. I've seen the skinheads and suedeheads drinking in the precinct on a Saturday, their skulls dinted by truncheons and baseball bats, their scalps like the skin of elephant seals – flawed by scratches and slashes and bites and God-knows-what. But Travis was perfect, not a mark on him. I will admit that the image of that strange alien creature supposedly pulled from a spaceship in Roswell, New Mexico, did flash through my mind, but only for a split second. 'You look like a pop star, boy,' I told him, as I dusted away the shavings from behind his ears and under his chin. 'You look like the next big thing.'

Kim did not think he looked like a pop star or the next big thing. She asked two questions. The first was directed at me but required no answer. It was rhetorical. As she stood in the doorway and stared hard at her son, she said, 'What have you done?' The second was shouted from the car window as she screeched out of the drive. 'Why didn't you just lobotomize him at the same time and be finished with it?'

21

In convoy, we followed Tony Football's Kawasaki along the unmade road between the canal and the railway line. Now and again a shock absorber thumped in the wheel arch as I drove at speed over a pothole, or the exhaust scraped on a bump in the track. There's something exciting about driving with the headlights off, like being on military manoeuvres, creeping closer to enemy lines under cover of darkness. TF pulled into the open yard of the Water Board depot, and we all parked under the high wall of the boathouse, Winkie in his Mondeo, Stubbs in his Volvo with Pompus in the passenger seat, like a prisoner under escort. We crossed over the little humpback bridge and followed the towpath around the basin to where the dark, still water of the canal disappeared through a massive iron grille in the side of the hill. Steam floated out of the black hole of the entrance. Over the wall was the huge, open mouth of the railway tunnel, and, to the left, a smaller service tunnel, enclosed by cast-iron gates with a heavy-duty chain looped through the ironwork and fastened with a single enormous padlock.

'What the hell are we doing down here?' said Winkie. 'It's nearly eleven o'clock, and this is private property. Isn't it?'

'All in good time,' said Tony Football.

From his holdall, he pulled out a camcorder and began fiddling around with the switches and buttons. Stubbs sat down on an oily old railway sleeper, drew out a cigarette from a packet of B&H and lit up. His face shone in the flare of the match, before he flicked it away into the water.

'I didn't know you smoked any more,' I said.

'Yeah, well, there's a lot of things I'm doing these days I thought I'd left behind. I'm regressing. I'll probably be wearing shorts next time you see me.'

'Don't tell me you're not enjoying yourself, though,' I said.

'Oh, sure, I'm having the time of my life.' He pulled hard on the cigarette and blew the smoke out of the corner of his mouth.

'OK, gents,' said Tony Football. 'Here's the deal.'

We gathered around him as he outlined the dare, Pompus with his chest puffed out and his arms folded, ready for his assignment.

'You won't need me to remind you that we're standing at the mouth of one of the longest tunnels in Europe. Just over three miles under the Pennines. Three separate shafts – the canal, the railway, and this service tunnel. So, Pompus, that's where you're going tonight, old pal. We'll be waving you off in a couple of minutes, and we don't want to see you again until you pop out in Lancashire. Shouldn't take you more than an hour, even a big lad like you.'

'So how do I get through those gates? I'm not Harry fucking Houdini, you know.'

From the pocket of his biking jacket Tony Football produced a big, chunky key that could have been the key to a dungeon in a fairy story.

'Where did you get that from?' asked Winkie.

'Let's just say I've got connections, and leave it at that.' He strolled over to the tunnel, and after messing with the lock for a minute or so, swung open each side of the iron gates.

Pompus stared into the black hole in front of him.

'How will we know if he's done it?' said Stubbs. '*You* might want to go and hang around at the far side till one in the morning, but I don't.'

Tony held up the camera for everyone to see. 'There's an hour's battery in this thing, including the light. We'll watch the film next Friday night to make sure you've been through, Pompus. And don't think about tinkering with it – if you switch it off the time code stops, so we'll know. And I've marked the cassette, by the way. So, one continuous film, starting with a shot of us lot and finishing with a shot of the signal box at the far end.'

He lifted the camera to his eye, panned across the four of us, then zoomed in on Pompus's face before handing it over. 'Off you go. Oh, and don't break it. They cost about a grand, them. It's only on loan, and I gave them your name and address. OK?'

'How am I supposed to get home afterwards?' said Pompus, in a flat, lifeless voice.

'No idea. Walk back through again if you dare, but remember the battery will have gone by then, so it'll be very, very dark.'

Pompus looked down at the camera whirring in his hand, then at the tunnel, then at Tony Football.

'Fifty-nine minutes left,' said Tony, tapping the face of his watch with the nail of his index finger.

Pompus looked at the tunnel again. Even in the dark I could see the nervousness and the reluctance in his body language.

'Piece of piss,' he said, shaking his head and forcing a laugh. 'Hardly worth the effort.'

He put the camera to his face and set off. We watched as the light illuminated the entrance, showing up the dilapidated brickwork of the walls, picking out weeds and roots hanging from the roof. 'Piece of piss,' we heard him shout from somewhere inside, like a voice at the bottom of a well. After a minute or so I walked over to the portal and looked into the long darkness in front, expecting to see Pompus's great bulk reduced to something no bigger than the end of my thumb, a squat, cut-out figure at the wrong end of a telescope, framed by the walls. But there wasn't even a flicker of light. Already the hill had swallowed him up. Tony Football was standing beside me in the clammy air, staring down the same barrel of darkness. 'Terrifying,' he said. Then he walked forward, and swung the iron gates back across the entrance, cere-monially almost, as if he were closing the gates of a stately home. Slowly and quietly he bound them together with the chain, and clipped the padlock between two of the links.

'Softly, softly, catch a monkey,' he said.

'Why have you locked him in?'

'Oh, you know, just a bit of encouragement. We all need a bit of encouragement, don't we, Barney?'

He dropped the key back in his pocket and smiled.

'So why this?' said Stubbs, as we walked back towards the cars. 'Why the tunnel for Pompus?'

Tony Football was grinning from one side of his mug to the other, and obviously couldn't wait to explain. 'Got to do your homework, haven't you? Got to use your noddle. I got a package through the post this week, a cine film transferred to video, us lot in the overflow duct that time. Courtesy of you, Barney, I suppose?'

'I sent one to everyone,' I told him. 'I found it in the attic and thought you'd all appreciate a copy. I thought it was the perfect time.'

'Oh, the timing was immaculate, especially for me. Because, when I sat down to watch it, I kept thinking there was something missing, something not quite right. And then it dawned on me – there were only four of us – me, and you three.'

'Well, that's pretty obvious. One person had to stay up top and do the filming,' said Winkie.

'Precisely, but why Pompus? He's not exactly Martin Scorsese, is he? Well, I'll tell you why. Because he volunteered. Because he was scared of the dark.'

'I don't think so, not Pompus,' I said.

'Oh, yes. Remember how he peed his pants on the ghost train at Southport and pretended he'd spilt his drink? I'm telling you. Big hard Pompus, scared of the dark.'

'But that was hundreds of years ago.'

' "The Child is father of the Man," ' said TF.

'Wordsworth,' said Winkie, quick as a flash.

'I didn't know you read poetry, Winkie,' I said.

'I don't. Me and Maureen are in a quiz team on Sunday nights. I read those trivia books when I'm on the toilet at work, and that was one of the questions. Go on, ask me another.'

Tony Football straddled his bike, pulled on his helmet and lifted the visor. 'I drove past his house a couple of nights this week – lit up like a fairground it was, inside and out. Well, goodnight, boys.

I really hope I charged that battery up properly. They can be pretty temperamental, those cameras.'

He roared off in a big, exaggerated circle, revving the engine and pulling a wheelie as he went past. I got in my car and followed him along the side of the canal, with Winkie behind me, and Stubbs bringing up the rear.

Out on the main road I had to think quickly and carefully at the same time. It's not easy. Like rubbing your tummy with one hand and patting yourself on the head with the other. Most people end up in a total mess. I was in a state of deep concentration, and must have driven at least two miles with no lights before a police car going the other way flashed me and gave me a blast with the siren. I nearly jumped out of my skin, as if I'd been fast asleep and some sadist had poured a teaspoon of icy water into my ear. It's a good way to wake a horse, apparently. I flicked on the headlights and held up my hand as a gesture of apology or thanks, and in the rear-view mirror was glad to see the cop car carrying on in the opposite direction, turning the corner out of sight.

I had to think fast. Like an airline pilot. If his plane develops engine trouble during take-off, he might have just three or four seconds to make a life-or-death calculation. He can abort, but only if there's still enough runway to play with, and the wrong estimation can mean ploughing through the perimeter fence into a container depot or council estate. Or he can try and gain altitude, dump fuel and bring the plane back in to land. But the engine failure might be catastrophic, in which case the thing is probably going to fall out off the sky and end up as a piece of smouldering junk with firemen crawling all over it looking for little black boxes and luggage tags.

Pompus, scared of the dark? Wasn't he just too fat for the manhole?

And why did Tony Football lock those gates?

I tried to do the sums, work out the equations, but it was all very confusing and spherical. Why was he taking it out on Pompus when it was Winkie he really wanted to whack? Also, if Pompus did try to double back and found the gates closed, he might shit himself, sure, but then he'd *have* to walk through the tunnel. He'd have no choice but to win the dare, and, four weeks later, Tony Football might be sitting down to a turd supper again, this time without sauce. Or did Tony Football really think he could out-dare the lot of us, work his way right around the circle, have his revenge on Winkie and even win the little green man, starting with this stunt tonight? In which case, *why did he lock the gates?*

Answer: he wasn't thinking straight. There was no motive for locking the tunnel. Only anger. It's all very well being logical and reasonable, being all equilateral and unemotional, but see it from the other side, I told myself. Forget the flash motorbike, the leather gauntlets and smoked-glass visor, the well-chosen words, the cunning plan, the cool exterior. *Put yourself in his position*, I said out loud. That's when I tasted the shit between his teeth and under his tongue. That's when I swung the car round.

Man, after all, is a predator, and like all predators, he goes for the easy meat. We pounce on the weak, prey on the feeble. We thrive on the self-destructive and their errors of judgement. That's not some piece of trivia you can learn from a quiz book sat on the bog in your lunch break. It's philosophical wisdom achieved through five million years of experience. Tony Football was all fizzed up about things. I could step in. I could capitalize. If Pompus made it through the tunnel, he'd be mad as a wasp in a jam jar, and I'd be on the receiving end. I didn't want another tattoo. But if Pompus bottled it and came back through the gates, he'd be out of the game. The circle would change direction, and I'd be in the clear for up to another three weeks. The great ideas in history, I've read, always come in one blinding flash – they don't need working out. In the same moment, I saw the tyre wrench lying in the boot of the car, and heard in my mind the sound – like the crack of a walnut shell – of a padlock being jemmied apart.

But down at the tunnel the gates are already open. The chain's thrown to one side with the padlock clipped to one of the metal links, fastened and intact, in one piece, not forced. By now it's truly dark, which is why I notice the red glow of a cigarette butt, smouldering on the towpath. It's summer. People should make sure those things are properly extinguished before flicking them away without a second thought. That's how fires start.

22

Of course, the great thing about calling Pompus 'Pompus' is this:
it's his name. Not the name on his passport, and not the name he
signs at the dole office every fortnight, and certainly not the name
his mother calls him. But his name, nevertheless. Not that I'm a
prude. Not that I'm in any position to go on about the sanctity of
marriage. And why should it bother me if one of my mates was
born the wrong side of the blanket? But it's a damned shame when
parents don't tell their kids something as important as who their
father is, especially when the rest of the world are yakking about it
over a cup of tea and a vanilla slice. Imagine how painful it would
be – to find out a thing like that from somebody else.

Let's say I heard it through the wall, the story about his mother
and a certain Mr Harold Pompus, no longer of the parish. Let's say
mum was never one for keeping things under her hat, and that if a
doctors' receptionist doesn't know what's going on in a small
northern town, then who does? Every night after tea she'd put her
feet up in front of the telly, and prattle on to my father about this
that and the other.

'And, Donald, you'll never guess . . .'

Donald wasn't listening – he was reading the *Telegraph*. Through
the serving hatch in the wall, though, I couldn't help but hear.

'I shouldn't be telling you this, Donald, but I heard something
today I couldn't believe.'

My ears twitched. Soap suds dripped from my rubber gloves.

Next Saturday we were all at the baths. It would have made a
great photograph, the five us on the diving board, all lined up ready
to take the plunge. Stubbs went first, a backwards summersault,
then Tony Football with a graceful swallow-dive that hardly made
a ripple. Winkie was stalling, adjusting his goggles, when Pompus

kicked him in the small of the back and sent him cartwheeling into the water.

'Nice one, Pompus.'

'What did you call me?'

The diving board was still reverberating from Winkie's surprise departure.

'Pompus.'

'What's that supposed to mean?'

'It's your new nickname,' I said. 'It means a person who's pretty pleased with himself.'

The board started to bend as he took a couple of steps towards the far end.

'Brill. Guess what, it's my uncle's name as well!'

'No kidding,' I said. The diving board twanged like a huge tuning fork as Pompus lunged head first into mid-air. Then waves of foam broke over the side of the baths. Looking down into the blue-green water under my toes, I could see the great, pink blob of his body moving slowly along the bottom. I put my hands in the air, bent my knees, and was just about to launch into the pool when, out of the depths, rising through the bubbles like some hideous, multi-coloured fish, came his ginormous, tie-dye swimming trunks.

We were kids. Twenty-odd years ago. I've got a pretty good memory as far as it goes, but you can't leave a matter as crucial as that to a chance remark overheard in the dim-and-distant, through a serving hatch. After all that time you need to check things out once and for all, get yourself down to the Family Records Centre in Islington and dig out the proof. If you ask me, it's a scandal that any old Freeman, Hardy or Willis can walk in off the street and order up a copy of someone's birth certificate for just six and a half quid and no questions asked. But I didn't make the law; I was just an interested party exercising a democratic right. And anyway I was in the area.

By half-nine on Friday Pompus hadn't shown up at my place, so we all piled into one car and drove to his house. The place was in darkness. Tony Football banged on the door and called his number using his mobile phone. We could hear it ringing out inside the house, but there was nobody home.

Down at the tunnel entrance, the gates were locked. Tony produced the key, and we set off into the darkness, each of us carrying a torch. Drops of water fell through the beams of light. Bats swung from one wall to the other. After ten minutes we passed the skeleton of a dead animal, a sheep probably, going by the size.

'One of yours, Winkie?' said Stubbs.

The distance was impossible to judge. We could have been two miles under the hill or just a couple of hundred yards when a train went hammering through the tunnel to our right. The racket was deafening as the sound ricocheted through the connecting passageways and against the brickwork.

'What if he went through on to the railway line?' said Winkie. He was holding on to the back of my jacket.

'Then we'd have read about it in the paper,' said Tony Football.

'Well, what if he wandered through into the canal? There's no towpath in there.'

'Oh, stop fretting. He can swim, can't he? Can't he?'

I crossed over into the canal tunnel and shone my torch on to the water. It was shiny and black, like a long channel of engine oil, absolutely still and undisturbed. Not even a water rat, or a pair of ginormous, tie-dye trunks.

The bricks eventually gave way to roughly carved rock, more like a pothole than a tunnel. If a caveman had lurched out of the shadows wearing a tiger-skin and wielding the tusk of a woolly mammoth, he wouldn't have been out of place. Then came the graffiti, names and dates going back to the nineteenth century, chiselled into the stone, and more recent additions in spray-paint, including the Stone Roses in metallic gold, and LUFC, expertly rendered in blue, white and yellow. To my way of thinking, it seemed a long way to come to express an affection for a particular band or allegiance to a football team, and for another thing, who was going to read it? More appropriate, I thought, was the ten-foot-high pentangle daubed in red paint. It filled an entire wall of a central cavern that must have been hollowed out to mark the halfway point. In one corner was a large animal skull. Stubbs jumped as his torch caused a giant shadow, like a scarecrow, to hurry across the stonework, and as we all angled our beams upwards, we lit up a large wooden cross, hanging upside down from a hook in the roof.

'Took me hours to get all this lot together,' said Tony Football.

'Come again?' I said.

'Have you ever tried buying a wooden crucifix? Well, Woollies don't sell them, I can tell you that much. And I had to go to a joke shop in Bradford for that plastic skull, then come plodding down here on Friday teatime to light the candles and get that five-sided star splashed on the wall.'

'You mean you set all this lot up?' I asked him.

This was sensational. A revelation.

'Sure did. Not bad, eh, for a poofter. I would have given anything to see Pompus's face when he got to this bit.'

'Well, you might just do that,' said Stubbs. He'd picked something up from the floor about ten yards further into the tunnel, and was walking back towards us, holding the video camera by its leather strap.

'It's that *Blair Witch* job all over again,' said Stubbs, as I fitted the Scart connector into the back of the video, and sat back in the chair with the remote. Tony Football stood up and dimmed the lights.

'These digital cameras are marvellous. The quality, I mean. You just watch.'

He was right. It could have been a fly-on-the-wall documentary. Winkie smiled at the camera like a total amateur. I stared into the lens. Stubbs pulled on his cigarette. Then the screen filled with Pompus's great phizog – like the moon through binoculars. Tony's voice was loud and distinctive from behind the camera. 'Off you go. Oh, and don't break it. They cost about a grand, them.'

'Whiz it on a bit. Let's cut to the chase,' he said.

I held down the fast-forward button. It was like a speeded-up film of an underwater salvage mission – remote-controlled probing of a sunken ship, nosing along corridors, glancing into cabins and cupboards, inching through funnels and flues. The walls of the tunnel zipped past the lens, the brickwork, then the roughly carved stone and graffiti.

'Woah. Do it from here.'

The time code in the top corner had reached thirty-two minutes as Pompus approached the central cavern. He was wheezing and panting, groping his way along the wall, and fell over several times, resulting in a series of close-ups of the gravel floor and the tunnel roof.

'Turn it up,' said Tony Football.

'Oh Jesus, oh Jesus,' Pompus was mumbling to himself. 'Oh Jesus Christ, oh Jesus.'

'Listen to him, the big lardy. He's going to mess his trousers in a minute, you just wait.'

Maybe Pompus thought he'd got to the far end, because he seemed to be rushing towards the light in the central chamber. Then he slowed, then stopped, and the automatic focus homed in on two candles shining in the eye sockets of the skull.

'Oh Jesus fucking Christ. Oh no, oh Jesus.'

The pentangle swung into view, then the cross. From the angle, I could imagine Pompus crouching on the floor, cowering from the nightmare. Then came the whimpering and the blubbing, the shouting for his mother, then the clumsy footsteps disappearing into the distance as he galloped off down the tunnel, dropping the camera, leaving a fuzzy, unresolved image of the tunnel wall or the ground. There were a few vague shuffling noises in the background. We watched in silence for another twenty minutes or so, until the picture blinked and went out.

'Gentlemen, we have our first loser. We are now four,' said Tony Football, standing up to make the announcement.

'But where is he?' said Winkie.

Tony Football spun round so quickly that Winkie actually flinched. 'Where is he? Where is he? How should I know, you little crap? All I know is he's out of the loop. Which means the circle changes direction. Which means it's my turn to dare you. So why don't you start sweating, you repulsive, nauseating, detestable little worm.'

23

All Winkie's colour had drained away. His face was just a small, characterless circle with two blank eyeballs behind his thick glasses. His mouth was a tiny hole, like someone had pushed a finger through a drum. Tony Football stood over him, menacing and tall. He was a mad dentist or a crazy priest. At any moment, he might have reached out with his thumb and fingers, dug them into the three useless openings in Winkie's face and used his head as a bowling ball.

'Funny how things work out. It's like one of those stories in the Bible.'

Winkie's Adam's apple rose and plunged in his throat. It stuck out so far you could have thrown your hat on it.

'It's nearly midnight. I'm going home,' he managed to say.

'You're going nowhere, my friend. This won't take a minute.'

Tony Football pulled out his wallet, and from the credit-card pouch, drew a gleaming razor blade, which he held towards Winkie's throat, reflecting the low, yellow light of the room on to the underside of his chin.

'Does he like butter? Oh, yes, he likes butter all right.'

Winkie gripped the arms of the chair and turned his face to one side. 'Come off it, Tony. Don't be a madhead.'

Tony didn't move. Just stood there with the razor blade, playing the reflected light across Winkie's face.

It made me think of the music lessons at school, in the classroom with the full-length, south-facing windows, with the old, gay music teacher whose life was one long uninterrupted misery. Each time he turned to the blackboard to explain the meaning of a semibreve or spell the name of a Russian composer, every boy in the class would turn his wrist towards the sun, and conjure up a laser beam of light from the face of his watch. It was amazing, like twenty or so tiny angels let loose in a room – brilliant little Tinkerbells bouncing off the walls, dog-fighting on the ceiling, buzzing around on the back of Teeby's jacket. One kid had read a physics textbook about a mountainside laboratory in Switzerland, where the light from several thousand mirrors could melt a diamond. He reckoned if we all focused our projections on the back of Teeby's head we could very easily burn a hole in his skull and zap his brains. But on the day of reckoning it was cloudy. And the week after that a big, beefy supply teacher strutted into the classroom and told us that Teeby had taken early retirement. In fact he'd been caught in a public toilet in Manchester – mum said so over a piece of Battenburg one night. And the last I heard, he was a choirmaster somewhere in the Lakes.

Winkie was avoiding eye contact with Tony Football, looking towards the wall and talking out of the side of his mouth.

'Come on. We've all had enough for one night. Barney, tell him it's got to wait until next week.'

The Adam's apple went again, this time in profile, like a piston under his skin. I was about to agree with him, not out of sympathy or anything like that, more on the basis that it would be even better to let things simmer for a week, bring them back to the boil next Friday. What was the rush?

Stubbs, though, had different ideas. 'I say we keep going. And so does Tony, by the look on his face. And you don't get a vote, Winkie, because you're in the chair. And Pompus is either floating in the canal or splattered all over the front of the Pennine Sprinter, or still legging it across Lancashire in a pair of brown undies. So don't think Barney here's going to turn into your fairy godmother, because even if he wants to postpone the agony, he's outvoted. So pipe down and accept it. Tony, he's all yours.'

'Yes,' said Tony Football, whispering into Winkie's ear. 'You be a good little boy. Take it like a man.'

Winkie didn't have to stay. He could have walked. Or he could have leapt from the seat, legged it out of the house and down the road. Maybe he thought mad Tony Football would chase him all the way home, slashing at his back with the blade. Or that Stubbs would deck him before he got to the door. Or maybe I should credit him with some pride or courage, the way he sat there in the armchair, pale and motionless, ready for the chop. He'd seen the lengths Tony had gone to in the tunnel – the camera, the candles, the pentangle daubed on the wall, the head with lights in its eyes. It must have taken hours, days even, and what had Pompus done to deserve it? Nothing. So whatever was coming now was going to be pretty special – you didn't have to be a computer programmer to work that out. It wasn't just going to be a case of saying the alphabet backwards or eating three cream crackers without water. This was going to be a proper Brahma, sheer gravy, the dog's cods, and Winkie knew it. So I have to give him credit for sitting tight, for staying put. Unless it was greed. Pure greed. The thought of all that money rooting him to the spot.

Tony Football had been gathering his thoughts for the big speech. 'When we were playing five-a-side a few weeks back, don't think I didn't see you staring at those scabs on my legs and on my back.'

He pulled up his trouser leg to show us a browny-red mark on his left calf, like a cross between a mole and a burn.

'I never,' said Winkie.

'I think so, too. Maybe you thought I'd fallen off my bike, or that all those sliding tackles were taking their toll. Well, I'm afraid these sores are a little more serious than that. You see, Winkie, there's a nasty little disease doing the rounds. Anyone can get it, but us queers have really cornered the market. Gets into the blood and it won't come out. You can take a whole bunch of tablets for your breakfast and keep your chin up and your fingers crossed, but it gets you in the end. Do you understand what I'm talking about?'

'I'm sorry,' whispered Winkie.

'I bet you are. Anyway, let me put it this way. You were kind enough to invite me for a meal a few weeks ago. The food was diabolical and the company wasn't much better, but as an experience it was unforgettable.'

Holding the razor blade in his left hand, he extended his right towards Winkie's face, then calmly and quickly dragged the blade across the tip of his own index finger. It was a deep cut. Blood welled up instantaneously from the wound, running back along his finger into the palm of his hand.

'I'd just like to offer you a little nightcap, Winkie. *Afore ye go.*'

He pushed the bleeding finger towards Winkie's face. Winkie curled his lips inside his mouth and manoeuvred his head gradually backwards. It could have been a rattlesnake or a cobra, rearing up at him.

'Come on, Winkie. One for the road. It won't bite you.'

If Winkie could have pushed himself through the back of the chair he would have. His lips were clamped shut, and behind them his teeth were locked together, reinforced by the barricade of his tongue, backed up by the clenched and knotted muscles in his throat. I thought of Travis when he was eight months old, refusing his food.

'No?' inquired Tony Football.

There was a pause. No answer.

'No? Not for Uncle Tony? Not even for the green man, locked away in the cupboard? Come on, you greedy bastard. Think of all that munka, all the fish and chips you could take home for little Mo. Get it down you.'

He jabbed at Winkie with the finger, smearing his cheek with blood. There was a longer pause. The dark, red liquid still oozed from the cut. It seemed like the only colour in the room.

'No,' said Winkie, finally. 'I won't.'

Tony Football stood back, dropped the razor blade in the bin, and waved at Winkie with his bloody hand. 'Bye-bye, Winkie.'

Winkie stares, not at the hand though, but through it, through the open fingers, across the room. He's staring at me. I wait for him to blink, but he doesn't. Just keeps on glaring through those glasses of his, as if I'm the one who's been trying to stick a fingerful of germs down his gullet. As if it's all my fault. He doesn't cry, though, I'll give him that. He gets to his feet, crosses the room, and is halfway through the door when he turns around and says, 'You people.'

Then he leaves.

'Well, I think that's quite enough excitement for one night,' I said. I blew out a long stream of breath that made my fringe flap up and down above my forehead.

'Stay where you are,' said Tony Football.

Like someone trying to get a splinter out of his finger he pressed down on the flesh with his thumbnails, working fresh blood out of the cut.

'Now it's your turn,' he said. He reached forward and dabbed me on the end of the nose.

'I, Solomon, having one spot, how many spots hast thou, oh Barnaby?' said Stubbs.

'What are you on about?'

'It's this game we used to play at home. You burn the bottom of a champagne cork and smudge someone on the face every time they get the saying wrong. You see, everyone takes a character from the Bible, and –'

'Shut up about the Bible,' shouted Tony Football. 'We're not playing *I, Solomon*, we're playing Barney sucks the end of this finger or he's out as well.'

Tony's bloody finger loomed in front of me, huge and blurred, too close to focus on, blotting out half the room.

'It's all a bit irregular. One dare straight after the last. Don't you think we should cool off for a week?' I said.

I was flustered. I felt my cheeks burning. I'd spent so much time thinking about what Tony Football was doing to Winkie I'd completely forgotten about myself. I'd forgotten the first law of friendship, the golden rule. And now everything was spinning, running out like water down a plughole, draining away to nothing. I couldn't stop it. It had a force all of its own. The music had stopped, and all the chairs were taken. It was the penalty for losing concentration for a split second, for taking my eye off the ball.

'Play on,' said Stubbs.

'What do you mean, "play on"?' I shouted. 'Like you're the fucking ref all of a sudden.'

He pulled a packet of B&H put of his pocket and lit up, then after a few drags said, 'Come on, Barney. Open wide. Say ahhhh.'

Livingstone, Campbell, Scott . . .

I open my jaw a little, then a little more, cranking it wider, one notch at a time.

Franklin, Raleigh . . .

My tongue retreats to the very back of my throat, recoils like a snail in its shell, and I squint as the finger closes in, squint till it hurts, squint so much I feel my eyes are meeting in the middle, crossing sides. I'm not a person who spends a lot of time contemplating death. I'm a survivor. Like some of the great adventurers and pioneers, I've got the survival instinct. It's in my genes. But in an instant, with Tony Football's manky finger staring me in the face, I see those heroes for what they really are. Failures. Failures, every one, and dead ones at that. Men who flopped and misfired and generally screwed up, and managed to get themselves killed into the bargain.

I rack my brains, go through the list. What about Shackleton – he lived. A year off the coast of Antarctica with the frozen sea crushing his ship to matchwood. Six months hopscotching it over pack-ice eating nothing but husky dogs and hoosh. Two weeks on godforsaken Elephant Island sleeping on a mound of penguin dung. Sixteen days in a glorified rowing boat in the Southern Ocean being hammered by tidal waves. Then land ahoy, at last, and a thirty-mile trek over the snowy mountains of South Georgia. He made it home again, lived to tell the tale.

But what if I'm not him? What if I'm one of the other hapless gits, like the chap who survived the same ordeal, then fell down the stairs in his house and died in a broken heap, all on his own. Or another one of the crew who was whisked off to war before the ice had even melted from his boots, and was shot through the head the first time he peered over the trench. Maybe that's who I am. Not the person in charge, the main man, the one at the summit holding the flag or the chap with his foot on the tiger's head, but the dumb sap bringing up the rear with frostbite in every

145

toe or the dental imprint of a wild beast in the stump of his arm. Mentioned
in dispatches. The Sherpa, the gofer, the also-ran.

The finger passes my lips, passes my teeth. And what is the mouth,
except a kind of escape valve for the brain or an entry wound caused by
the outside world, a porthole of raw, tender flesh, a breach in the skin
where most of the hurt comes out and most of the harm goes in. I close
my eyes, imagine my tongue meeting the taste of blood, remember the
flavour of blood – nosebleeds, cavities, paper cuts – the taste of copper or
old coins. I imagine closing my lips, resting my teeth against knuckle or
nail, sucking on the bloody teat, feeling the first drop spill from the cut
and trickle down my throat, into my gut.

Me, Barney, the dentist's son.

'Don't,' he said.

I opened my eyes. Tony Football had taken away his hand and
was wrapping his finger in a white hanky. Then he picked up his
leather jacket, put on his gloves and helmet, and left.

Later, outside on the step, Stubbs tipped a can of lager above his
lips, letting the last few drops dribble into his mouth. Then he
mangled the metal with one hand and drop-kicked it over the fence.

'One question,' he said. 'Would you have done it?'

'Done what?'

'You know, Tony's blood.'

I took a gulp of my own drink and said, 'It doesn't matter now,
does it. He defaulted, so he's out of the game. End of story.'

'I thought you were in some sort of trance for a minute, sat there
with your gob wide open and your eyes closed. You looked like
one of those space stations, waiting for a rocket to dock.'

'I'd nodded off. Anyway, it's a terrible thing. About Tony, I
mean. We should do something, you know. A bit of moral support.'

Stubbs zipped up his coat and ground the butt of his cigarette
into the tarmac with his heel.

'But would you have done it? Hypothetically speaking, would
you have swallowed his blood?'

The first gulps of lager had been cool and quenching but the dregs were warm and flat. I had to force the last mouthful down.

'Hypothetically speaking?'

'Would you?'

'Hypothetically speaking, I'd have bitten his finger off at the root and spat it back in his face,' I said, before walking across the drive and putting the beer can into the dustbin, tidily.

And maybe those cans were past their sell-by date, because in the middle of the night I woke up drowning in sweat, dreaming all sorts of weird and wild things, and had to run to the bathroom to puke.

24

The secret of a good lie is this: it should contain some aspect of the truth as well. Either that, or it should be such a whopper, such a humdinger of a porky-pie, that no person in their right mind could have made it up.

The Americans, I reckon, are pretty confused about lying. They're pretty confused about most things, to be honest. They're a third-world country with money. My father said so. I've only been there once myself, to Disneyland on honeymoon, which was great, except Kim wouldn't go on any of the rides. She was pregnant with Travis at the time. Thinking back, what more harm could it have done? On the plane we had to fill in immigration cards. Questions like, 'Are you a terrorist or have you ever participated in terrorist activities?' Or, 'Are you plotting to overthrow the democratically elected government of the United States of America?' Questions like that. Maybe lying carries a stiff penalty in the United States, but presumably not as stiff as the punishment for blowing up the White House. So why ask in the first place? 'Ha, he's a liar as well. Take him away, Bubba, and plug in the electric chair.' I did a lot of thinking about it at 30,000 feet over the mid-Atlantic and never came up with an answer. Maybe it's all to do with George Washington and that business with the tree.

Mum tells lies. Just small lies, to make life easier. White lies, I suppose. But when she tells them her face goes beetroot red. Even if she's looking the other way. It's a kind of honesty, because the lies are impossible to conceal, and she knows it.

My father isn't a liar, but he is an embroiderer. An enhancer. Lying would be bad, unfair. He's a decent man, and decency was handed down from his father and from his father before. Like a tradition. Like an heirloom. Like the pistol wrapped in oilcloth in his bedside cabinet. Like the kitchen clock. It's something to do with England and the war. To his way of thinking, telling a lie is cheating, which is as good as accepting defeat. It's wrong. But he certainly doesn't mind a good embellishment now and again. 'And this is God's honest truth,' he'll say, as he reaches the punchline or conclusion of some improbably tall story, or, 'And that's no word of a lie,' as he puts the icing on the cake of a huge exaggeration. Or when an overstatement has been stretched beyond all credibility whatsoever, he'll conclude with, 'And Barney will back me up on that, won't you, son?'

'Trust me' is another of his little phrases, thrown into any family dispute before things go any further. You can't argue with 'Trust me'. It would mean we couldn't trust him, which would mean he was a liar, which would be wrong.

But the pistol stayed in the drawer and decency didn't bridge the generation gap. So for me, lying was always an option, and for my brother, a kind of artform. He lied his way into trouble, then back out of it. He told so many lies he had no idea what he'd lied about, or who he'd lied to, or when, or, most dangerously, why. He wouldn't have known the truth if it had walked up to him and slapped him in the face, which it did on a daily basis. So he told another lie, which smoothed things over until next time. My brother was not a bad person; lying was just his thing. He did it because he was good at it and it was fun – isn't that what we're all looking for in life? It was just his way, how he was. Some people grow a moustache. My brother told lies. He was a troublemaker, too. A shit-stirrer. Every time we walked along the Old Coal Road, near Christmas, he'd stop on the banking and look down at the Christmas tree in the grounds of the Parish Church.

'All those light bulbs. One day we should climb up that tree and nick the one at the top. That red one, see it? Maybe we should climb up and nick the lot.'

Whenever he used the word 'we' he was mostly talking about me, setting me little jobs or labours or tests, as if I was serving some kind of apprenticeship, reminding me I could never be him.

The night I climbed the tree it was very cold and still. I wouldn't have gone up in the wind, like a sailor climbing the main mast. Even in good weather it didn't look too sturdy, planted in what must have been an empty grave and held up with a couple of hawsers, one of them lashed to the lych-gate. I thought I'd chosen the right time to go undercover, the few minutes of darkness before the light meter triggered the lamps. But I was only two or three rungs up when the bulbs flickered into life on every side, blue, orange, yellow, white, green. I held on to the trunk of the tree, waited for a while, until it occurred to me that I was even more invisible inside the ring of lights, same way you can't tell who's driving a car when it's heading towards you on full-beam. It's something I've practised a lot, looking at myself from where other people are standing.

I carried on climbing. It was like wrestling a bear, thick fur covering the heavy limbs, like being in one massive bear-hug. At the top I reached out for the bulb, which stung my hand, and I had to pull the sleeve of my jumper over my fingers before gripping and unscrewing it. Almost instantly, the energy in it cooled and died, and the filament darkened and shrank, and suddenly the bulb was ordinary, weightless and empty. Like nothing. From up on the Old Coal Road the lights had looked like brilliant globes, like shining orbs. But the thing in my hand was no more than an empty glass ball brushed with a coat of paint. I pocketed it anyway. On the way down I edged out along some of the thicker branches, unscrewed more bulbs, and lobbed them over the wall into the school play-ground. I was thinking about hand grenades. I was imagining each explosion of glass against the concrete floor, the burst of each little bomb of dry, scorching air against the cold, hard ground. Splinters of wafer-thin glass skittered over the frosty surface. I told myself that if I unscrewed a bulb and it still glowed hot and bright in my hand, like a miracle, then I'd stop. But every one was a dud. I must have thrown fifteen or twenty of them over the wall, working my way down, and I didn't turn round to look back at the tree on the way home. I could imagine.

About half-ten that night there was a hefty knock at the door – the kind of knock that means trouble – and my father showed a police constable into the living room. I heard the two of them going upstairs, then coming back down, talking. I was doing some artwork on the kitchen table, a poster on a large sheet of cartridge paper. The copper came into the kitchen and closed the door.

'Your dad says it's OK if I talk to you for a minute. Do you know anything about the Parish Church Christmas tree?'

'Like what?' I said, and carried on drawing.

The policeman put his big leather hand over my own hand and flattened it against the paper.

'Like the fact that most of the bulbs have been thrown over the churchyard wall. Like the fact that when I was driving along the road here I noticed a bright-red glow coming from a bedroom window, and like the fact that, when I went upstairs just now, there's an industrial-quality external light bulb attached to a domestic fitting in your bedroom. Stuff like that.'

Maybe I started to blub. Maybe the odd tear dropped on to the paper and smudged.

'Look, son,' he said, withdrawing his hand. 'You've got no record and your father tells me nothing like this has happened before. Says it's out of character. So what's going on? Is there somebody else involved? Was it someone else's idea?'

Another tear fell on to a blank part of the sheet, and sat there like a clear, empty eye, raised up, trembling with surface tension, not able to soak down through the skin of the paper. I looked up, and that's when I saw my brother's face in the window, over the copper's shoulder.

'Tell him it was me,' he was mouthing, pointing to himself. 'Tell him it was me.'

In films and in books, people never *rat* or *grass*. They never *dob someone in*. It's a kind of pact between criminals, honour amongst thieves and all that stuff. But we weren't criminals or thieves, we were brothers.

'It was Troy,' I said.

'Troy?'

'My brother. It was his idea.'

'Older or younger?'

'Older,' I said. More tears fell on the paper. I glanced towards the window again, but he'd disappeared.

The copper went back into the living room to talk to my father. I could hear what they were saying, even without listening.

'I'd like to speak to Troy.'

'Troy?'

'The boy says it was his brother's idea. Is he in?'

'No, officer. Troy's dead.'

'I beg your pardon?'

'He was killed in Northern Ireland, in the army.'

There was more talking, more words. Roadblock. Friendly fire. Terrible mistake, terrible waste. I heard the policeman say something about duty, something about pride.

'Has he gone off the rails before? It's just that this thing with the tree – there's glass all over the schoolyard. It's quite serious, really.'

'No, never,' said my father. 'Although, today . . . it's the anniversary. A year ago, when Troy died. Maybe . . .'

I looked down at the poster. The tear stains were beginning to disappear. Some of the blots had lifted the surface of the paper, but nothing fatal, and the smudges could be gone over again.

'Under the circumstances, then,' the policeman was saying. Et cetera, et cetera. He passed through the kitchen without looking at me, and I heard his car turning round in the drive. The next time I looked up my father was standing there.

'It *was* his idea,' I said. 'Before he went.'

'All right.' He sat down on one of the stools at the breakfast bar, and was quiet.

'Thanks,' I whispered.

'For what?'

'Saying it's the anniversary, when it isn't.'

'Isn't it?'

'No, not today.'

'Trust me, Barnaby, it is. It's every day.'

He dead-headed one of the plants on the windowsill, went back into the living room and closed the door. I wanted to ask him if it was OK to keep the bulb, but one thing I've always been good at is knowing when to open my mouth and when to keep it shut.

Mum had been out, at choir practice, which was just as well really. She would have flipped.

I'm remembering all this as clearly as I can, but it was the Seventies, and in the Seventies, things got covered up. Walls were draped with woodchip, antique doors were boarded over and panelled off. Mantelpieces were torn out, fireplaces bricked up. Bricks and stone were daubed with Artex or emulsion. Ceilings were clad with polystyrene tiles, floorboards with lino and wall-to-wall foam-backed carpet. Every inch of wood was treated and primed and slapped with coat after coat of shock-resistant, blindingly shiny gloss. After so many layers, it's hard to get back to the true grain.

25

I sit in one of the coffee shops, away from the crowd. Hordes of Scousers in tracksuits and trainers drift into the departure lounge for a full English breakfast, a trolley dash through duty-free and as much beer as they can sink before the flight. Herds of Mancunians emerge through the arrival gates, women in espadrilles with raffia-work donkeys under their arms, men in ponchos and three-quid sombreros, pissed-off kids, young lads with burnt faces and the bruises, grazes and broken limbs of bar-room brawls and moped accidents. Three wheelchair passengers come through, one on a drip, and one with plastic tubes up his nose and an oxygen mask. Followed by a gaggle of seven or eight girls in their early teens, all wearing clothes consisting mainly of straps and holes that show off their Celtic-design tattoos to best effect. Followed by a pregnant woman with four little brats buzzing around her purse like flies around a dead rat.

Taxi drivers wait with signs written in scribbled biro on the torn-off flaps of cardboard boxes: Cooper, Duffy, McTaggert, Hunt. To think that air travel was once considered glamorous. To think I used to come here with Uncle Sid and stand on the observation deck with a short-wave radio, watching the jets come and go, ogling through binoculars at the men and women on the escalators and moving walkways, the passengers gliding between terminals, ascending and descending between floors. Or how I goggled at the pilots as they strolled out to the planes in the summer heat in their shirt-sleeves, with their soft-leather attaché cases in their hands and their caps under their arms. How I spied on the private jets on the far side of the runway, waiting for the rich and famous to be escorted across the tarmac and whisked through customs. Now look at this place. Nothing more than a mall. A covered precinct. A cattle-market. And the planes themselves – oh, my God. Accidents waiting to happen. Flying snack-bars. Dustbins with wings. When one lands, basically they mush *the passengers out of the front door, rake all the crap out of the back, take on another batch of hospital food, rev up, and whoof, off again. And the cabin crew or whatever title they go under these days. They're not glorified waiters at all – they're toilet attendants by another name. Cleaners, with a sideline in sales chat and a first-aid certificate in their back pocket. Because when a plane bursts into flames on impact, where would we be without half a dozen make-up-encrusted trolley-dollies to prop us in the recovery position?*

I get another cup of coffee, read the adverts in the free paper. People wanting the world, for nothing. People flogging items of worthless shit for as much as they can possibly get, or the nearest offer. People shafting each other left, right and centre for a few measly quid. People climbing all over each other, trying to get a few millimetres ahead.

I was tired. It was eleven o'clock at night and the flight was delayed. Eventually, they came on to the concourse with just a small holdall each, mum with a bandage on her knee. My father let her come forward so she could give me a hug, then he shook me by the hand and I carried their bags to the car.

'Do you want to drive?'

'I won't, if you don't mind. I'd probably end up on the wrong side of the road, and anyway I had a brandy after the meal.'

It had started to rain. Mum sat in the back, but hunched up between the seats so she could put her hand on my shoulder and talk. The windscreen was greasy, smeared with dead flies and the stickiness of summer. As the wipers swished intermittently across and back, I thought of Travis before he was born, the doctor slopping a dollop of gel on to Kim's stomach, then the scanned image on the screen, like a butterbean in its pod, and the Polaroid they gave us to take home. Everything was fine, they said. Everything was tickety-boo. We should go home and wallpaper that nursery.

'England. It never changes. It's nice to come home, but whenever I do, I can see why we went away.'

'Thanks.'

'Oh, I didn't mean it like that. You know I didn't mean it like that.'

'What's the bandage for?'

'A mosquito bite that went wrong.'

'Exactly. Give me the Pennines any day.'

She laughed and gave me flick on the ear.

'So what kind of a summer have you had anyway?'

'Oh great, really great,' I said. Then I said, 'Or were you talking about the weather?'

I counted three Eddie Stobart lorries on the way home, two less than on the journey out to the airport, although it was later in the day. A professor at some university or other has worked out that the state of the economy is directly related to the number of Eddie Stobart vehicles passing a particular motorway junction on any given day, which I can believe. Certain statements have the ring of truth. Whereas research that proves a person has more chance of winning the National Lottery if he doesn't buy a ticket strikes me as a philosophical position on life itself, rather than a mathematical fact. Sometime after we'd split up, Kim told me an urban myth about a woman who'd thrown her wedding ring down the toilet, and the ring made its way along the soil-pipe, through the sewer, into the river and out to sea. Ten years later she bought a cod in the market, and when she cut into the fish, out popped the self-same wedding ring, as shiny as the day it was bought, all polished and oiled.

'So you're saying it's money down the drain, basically?' I said.

'How do you mean?' asked Kim.

'I mean, if the odds of that happening are the same as picking the winning numbers, you might as well flush your ticket down the bog. That's essentially what you're saying, yeah?'

She looked at me with her eyes closed and said, 'Barney, it isn't a story about the National Lottery. It's a story about married life.'

Just for once, I thought I'd have the last word. 'Well, to me, it doesn't stack up. Nobody buys wet fish these days. It's all pre-packaged stuff.'

*

By the time I pulled up in the drive my father was asleep, slumped forward like a crash-test dummy after impact. Mum was snoring, laid out across the backseat. I went inside, checked the answerphone for messages and put the kettle on. Looking at them through the kitchen window, I remembered our first holiday by car, when we were kids, setting off to Cornwall in the dark, arriving all sleepy-eyed in a deserted town, walking on a spooky harbour wall before dawn. Without a railway timetable to go by, my father had miscalculated by several hours.

I could have left them there all night or until they got cold, instead of going outside to wake them and tell them they were home.

Next morning my father went through his routine. Checking the gutter for leaves, making sure the coal-house door was bolted from inside, pushing a long stick down the drains, reading the meters, mowing the lawn, having a word over the fence with the man next door, opening the pile of junk mail.

'Well, everything seems to be in order,' he announced, sitting down at the kitchen table with the paper, a mug of tea and a round of toast.

'All present and correct, is it, sir?' I saluted him. One of those over-the-top salutes with the outside of the hand.

'Yes, you might be a bit of a layabout in some respects, but you keep a tidy house, I'll give you that.'

'Is that why you come home? To check up on me?'

'Don't be silly, Barnaby,' he said, and lifted the paper in front of his face.

Mum had come downstairs in her dressing gown and slippers. 'Is that blood on the carpet?' she said.

'Where?'

'In the lounge.'

'Oh, yes, I cut myself shaving.'

'In the front room?'

'Er, yes, the telephone was ringing so I had to come running downstairs.'

'I thought you used an electric shaver.'

'I do. Usually. That's why I cut myself with the razor.'

She went into the front room with a damp cloth. I could hear her scrubbing at the carpet, attacking the little red stains, the same way she used to come at my face with a blob of spit on the end of a hanky.

'Salt,' said my father.

'What is?'

'Salt. For soaking up blood.'

'That's for red wine,' I corrected him.

'Oh, could be. Vinegar, then.'

'Cold water, I think you'll find.'

'Really? You know, an anaesthetist I once worked with was a haemophiliac. Blood wouldn't clot. I was always scared he was going to do himself some minor injury and bleed to death in front of me. The man was a liability. A splinter from a desk or a nail under a chair, and he could have sued for millions. He was the sort that would have, as well.'

'Especially if you started throwing salt at him.'

'Couldn't even have a tooth out. Terrible business.'

I was cleaning the kitchen clock, or pretending to. In fact, I was mending the damn thing. It had been my grandfather's, and his father's before him, and if the story was to be believed, had been a present from the royal family way back in the days of yore. Apparently my great-grandfather had once found a pigeon with a damaged wing floundering on the roof of the house. He went up with the ladder, and it happened to be ringed, tagged with an address somewhere in Norfolk. So he sent a letter, and in the meantime fattened the thing up on corn and bread, and generally nursed it back to health, even though he'd never kept a pigeon in his life. Then one day a car pulled up outside. And this was in the days when there weren't too many cars around. And it was a man from Norfolk, who turned out to be Keeper of the Queen's Pigeons at Sandringham, who said this pigeon was a particular favourite.

'The bird has a place in the royal heart. Your kindness won't go unnoticed.'

Then he took it away in a wicker basket, and two weeks later a van pulled up at the door, and out came the clock.

It's a good story. It's a good clock, as far as timekeeping goes, but the chimes drive me to distraction, especially if I'm concentrating, working something out. Ting ting ting ting every fifteen minutes. At twelve o'clock it just about has an epileptic fit. The first thing I did when they went away was let it wind down to a complete halt. But then I got worried it might seize up, so I took to covering it with cushions and paper bags, but the sound of it whining and moaning like a cat under the floorboards was even worse. Then one day I blew a gasket and threw a pair of rolled up socks at the thing, and it stopped, stone dead.

Spreading the cogs and springs across the kitchen table was killing two pigeons with one stone. One, covering up the fact I'd nobbled it in the first place, and two, scoring Brownie points for keeping my father's prized possession in working order.

'Are you sure you know what you're doing with that?'

'It's only a clock. Not a time bomb.'

He folded down the upper half of the newspaper, looked at me over the top of his glasses, raised his eyebrows, then carried on reading.

'I don't bother with a paper any more out there. Costs me two pounds fifty for the *Telegraph*, it's always three days out of date and usually looks like someone's slept in it. Anyway, we get all the news on the World Service.'

Mum had stopped scratching around in the living room and had gone upstairs to get dressed. There was a pause, and I suddenly realized he'd been biding his time, waiting for one of his little chats. I was hemmed in between the table and his newspaper. Also, there was the clock. If I walked away from it now I'd never remember how to put it back together. It might end up looking less like a gift from the royals and more like one of those Wilf Lunn contraptions from *Vision On*. You turn a handle over here, and somewhere over there a dog comes out of his kennel and barks at the moon.

I was trapped.

'So, how's that son of yours doing?'

'Fine.'

Curly Wurly, Love Hearts, Treets, Revels (but not the peanut ones), Swizzles, Twix . . .

'Because strangely enough we were watching a documentary one night, which turned out to be about autism. We just turned on halfway through. It was dubbed into Portuguese, so we didn't get the whole thing.'

I sprayed oil on to three little cogs and laid them down on a piece of lint. I picked up the glass face, breathed on it, and began buffing it with a duster.

'Anyway, in the Fifties they used to blame the parents, apparently. That was the thinking. Some Jewish psychologist who'd been in one of the death camps came up with the idea that autism was a kind of retreat from unbearable reality. The same way the Jewish prisoners became insular and withdrawn. Terrible, really, as a parent, to be told that.'

'I know all this.'

Fizz Bombs, Dr Deaths, Refreshers, Bazookas (with the powdery, pink bubbly and waxy cartoon strip, like a puncture repair kit), Spangles, Polos, Trebor, Space Dust, Sherbet Fountains, Flying Saucers (communion bread full of sherbet), Ice Pops, Midget Gems . . .

I put down the glass and picked up another part of the mechanism, jabbing at it with a jeweller's screwdriver. It rode over the top of the screw-head and into the cuticle, making me wince.

'Obviously things have changed since then. Something to do with the back of the brain, they reckon now. The "cerebellum", I think they were saying, like a big mushroom in the back of the head that controls the senses. Apparently about half the neurones are missing at birth. Anyhow, there's this place in Ontario . . .'

'I KNOW, ALL RIGHT. HOW MANY MORE TIMES? I KNOW.'

It took over an hour to pick all the pieces up, with both of us down on all fours, my father scooping the cogs and screws into an envelope with the edge of a postcard, me with a dustpan and brush. Under the table, we bumped heads.

'Sorry.'

'What about using a magnet?' he said.

'I wouldn't. Might magnetize the working parts.'

'Of course. Why don't I put the kettle on?'

'At least this didn't break,' I said.

I looked through the fish-eye lens of the glass face at the hundreds of bits of metal spread out on the table, all of them magnified and seemingly warped and stretched.

'Yes,' he said. 'There is that.'

Mum came into the kitchen.

'What have you done to your thumb? Come here, you need a plaster on that.'

One hundred and two pounds, thirty-six pence is a lot of money for putting a clock back together, if you ask me. But it's the sort of sum you can't really argue with. Not ninety-nine pounds, ninety-nine pence, and not a hundred for cash, but one hundred and two pounds and thirty-six pence exactly. Painstakingly calculated by a man who tots up his bills in the same precise, methodical way that he mends a clock. A con, almost certainly, but a good one.

Not to worry, though. It wasn't my money.

I crossed the road from the jeweller's and stopped to look in the window of the old toyshop. Airfix aeroplanes swung from the roof, Matchbox cars shone in their perspex boxes. An electric train made its way under the fluffy tail of the owner's Persian cat, twelve freight cars and a guard's van at the rear, oo scale. As it passed the junction box, the signal changed. I watched it disappear into the shop, and was waiting for it to emerge through the covered, wooden bridge, when I saw the reflection of Kim's car parked across the street, with Travis asleep in the back. I stood outside the café for a couple of minutes but didn't go in. Kim had company. Male company. He offered her a cigarette and she drew one out of the packet. He was sat with his back to me, so it was only when he leant over to another table for an ashtray that I saw his face. Well, well, well. Mr Cigarette himself. I should have guessed.

26

'Why Scarborough? Why don't you take him to Alton Towers or somewhere like that?'

'I don't know the way.'

'What do you mean, you don't know the way? You go down the motorway, and when you see the sign for Alton Towers, you turn off.'

'I wanted to take him on the train. I thought he'd like that.'

Kim put her hands on her hips and sighed. 'The train doesn't stop there any more, Barney.'

'Yes, it does, I checked.'

'I'm not talking about Scarborough,' she said. 'I'm talking about Memory Lane.'

Travis appeared at the top of the landing and made his way downstairs like a monkey, assaulting the spindles and banister rail, then swinging across the coat hooks at the bottom and dropping on to the windowsill in the hall.

I said, 'It's not like I'm the only one who's been visiting that place.'

'What's that supposed to mean?'

'Nothing. Come on, Travis, get your coat.'

'No coat, pweese. No coat.'

'Anyway, have a good time,' said Kim. 'He starts his summer classes on Monday, so this is his last big treat. Come here, sweet-heart, and give mummy a kiss.'

She opened the front door, and Travis shot off down the garden path and climbed on the gate. In a baseball hat and bomber jacket, he looked like he was dressed for an audition for *Peanuts: The Movie*.

'What's with the Charlie Brown look?'

'It's not Charlie Brown, it's Oxfam,' she said, and closed the door.

The train was late. On the platform, Travis stood in front of the chocolate machine, pressing the buttons and rattling the metal flap.

'I think he wants some chocolate, luvvie,' said a fat woman in a plastic anorak. I smiled at her and nodded.

'Here,' she said, pulling a red, leather purse out of her pocket and undoing the clasp. 'Get him a bar of Fruit and Nut, from me.'

'He's allergic,' I told her.

'Don't be silly. Get the poor little mite a bar of choccy. It'll do him good.'

She pressed the money into my hand. Travis pointed at the coin slot and then at the almighty, purple chocolate bar on the cover of the machine.

'Dat tocolate. Pweese dat tocolate.'

I dropped the coins in one at a time but she hadn't given me enough. Luckily, though, the train pulled in, and I let her waddle off towards the front carriage before bundling Travis down to the other end and shoving him into a seat.

'PWEESE TOCOLATE. PWEESE TOCOLATE.'

'No chocolate, Travis. Look, look up there at the people on the bridge.'

'NO BWIDGE. TOCOLATE.'

He slithered off the seat and crouched on the floor, covering his eyes with his hands. It was a bad start, but once the train began to move he stood up and stared through the window. Another train went past in the other direction. Travis let his head fall to one side, resting his cheek on his shoulder, then squashed his nose against the glass, watching the doors and windows of the other train flickering across his stare.

Trains are a good thing. So said my father – on many an occasion. Roads are just roads – they're everywhere. If there's a house, there's a road, and if there's a road, there's a car, and for every car, there are a dozen more. There's nothing special about roads. Stick a pin in a map, and odds on you can get there by car, and when you arrive, a hundred other cars will be clogging up the junction or parked on the verge, spoiling the view. The railway, though, like the canal, follows a different map. 'The iron horse steers its own course.' Or so he'd say, as we waited on the platform with our suitcases, watching for the snub-nose of the engine to materialize in the far distance, listening for that peculiar tingling noise in the metal rail, like the fracturing of ice. Our holidays always began with that scene, and were plotted around timetables and connections to seaside resorts at the end of the line, rather that a desire for any particular location. Deep down, mum resented it, I'm certain of that, but my father was deaf and blind to her wishes. He had steam in his eyes. He heard the stationmaster's whistle in his inner ear. And a train pulled him along, following the contours of the land, sniffing out gentle gradients and slopes, flying over valleys, burrowing under hills and mountains, passing among backwaters and trundling through the quieter side of towns and cities, not deviating one degree from the natural route, following the line of desire. If I'd have turned out to be one of those defectives stood at Crewe Junction in a snorkel parka and Clarks' shoes, with a notebook in one hand and a Thermos in the other, I wouldn't have failed. Not in his eyes.

Kim had made a packed lunch for us both, politically correct sandwiches filled with an unidentifiable enjoyment-free paste. I put the top back on the box. We were late. The buffet was closed. The toilet was flooded. The seat was plastered with chewing gum and riddled with cigarette burns. But trains are a good thing. Even Travis thinks so. He tipped out his little bag of toys, including Thomas the Tank Engine and pals – that gang of shiny, enamel locomotives with the creepy faces – then set about coupling up the carriages and freight cars. For the rest of the journey, he sat with his chin on the table, driving the long, snaking train across the grey plastic surface, hauling a cargo of spent matches and sweet wrappers from the window to the aisle, and back again.

From the station we wandered into the town centre. I bought him a helium balloon in the shape of an astronaut and tied it to his wrist. In the precinct he wanted to walk along the tops of the flower beds, brick-built oblong troughs about two- or three-courses high but rising to three or four feet as the street descended the hill. Like one of the lost boys walking the plank, at the end of each bed he tightened his face and stepped off into mid-air. I held out my hand but he wouldn't take it. Instead, he seemed to drift back to earth, with the inflatable silver spaceman floating above his head. For all the terror Travis carries with him, in other respects he's fearless. No drop is too high. No gap is too wide. Somewhere in her mind's eye, Kim sees a future of social workers and residential care, of life-skills and sheltered housing. She has a strategy and a long-term plan. But lying awake at night, I see an accident or a fall. I see a policeman at the door. I see misadventure. An open verdict. One leap too far.

Nothing had changed. That's the great beauty of English seaside resorts. Nothing ever does. We walked down to the prom and into the amusement arcades. Travis wasn't interested in winning, just wanted to watch the reels go round, or follow the path of a coin as it zigzagged through the metal pins and into the penny-falls, or press his eyeball to the video screen as the space-invaders exploded into a thousand fragments of coloured light. When the loose change ran out he cried, but only as far as the funicular railway. It's a strange contraption, more like a garden shed on a tow rope, designed to ferry fat-arse guests at the big hotel down to the beach and back. After six return journeys, and more tears, I pulled him along the front as far as the north shore. Then came some serious skrieking when the balloon came untied from his wrist and floated off into the ether. It was a crisis, but there was an ice-cream van parked only fifty yards away. I stuck a lolly in his hand and pointed him at the sea. He skipped down to the shoreline. And immediately stripped off.

'No, Travis, it's too cold.'

But Travis doesn't feel the cold, and doesn't fear the ocean, and doesn't listen when he doesn't want to hear.

The shoes came flying over his shoulder, followed by the socks, then he pulled his coat, sweatshirt and vest over his head in one neat move. Stepping out of his trousers, he glanced back at me, but before I could shout at him to leave his undies on he'd dragged those off as well, and was already ankle-deep in the North Sea.

There was no danger. The sea was calm and shallow, and he wanted nothing more than to kick and splash and scoop handfuls of water into the air, past his eyes. I sat on one of the wooden groynes, watching him carefully. People walked past, pointed at him and shivered. He looked liked something out of a fairy story, a skinny little sea-elf with blond hair and blue eyes, who'd come ashore from the deep. At any moment he might slide back under the waves and disappear into the otherworld. A dog carrying a lump of driftwood in its mouth paddled out to him, sniffed his backside then came splashing back to the beach. After about half an hour, and just when Travis was beginning to turn grey with the cold, the man from the ice-cream van was suddenly standing behind me with a threadbare roller-towel over his arm.

'Looks like you might need this. Drop it back when you've done.'

In his white smock, he could have been a nurse or a doctor, come to take us away.

I had to pull off my shoes and socks, roll up my trouser legs and wade in as far as my calves to pull Travis out, then lasso him in the towel to rub him down. For a while, he stood in nothing but the towel, drawing shapes in the sand with the ball of his foot, and absent-mindedly tugging the end of his dick, pulling and stretching it like a rubber band. I had to turn away not to laugh.

For dinner we bought two giant cones of chips, and ate them on the front, surrounded by a posse of vast, plug-ugly seagulls with

nicotine-coloured beaks and dinosaur feet. Every now and then
Travis ran and kicked out at them, sending them waddling off in
all directions before creeping back towards our feet, closer and
closer every time. They weren't as stupid as they looked. When
we'd eaten enough I tipped the cold, greasy chips on to the sand,
and within a few seconds they were gone. One evil-looking bird
waited by the litter bin, then dragged one of the soggy cones to the
ground, stood on it with both feet, and pecked away at the waxy
paper soaked with vinegar and fat. In St Ives, I once saw a seagull
swoop low across the beach and grab the top half of a Cornish
pasty out of a little girl's hand. She screamed, and her father shook
his fist at the bird as it landed a couple of hundred yards out to sea
with the big hunk of pastry hanging from its beak. Kim said it
wasn't the bird's fault.

'Whose fault was it, then? The little girl's?'

'If we didn't leave litter and food all over the beach in the first
place, they'd have to fish for their food, rather than scavenge. It's
like foxes in the cities and towns, going through the dustbins. It's
only natural.'

'What if that feller went and got a shotgun and blew the crap
out of the seagull, for stealing his daughter's pasty? Wouldn't that
be natural?'

'No. That would be pathetic.'

'What, like a seagull stuffing its face with minced beef and diced
potato isn't? Or is that natural as well?'

'Oh, for God's sake, you could start an argument in an empty
room, you could.'

'I'm not arguing. I'm just saying.'

'It's the same thing with you. You're always jumping down my
throat or sniping at other people behind their back. You're a
troublemaker.'

'I don't think so.'

'Well, you wouldn't, would you. You should listen to yourself
sometimes. Even your name means trouble.'

'What are you talking about?'

'Barney. Having a barney. Your parents knew what they were doing when they christened you, didn't they?'

We sat there for a while, under the sunshade, while Travis toddled down to the sea and back with a blue plastic bucket, filling the moat of his sandcastle with water. It was our last holiday together. As a family.

'So what does Kimberly mean, then?' I said. 'Queen of the peacemakers, I suppose. Centre of all stillness. She of great calmness and infinite wisdom. Oh saintly one.'

It was time to go. On the train I nodded off for twenty minutes. When I woke up, Travis was playing Happy Families with the woman on the other side of the table, a woman with died-black hair and a printed leopard-skin scarf around her neck. She wore a leather jacket with the fleecy collar turned upwards, and when she spoke, something like a pearl or a metal pea flashed in her mouth.

'He's a clever boy,' she said.

I looked into her mouth and saw that her tongue was pierced with a small, silver stud. She placed the thunder-thighs of Mrs Bun the Baker against the geeky face and puny chest of Master Pill the Doctor's son, and Travis laughed and rolled his eyes.

'How old was he when he was diagnosed?'

'What do you mean?'

'When you found out about his autism. What age was he?'

'Three.'

'Did he have the MMR?'

'Yes.'

'Hmm,' she said, and shook her head.

She was waiting for me to ask. How she knew. But I didn't. After another couple of cards she said, 'I teach. Special needs. How old is he now? Eight?'

'Seven.'

'Yes, he's very bright. And very cute.'

I looked out of the window, but she wasn't going to be put off. We ended up chatting. Every now and again she tapped the

169

tongue-stud against the underside of her front teeth, then licked her lips.

'Does that hurt?' I asked, touching the tip of my finger against my own tongue.

'No. It's nice.'

'Didn't it hurt when you had it done?'

She laughed and re-adjusted the scarf around her neck. 'You sound like my mother!'

We talked some more. About the weather. Mobile phones. Blood sports, which she was against. I told her about the Border terrier in the woods that night, the badger-baiting that went on in the name of sport.

'It's sickening,' she said, shaking her head.

I thought about Winkie in the cellar, the black sheep with its brains hammered in.

When the trolley came through, I paid for two teas and bought Travis a packet of cheese and onion. He scrunched it in his hands until the crisps were broken into a million pieces, then opened the bag and poured the contents down his throat, like a drink.

'It's so he doesn't have to hand them around. He's not good with sharing.'

'That's very typical. Especially with the boys. And it is predominantly a male trait. About three to one, right?'

We talked some more, and she rattled on about autism and other medical conditions while I listened and sipped at the tea and chewed at the rim of the plastic cup. All the while she carried on the game of cards with Travis, laying them down, making him squeal with laughter every time some misshapen character came into being on the table.

The next time the train stopped, she stood up and pulled a canvas duffle bag from the overhead rack. 'This is my stop.' Then she opened her Filofax and pulled out a lilac-coloured business card, and passed it to me.

'Do you have one? A card?'

'No. Not on me. I'm Barney.'

She shook my hand and made her way out of the carriage. Then from the platform she tapped on the window with her signet ring, and waved at Travis.

'Wave bye-bye to the lady, Trav.'

'Bye-bye, Yorg.'

I looked at the card. *Samantha-Jane Opie, Child Development Consultant*. There was an address, and a phone number.

'She's called Samantha, Travis,' I said, lifting his arm to make him wave again.

'Bye-bye, Yorg,' he repeated.

Samantha-Jane Opie had disappeared through the barrier, but Travis was still waving. I thought he was having one of his fixations, but when I followed his line of vision and suddenly found the thing he was staring at, I was stunned. The name of the station was hanging from the roof. Big black letters on a white background. York. I couldn't believe it.

'Bye-bye, Yorg,' he said again, and waved at the sign as the train pulled off.

I really couldn't believe it.

Someone had left a copy of the *Sun* on the opposite seat. I reached over, then pointed at the front page.

'Travis read this word. Travis tell daddy what this word says.'

'Mad.'

'Mad. Good boy. And this word.'

'Coows.'

'Cows. Good boy, Travis. And this word. What does this say?'

'Bur-gar.'

'Burger.'

'Burger.'

I just couldn't believe it. Like I'd discovered the north-west passage, or the secret of eternal life. I felt exhilarated and proud. I went all through the paper with him. He could read the small print, too, as well as some of the longer words by running the sounds together. He wasn't just remembering or making it up, he was reading. He was bloody well reading.

'Biff. Beef. Bones.'

'Good boy, clever boy.'

I could have gone on and on for hours, but for Travis it wasn't exciting at all. After a while he wanted to escape. He pushed the paper to one side and climbed over the seat, on to the next table. Apart from the two of us the carriage was now completely empty, and he clambered from one seat to the next, opening the little square windows and throwing out the crisp packets and empty cans and paper cups. I let him. He was a genius, and he could do whatever he pleased. I put my head against the seat, and closed my eyes, and thought about telling Kim the news, about all the things me and Travis could do together, all the games we could play.

The guard woke me, looming overhead, asking to see the tickets. Travis was curled up in a tight ball with his hat pulled down over his face. It was cold, because every window in the carriage was wide open. Not only that, every single thing that wasn't nailed down had been thrown out. Including Mr Turnip the Grocer and all his kith and kin. Including the lilac-coloured business card of Samantha-Jane whatever-she-was-called. Including two day-return tickets to Scarborough I'd tucked in the arm of the seat.

'I'm sorry,' I said to the guard. 'He's autistic.'

Outside the station, the first phone was jammed with a lolly stick, and in the second someone had stuck a lump of chewy over the earpiece. It was still warm. The third kept spitting the money back out, so in the end I dialled the operator and reversed the charge.

'Will you accept an operator-controlled call?'

I could hear Kim's voice way off in the background. 'A what? Who from?'

'Kim, it's me,' I shouted.

'What's happened? What's wrong?'

'Will you accept the call?'

'Yes, yes.'

'Thank you, I'm connecting you now.'

'What's wrong?'

'Nothing's wrong. I've got something to tell you.'

'What?'

'He can read. Travis can read.'

There was a pause. Like she couldn't take in what I'd told her. Like I was talking a different language. 'What do you mean?'

'I mean, he can read. Words on a page, writing, signs on the wall. He can read. It's amazing, don't you think?'

There was a longer, deeper silence. 'And you've just discovered this, have you?'

'Yes. Well, it's not about me, is it, it's about him. It's a breakthrough.'

Kim's voice went very dry and very cold. 'I know he can read, Barney.'

Travis was tugging at my sleeve, wanting to run off and climb on the bronze statue of Harold Wilson.

'Since when?'

'Since about six months ago. More.'

'So how come nobody told me?'

'If you looked at his school report once in a blue moon you'd have bloody well known,' she shouted.

Travis let go of my arm and went spinning across the flagstones, banging his elbow on a metal bench. He let out a soulful yelp.

'Is that Travis? Oh, for God's sake, just get a taxi and get him HOME.'

Later that night, I phoned her again. To apologize.

'I'm sorry.'

'Did you think he was some kind of Rain Man? You're hopeless.'

'I am.'

'By the way,' she said, 'what's that red mark around his wrist?'

I told her about the astronaut balloon and the string, how it had come undone and gone sailing away into the clouds and out to another galaxy. I made it sound very poetic. A spaceman, returning to space.

'Oh, *spaceman*, that explains it,' she said. 'It sounded like he was asking for his special man to come back, and for one stupid moment, I thought he was talking about you.'

27

Stubbs was already in the sauna when I opened the door, sitting on his own on the wooden slats with a towel around his middle and a pair of flip-flops on his feet.

'It's like our garden hut in the summer,' I said.

'Which summer was that, Seventy-six? Anyway, you should put something on your feet.'

'Why, does it burn the soles?'

'No. Verrucas. People from the council estates come here, you know, because it's cheap. I know how sensitive you are about things like that.'

I sat down at the opposite side of the bench and took a drink from a bottle of water. I'd never been in a sauna before. The heat seemed to make straight for my face, biting into my cheeks. Like mosquitoes, going for where the blood runs close to the surface of the skin.

'In Japan,' I said, 'they do a lot of communal bathing and that type of thing. Most people don't even have a shower at home – they go down to the bathhouse and jump in a pool with all the other blokes from the neighbourhood.'

'Go on,' said Stubbs. Like he knew there was more to come.

'Hot pools, cold pools, pools with electric current passing through them, very tingly, apparently. Weird, if you ask me. Anyhow, as a result of all this splashing around in the buff together, some kind of fungus gets passed from one man to the next. Embeds itself in the base of the spine, and a wart that looks like a button mushroom starts growing, right there, at the top of the arse. Looks like the devil's tail. So you'd be wearing more than flip-flops if this was a sauna in Kyoto. A pair of lederhosen, more like.'

'And you've seen these warts, have you?'

'Well, obviously not. I've never been to Japan, have I?'

'You've never been anywhere, Barney. You've never been anywhere, and you've never done anything, but it doesn't stop you going on and on like you're Alan Wicker or Clive James or some other clever-clogs.'

'I read a lot. I'll tell you something else about the Japanese. They think we smell, because of all the dairy products we eat. I mean, to them, we literally stink. And the gangsters are tattooed from their necks to their ankles, but they're all businessmen, and the tattoos are hidden beneath their suits. So you might think you're being introduced to the general manager of Mitsubishi, but below that collar and above that cuff, there's a fiery dragon waiting to chew you up and spit you out. Oh, yes, and for the Japanese golf is all in the mind. They don't even need a ball. And the young kids are eating more hamburgers but not enough calcium. So in a decade they've gone from being a race of midgets, basically, to a race of lanky, spindly people with really brittle bones that snap when they shake hands, which is why they go in for all that bowing and nodding, I suppose, and . . .'

'Have you finished,' he growled. A bead of sweat ran down from the bridge to the end of his nose and trembled there for a second before dripping into the grooved channel above his top lip and into his mouth. 'Because, if you hadn't noticed, it's just the two of us now, so why don't we stop beating about the bush and get on with it.'

'Get down to brass tacks, you mean?'

'Stop going on about little yellow men and start talking about little green ones instead.'

Funnily enough, I'd almost entirely forgotten about the green statue locked in the bureau at home, so much so that I hadn't given the actual prize a moment's thought for weeks. For Stubbs to mention him took me by surprise, sort of. Undignified, sort of. Kind of crude. 'Oh, that thing.'

'Exactly, that thing. That thing we've all been tearing ourselves in half for, so don't pretend you don't give a stuff about it all of a sudden.'

'It's not that. It's just . . .'

'Just what?'

'It's just that I feel things have already been decided. Like the little green man's got my name on him, and he's coming to me. Doesn't matter what anyone else does or doesn't do. It's destiny. Fate.'

'It's bullshit, more like. And if that's your way of telling me to back off, you can forget it, Barney. I haven't come this far just to be side-tracked by your mumbo-jumbo, do you hear me?'

Of course I hear him. We're sitting next to each other in a wooden hut in the concrete basement of a sports centre at eight o'clock at night. It isn't as if he needs to shout. I can feel the air singeing the hairs on my arms. The underside of my top lip stings with the heat, as if I've scalded my mouth on a hot drink. I have to draw air in slowly to stop it burning my tongue, and I feel stupid, like someone trying their first-ever curry, choking on a mild chicken korma. How do people stand it, I'm wondering. But I'm damned if I'm going to say anything. I'm damned if I'm going to ask for the English menu.

'So here's what you've got to do,' said Stubbs.

'Excuse me?'

'The dare. I'm telling you what the dare is.'

There wasn't a crack in his face. He was serious. Totally serious.

'What do you mean, "I'm telling you what the dare is"? It's my turn to dare you, Stubbs.'

He looked genuinely astonished. Hot, and astonished. 'No way. Tony Football capsized, so the circle changes direction. Now it's me to dare you.'

'Tony Football capsized when he was daring me, so now it's my turn, and you're the only other person left.'

'No fucking chance, mate.'

'Every fucking chance, MATE.'

Strange word, that. Describe someone as your mate, and they're a true friend. But say it to their face, and you're probably squaring up to them, especially if you pronounce that 't' at the end like you're spitting out a bit of meat stuck in your teeth.

Stubbs had risen to his feet. He seemed to be waiting for me join him. His nipples were level with my face. Ringed with hairs, they looked like the eyes of a cow, all starey and strange. And that blotch on his neck in the shape of South America – I'd seen it before, poking over his shirt. Now I could see it all, mottled and angry, with a long tail running down to his collar bone, running all the way to Tierra del Fuego.

'Well, I'm not fighting over it,' I said. 'Not in this heat, and not in the nude. It might look like something's going on.'

'Come on, Barney, why don't we sort this out once and for all, right now?'

Pomfret cakes, Cola bottles, humbugs and barley sugars (but only in mum's handbag on long journeys, stop you getting carsick), dolly mixtures, Iced Gems, Blue Bird Toffee, Highland Toffee, Toffee Crisp, coconut mushrooms, Lucky Bags, apple custards, apple tarts . . .

The door opened and a man with silver hair popped his head into the mist. 'Sorry, sorry.'

The door shut, and the darkness closed in again, and the heat started to swarm, worming its way into the pores of my skin. Stubbs sat down and pushed his hair above his face. I gulped down what was left of the water.

'I know. What about paper, scissors, stone? The winner gets to do the dare.'

He didn't look at me. Just huffed, and said, 'A bit playground, isn't it?'

'Well, we could flip a coin, but only if you've got one tucked up the nick of your arse.'

In fact I'd never played paper, scissors, stone. Only seen it on telly or read about it in stories – something that kids do in the dormitories of public schools. There was probably a nailed-on strategy for winning, like with noughts and crosses. But before I had time to work through all the permutations, Stubbs had placed his closed fist in the space between us. We banged twice on the wooden slat. On the third beat, my hand just sprang open, my index and middle finger flicking out – two blades, ready to cut. But Stubbs's hand was still a fist. Solid. Tightly closed. Hard as a rock.

'Go on then,' I said. 'Before we both spontaneously combust.'

'Two questions. That's all. First question: all this do-or-dare stuff, this whole thing with Pompus and Winkie and Tony Football and me – what's going on, Barney?'

'How do you mean, what's going on?'

'That isn't an answer, it's another question. I want the truth. What's this all about?'

His right hand was still in the shape of a big, heavy fist. I don't think he wanted to hit me, but it was so hot, anything could have happened. It wasn't a good time to be boxing clever, or even for building walls, blocking out the world with lists of toys or sweets. It was honesty time. Time for a heart-to-heart. 'I was lonely,' I said.

'What do you mean?'

'I mean I was lonely. Look at me, Stubbs, I'm thirty-five, unemployed and separated from my wife. I've got a dead brother, ex-pat parents and a son who doesn't know dog shit from Easter eggs. Do I need to spell it out? Do you need to look it up in the dictionary?'

'I know all that. I understand. But why us lot, eh?'

Technically speaking that was question number two, but I let it go.

'I thought we could all be mates again. Like in the old days. When I found the little green man after all those years, it felt like a sign, a way of bringing us together. Maybe it backfired, but at the time it made perfect sense.'

'Well, that's strange, Barney, because I bumped into Kim the other day, and she told me that when you were with her you never mentioned us. Like we didn't exist. So what do you say about that?'

Question three.

I drew a long breath of air into my lungs. It was like eating fire. 'You know what it's like when you get married. They want you to leave all that stuff behind. Everything you've been – they turn you

179

against it. Maybe I should have been stronger, then I wouldn't be on my own.'

I thought I'd finished, then another thought came into my head. 'I was angry. And I missed you. That's all.'

'I don't know, Barney,' he said.

There was silence between us for a minute or so.

'What else did you want to ask me?'

The fist had uncurled now, and his hand lay flat on the bench.

'Let's call it the 64,000-dollar question. The little green man – is it real?'

'Of course it's real. Jesus Christ.'

'Don't play games, Barney. I'm asking you in plain English. The little green man, and the valuation, are they real? And I want the truth, don't forget, because if you lie, that's it.'

'He's real. I swear.'

'On Travis's life. Do you swear on Travis's life?'

'I swear, on Travis's life.'

He shook his head and breathed out, slowly. 'Yes, but you would, wouldn't you.' He stood up, walked towards the door and lifted the latch.

'Can I tell you what the dare is, for next week?' I said.

He stopped, but he didn't turn round, and he didn't say anything.

'I just want you to show up. At my place on Friday night. That's all. I want us to be friends, Stubbs.'

The light from outside streamed in between his legs and under his arms and around his head, and he shimmered, the whole of his body, shimmering with light and heat and steam. Like a god. A burning, smouldering god.

'See you next week, then?' I said.

'Sure,' he said, and went out, and closed the door behind him.

28

For one terrible moment I thought he was going to throw a ladle of water on to the coals. As a parting shot. I'd never been in a sauna before and I'll probably never go in one again. But I've seen that trick with the ladle in about a million films, and it's the corniest thing on the planet. He didn't, though. He stood in the light of the doorway with his back to me, glowing and fuming. For a week I carried that picture around in my head. It's like looking at the sun, then closing your eyes. It's like a stain that won't disappear, that floats in front of you when you try to sleep, that jumps into view every time you blink.

I could hear the phone ringing from outside in the drive, and in the hallway the light on the answering machine was flashing like a Belisha beacon. I picked up the handset, and Kim's voice bulleted through my eardrum.

'Have you got him? Is he with you?'

'Who? What are you talking about?'

'Travis. Is he there with you?'

'No. Why?'

'Oh no, oh please, no.'

'Kim, what's the matter?'

She was breathing so hard she could barely speak. 'Somebody's taken him. Someone picked him up from school, I thought it was you.'

'No, I just took my parents to the airport. What happened?'

'I got to the school and he wasn't there. Someone's stolen him, Barney. Oh God, what am I going to do?'

'Did you phone the police?'

'No, I was waiting to speak to you – I thought he must be with you.'

'All right. I'll phone them now. Then I'll call you back.'

'Barney, he can't even say his own name properly. Anything could happen. What are we going to do?'

'It's all right, Kim, try and stay calm. He's probably just wandered off across the road. I'll phone the police.'

'Someone's taken him, I know they have. Some bastard . . .'

'Kim. Put the phone down. I'm calling the police.'

I'd no sooner pressed the red button on the receiver when it rang again, trilling madly in my hand.

'Kim, I'm dealing with it, OK? I can't call the police if you're on the phone, can I?'

No one spoke. The line buzzed. There was silence, but the kind of silence made by somebody keeping quiet, listening, waiting to talk.

'Kim?'

The line crackled and hummed.

'Travis?'

I could hear breathing now. Slow, relaxed breathing. Someone taking their time.

'Phoning the police? Outstanding, Barney! Maybe it's something I could help you with?'

It took a few seconds to put a name to the voice. 'Pompus?'

'At your service.'

'Look, Pompus, it's good to hear you, mate, but there's something I've got to sort out, so I'll call you back later, all right?'

'You're not listening, Barney. I'm offering to help.'

'What? What do you mean?'

The earpiece was hot and sweaty. I could hear the blood beating in my head. I could hear myself thinking, and if you can hear yourself thinking, so can everyone else. You might as well have a loudspeaker wired up to your brain.

'What's going on, Pompus?'

'You want your noodle-brained son back, you'd better come and get him.'

Then the line fizzled out. Went dead.

It takes about twenty minutes to drive to Pompus's house from mine, on a good day. It was four-thirty, a Friday, so the traffic was bad. At least it gave me time to think, but nothing I could think made any sense. Pompus wasn't the kidnapping type, was he? Maybe a night in the tunnel had sent him round the twist, but even so he wouldn't harm a defenceless seven-year-old boy. Would he? More to the point, what did he want? The little green man? In which case, why hadn't he said so on the phone, why hadn't he told me to bring him with me, to do the swap? Surely he wasn't this reckless, was he? Or this stupid? Or this bright?

Although there was something I hadn't factored into the equation – desperation. Not greed, but need. I hadn't seen his place in daylight before, and it was a tip. A proper pigsty. I pulled up on a levelled area of hardcore strewn with rusty engine parts and dented bodywork. Old, bald tyres were stacked against the wall of an outside toilet. Sump oil and petrol had stained almost every inch of the ground, but hadn't stopped nettles and other weeds growing to a height of four or five feet. A couple of ancient, scraggy hens were picking and piking amongst a pile of greasy railway sleepers. I looked up, thinking I might see Travis waving from a bedroom, or catch the blur of his blond hair through the frosted glass in the bathroom. But the windows of the house hadn't been cleaned for a million years. Poverty. Failure. Smoke puffed from the brick chimney. The door was half-open, so I went in.

I could see Pompus's muddy boots resting on a cardboard box. He was slumped in a tatty Dralon-covered chair watching the telly, with a beer in his hand. Coal glowed in the grate, and the room was hot and stuffy, and stank of cat piss. A dirty plate, smudged with brown sauce, poked out from under the settee. Beer and lager bottles of various sizes, shapes and brands were displayed on the mantelpiece like trophies, some encrusted with candle wax, and one stuffed with a plastic joke banana, half-peeled with a bell end and Jap's eye at the tip.

'Come in, make yourself at home.'

'Where is he?'

'No so fast, Barney, old pal. Why don't you have a drink, since you're here?'

'I don't want a drink. I want Travis.'

'Don't be offended if I have one, will you?'

He pulled himself out of the chair, brushed past me and produced a bottle of Beck's from the middle cabinet of the sideboard. Then he took off the top with his teeth. 'I can strike a match with one hand as well,' he said. He lifted the bottle to his mouth and downed half of it in one long gulp.

'I mean it, Pompus. Where is he?'

'Don't get fruity with me,' he said. 'I'll crush you.'

He sat down again and turned off the telly with the remote. 'So what do you think of this place?'

'It's OK.'

'It's a shit-hole. Needs a pot of money spending on it, and I'm skint. I could have really used that cash. That would have been very handy, all that moolah.'

He pointed at the Primus stove in the corner. 'See that? Got cut off.'

I sat down on the arm of the settee. If this was what the living room was like, what state were the other rooms in. The attic, the cellar, wherever Travis was. Pompus scratched his face with his finger, the bullet mark on his cheek, like a borstal spot.

'Aren't you wondering where I've been, last few weeks?'

'Surprise me.'

'Mallorca, mate. Blinding, it was. Outstanding.'

'You're not very brown.'

'Sun doesn't shine in the pubs. Better than being stuck in a fucking tunnel, though.'

'Don't blame me, blame Tony Football. He was the one who sent you in there.'

'Yeah, because of your sicko games.'

'Pompus, listen. I know you're angry, and I know you're upset, but we're talking about a serious offence here, and if I don't see my

184

son in two minutes flat, I'm calling the police.' My voice sounded as if a baby bird was trapped in my throat, trembling and flapping about. 'Do you understand? You could go down for this. He's autistic, for God's sake.'

'Look at me, Barney. Am I angry? Am I upset?' He drained the bottle, placed the empty on the mantelpiece next to the other empties, and helped himself to the next. 'This is no place for a kid, anyway. I was just passing on a message.'

'So where is he? Who's got him?'

He spat the silver bottle top into the hearth.

'Someone with no kids and a little dick that doesn't work. Someone who really is pissed off. Know what I'm saying?'

I had to stop at a phone box to check Winkie's address in the book. I couldn't ring Kim, though, not yet. Then the fuel light came on in the car and I had to buy petrol. And when I got to the right part of town I had to wind the window down five times to ask for directions. An Asian kid in a Leeds United shirt was the only person who knew the way. 'Turn right by the swings. If you get to the church you've missed it. Yeah?'

Winkie's car was outside. The house was a semi with a wooden porch on the front. I rang the bell and banged on the glass panel. Inside, a hand came through a curtain of coloured plastic strips – one of those things for keeping flies out – and I heard bolts being undone, and the turning of a key. It was Maureen.

'Yes?'

'Is Wi— er, I'm a friend of your husband's. Is he in?'

'No. He's out.'

'Right. Right.'

'Is it anything I can help with?'

'No. Er, I'll leave it. Can you ask him to call me when he gets in?'

'It's Barney, isn't it?'

'Yes, it is.'

'Your son's not here.'

'I beg your pardon?'

'You're looking for your son. He's not here.'

Behind her in the house, through the curtain, I saw a figure dart from the bottom of the stairs, across the hall and into the living room. A small figure, but not a boy. Someone wearing glasses.

'I'll tell you where he is on one condition. You never get in touch with my husband again. You don't phone him, don't write to him, you don't speak to him if you pass him in the street. Is that clear?'

I looked at the ground and nodded.

'You're a sick person. You make people ill. You poison them.'

I kept my head down until she'd had her say. She was wearing open-toed slippers with fluffy blue pom-poms on the front. She painted her nails but she didn't shave her legs.

'19b Granger Street, in town. Now scram.'

She pushed the door shut in my face and disappeared through the plastic strips.

I walked along the alleyway where I'd dragged Tony Football by his collar that night, and knocked at the door where I'd dumped him in a drunken heap. A light came on inside and a tall man in a polo shirt and jeans opened the door.

'Is Tony in?'

'Go on up,' he said, then stepped past me and walked off towards the street.

The light went out when I was halfway up the stairs. I had to follow the banister rail to the top and grope around for a door handle on the landing. Inside, the kitchen was all polished wood and gleaming chrome and shining glass. Travis was sat on a stool at the breakfast bar watching a portable telly and eating a Toblerone.

'It's all right, Travis. Daddy's here.'

He glanced in my direction with a mouthful of chocolate, then turned back to the television, swinging his feet under the stool.

'Skoody Doo. Skappy Doo.'

'It's all right, Travis.'

'Skoody Doo. Delma. Feddy. Chaggie. Dapnee.'

'"And if it hadn't been for you meddling kids, I would have got away with it,"' said Tony Football, in a cod American accent. He was leaning against a bookshelf, drinking a glass of fruit juice.

'This isn't funny, Tony. Don't think this is funny, because it bloody well isn't.'

'He seems happy enough to me.'

'I was that far from calling the cops. Jesus Christ, his mother's going mental. He's not even supposed to eat this rubbish.'

I tried to pull the chocolate bar out of Travis's hand but he clung on to it, swinging on my arm until I let go. 'Pweese tocolate. Pweese tocolate.' Then he climbed back on the stool and rested his nose against the television, and rolled his cropped head against the screen.

'He's been having a good time. He hasn't been a moment's bother.'

'Just because you're out of the game doesn't mean you can pull a stunt like this. You and Pompus and Winkie, you're a regular little conspiracy, aren't you?'

'Calm down, Barney.'

'A right little confederacy.'

'We just thought we'd give you a bit of respite care. We appreciate what a trauma it must be for you, having three strange little boys to look after.'

'What's that supposed to mean?'

'Well, there's Travis here, poor soul, and there's that little green man you seem to spend so much time thinking about. And then there's yourself. You're the biggest kid going.'

'That's priceless, coming from you.'

'Meaning?'

'Meaning, if you're not prepared to take it on the chin, like an adult, you shouldn't play in the first place.'

'Oh, like I'm not *man* enough, yeah? That kind of thing?'

'More pweese tocolate. Pweese tocolate.'

'No, Travis. There's no more chocolate.'

'PWEESE TOCOLATE. PWEESE TOCOLATE. PWEESE TOCOLATE.'

'I said NO.'

Travis threw himself to the floor, banging the soles of his shoes against the polished lino. Tears welled up in his eyes, then he began thumping one of the kitchen units with the outside of his fist. I lifted him up to the tap and tried to wash the chocolate from his face, but he squirmed and lashed out with his arms, catching hold of a dried flower on the windowsill and bringing a glass vase crashing into the sink. I sat down with him on the floor and held him tightly, whispering in his ear and stroking his head, until the screaming turned to sobbing and weeping. His whole body convulsed with anger or fear. I pulled his knees up under his chin, and held him like a baby, in a tight ball, and let him cry and cry and cry.

Tony put his glass down on the drainer and lifted his leather jacket from the back of a chair.

'Well, I've got to go, so I'll leave you to it. Don't bother about the mess. Drop the latch when you leave, won't you?'

The chocolate was coursing through his bloodstream, but strapped in the car seat the most he could do was kick me in the back and use the headrest as a punchbag. I scrabbled in the glove compartment for a tape, slammed it in the cassette-player and cranked up the volume: 'When I See an Elephant Fly'. After a few miles the toe pokes to my spine and thumps to the back of my neck became more rhythmical and less violent. Eventually they gave way to some tuneless babbling. 'Vovolo, Vovolo,' he kept muttering. I kept driving, until I looked in the rear-view mirror and saw his head tipped to one side and saliva dribbling from the end of his chin. His eyes weren't closed exactly and he was mumbling to himself, but he was as good as asleep.

'Vovolo. Vovolo.'

I leave the engine running and step into the phone box. Before I put the money in I rehearse the story, number by number: 1 – I thought it was my day to collect Travis from school; 2 – but I had to take my parents to the airport; 3 – so I'd asked one of my mates to pick him up instead; 4 – then I forgot all about it. That sounded good, but why didn't I phone before now? 5 – because, would you believe it, I only went and got a puncture.

No, ran out of petrol. No, I was stopped for speeding. I was speeding because I panicked. Because I love him. Because I care.

I go through it again, joining the dots. It's a good story. Absent-mindedness is the only crime – hardly a hanging offence. She'll go off the deep end, sure, but Travis is safe and that's the main thing. Barney made a mistake, then Barney put it right. Everything is normal again. Yes, he's with me now. In the car. Asleep. There's chocolate on his shirt, but if a dad can't treat his son to a wedge of Toblerone once in a blue moon, what kind of world are we living in? So I messed up. So shoot me.

The dialling tone purrs in my ear. In the car, in his sleep, Travis flinches and mumbles the odd word. Truth is, he could have been to Jupiter and back and no one would be any the wiser. Any other seven-year-old would get home and spill the beans, sing out about the house with the beer bottles and the woman with the painty toes and the man with the broken vase. But not Travis. The cast of Scooby Doo might get a roll-call, but after that, nothing. Except for this 'Volovo, Volovo' business. What's all that about? Must be a car. Those big, boxy Swedish jobs with the side-impact protection system and the letters stamped in the cross bar of the steering wheel and the sidelights on all the time, like the army. I only know one person with a car like that, and that's . . .

It's Friday night. It's too late.

I drive like a maniac back to the house, but it's too late. The door is still locked but the kitchen window has been forced. The air inside is disturbed, bruised. In the living room, the bureau looks closed, but the door falls off in my hand, both hinges wrenched from the wood. Papers and pens are scattered, small wooden boxes lie on their side or upside down. An envelope has been ripped apart and filleted. The secret drawer at the back is open and empty. It's too late.

Friday night. Stubbs, keeping his word. Turning up as arranged. Doing the dare. Stubbs, suddenly one step ahead, somewhere out there, in the world, with the little green man.

Travis was still asleep in the car outside. I picked up the phone. Kim came at me like a guard dog, like an alarm going off, like a harpoon with a barbed tip. But Travis was safe.

'He's safe, that's the main thing,' I said.

And after that it wasn't so hard to calm her down, to tell the story, explain why I hadn't phoned. There were lots of things in my favour. I'd even been burgled now.

She said, 'What did they take?'

I said, 'Nothing. Just crap. Probably some kid looking for money or sweets.'

29

'Peace offering?' I pushed the bottle of wine and the flowers and the present into her hands and looked away.

'Do you want to come in?'

'Only if you're not busy.'

'Oh, let me think. I'm expecting a telephone call from Nelson Mandela in half an hour and Paul McCartney said he'd call round later but, apart from that, I can probably fit you in.'

'I thought you might have gone out for a birthday drink with the girls from work.'

'The girls from work go out on Friday and Saturday wearing see-through dresses and high heels. They get pissed, go to night-clubs, take drugs, have sex with anyone who fancies it, and turn up on Monday morning looking like nothing's happened. Most of them are seventeen or eighteen. They talk to me like I'm their mother.'

I'd followed her into the kitchen. She sliced through the flower stalks with the bread knife and dropped them in the bin. She poured a sachet of plant food into a glass vase, stirred the water with the handle of a wooden spoon, then inserted the tulips one at a time, until the heads were evenly spaced in a circular arrangement. Through the glass the stems looked like the frame of a little green wigwam.

'I grew them myself,' I said.

'Liar. Anyway, they're out of season.'

'Honestly, I did.'

A travelling market had come through town last year, stallholders from all over Europe, selling everything from truffles to engine parts for Ladas and Skodas. The council had allocated a street to each country, so every time I turned the corner it was like crossing a border, with bunting and flags hanging from lamp-posts, and the smell of garlic sausage or pickled herring or pizza filling the air as I wandered from the bus station to the park, crossing through France, Norway and Italy. The English section was the grottiest and the smelliest. Nylon shirts, pork pies and blow-up Santas. In the Dutch section, I won half a dozen bulbs in a tombola, 'Black Tulips', then forgot all about them, until I found them going mouldy in a paper bag in the back of the car. Thinking they'd had it, I slung them on the compost. I'm no gardener in any case, and I've got a secret, long-term plan involving either concrete flagstones or a lorry-load of tarmac that could make lawn-mowing and weeding a thing of the past. But then last Thursday, hanging out the washing, I saw them in the corner of my eye, six perfect blooms at the end of the garden, like six tiny life forms from another planet. Seemed a pity to waste them.

'What colour would you say they were?'

'I don't know. A sort of browny-purple.'

'They're supposed to be black.'

'How come?'

'It said so on the packet.'

'Well, it says "Wonderbra" on the side of the buses, but they don't sell them. Anyway, there's no such thing as a proper black flower, is there?'

'I don't know. You get blue Smarties.'

She looked sideways at me from under her fringe.

'Mind if I use the loo?'

'You might be a big kid, Barney, but you don't have to ask if you can go to the toilet. Only don't wake him up. I've just this minute got him off.'

Upstairs, I push open the door of his bedroom. Like a shrine to the animation industry, every inch of wallpaper is covered with a poster or cut-out of some cartoon character, from Mickey Mouse to more modern, new-fangled creatures, whose names I don't know. A mobile of Snow White and the seven dwarves hangs from the ceiling – she seems to be free-falling through the air using her skirt as a parachute. On the windowsill, Pocahontas and her feller are smooching, with a whole bunch of Happy Meal figures standing in a circle, watching. Mowgli swings from the light shade. If Walt Disney really is being kept in a deep-freeze somewhere in Beverly Hills, the first thing he'll do when they thaw him out is rub his hands. And it won't be because of the cold.

Inanimate objects, caught in the act. Just one living thing – Travis – curled up under the duvet, sleeping his sleep, dreaming his dreams, his face pale and expressionless against the blue pillowcase. The day I took him to see Toy Story *he hid under the seat and put his hands over his eyes. It was too bright, too fast, too big, too loud. Maybe it was too real. And that night he couldn't sleep, or slept like a cat – with one eye open – in case everything came to life, in case Dumbo swept low over his face, or Bagheera dropped from his perch on the curtain rail and pounced.*

I close the door and leave him be.

Kim was still in the kitchen, looking beyond the flowers on the windowsill, staring into the sky.

'You're still mad with me, aren't you?'

'I'm just confused. How could you forget that one of your friends had gone to pick him up from school? I mean, it wasn't even your turn to collect him in the first place. So either you've gone stark-staring bonkers, or you don't care.'

'Of course I care. He's my son, isn't he?'

'Well, you've got a funny way of showing it. I only ever let him out of my sight to go to school or spend time with you, and now I can't trust anyone. I'm completely on my own.'

'No, you're not.'

'Yes, I bloody well am. You only see him because you have to. Not because you want to. You don't love him. He annoys you, doesn't he, because he isn't normal, because he can't be a proper son, and do all the things you did when you were a boy? I don't even think you like him.'

'You're talking nonsense now.'

'I'm telling the truth and you know it.'

She was crying, biting her lip and sniffing back the tears. Then she produced a tissue from the cuff of her cardigan and blew her nose and wiped her eyes. All the time she was looking through the flowers, looking at nothing.

'I'm sorry, Kim. It won't happen again. Why don't you open your present?'

'What is it?'

'It's a new E-type Jag in British racing green.'

She looked at the little oblong parcel and half-laughed.

'Sure. With a child's booster seat in the back, I suppose.'

Slipping her finger under the Sellotape, she tore open the wrapping and pulled out a VHS cassette.

'I was going through some old films the other day and thought you might want a copy of this. I had it transferred on to video. Anyway, if you don't want it, just chuck it.'

'Thank you.'

'Pleasure.'

She blew her nose again and tucked the hanky back in her sleeve. We stood for a minute not saying anything, then I turned towards the door.

'Barney, have you eaten?'

'No.'

'I've got nothing in the house. Why don't you fetch a takeaway? Help me drink this wine?'

'OK.'

'I'm sorry. I'm just feeling a bit lonely.'

The telly was on in the Chinese, a colour portable bolted to the wall, with a smear of grease where someone had thrown a spring roll at the screen. The only other customer, a construction worker in a padded shirt and a yellow hard hat, leant on the counter, smelling of beer. The telly droned on. A cable channel. A programme about the human body – consciousness, reflex and instinct, that kind of thing. A woman had been wired up to a computer. Every time she made a particular movement with her body, the computer recognized it, and a counting machine in front of her recorded the score. But she hadn't been told what the particular movement was, and after ten minutes, with the score at 178, she still had no idea.

'Is it every time I breathe?' she said.

'No, I'm afraid not,' said the presenter, and the counting machine clicked over again, then again, then again.

'Every time she farts, more like,' said the man in the hard hat.

It turned out to be blinking. Every time she blinked.

'Which just goes to show', said the presenter, clapping his hands together, 'that the mind doesn't always know what the body is doing, even when the evidence is right there in front of our eyes.'

'I had no idea, no idea,' said the woman, as she was shown back to her seat.

The next report was about drugs in sport. Anabolic steroids. Food supplements. Ginseng. Nandrolone. A scientist mixed some powders in a flask, and talked about 'masking agents', with his protective goggles pushed back over his hairline. Then came some serious music, and Ben Johnson running the 100 metres, in slow motion. Then a close-up of his face – his eyes and his teeth.

'It's all bollocks anyway, in't it?' said the workman.

'Is it?'

'Let 'em get on with it, that's what I say. Take what they want.'

I nodded, but he hadn't finished.

'You think about it. In fifty years from now, we'll all be taking those drugs, right? Because we will. So these athletes, who don't take 'em, they'll be a joke, right? They'll be doing their 100 yards or whatever in ten seconds, and we'll be walking past 'em, saying, see you later, pal. Don't you reckon?'

He had a point, even if he was pissed, but luckily I didn't have to discuss the fine details with him. The face of a Chinese man appeared in the serving hatch and an arm came out with a large brown-paper bag at the end of it.

'Thank you, Charlie Chan. Same again tomorrow. Same time.'

The worker took off his hat, turned it upside down, put the bag in the hat and carried it out, using the chinstrap as a handle. I heard a large vehicle start up outside, and seconds later he drove past the window, high in the seat of a yellow JCB preceded by a giant claw. Like the king of the diggers, on his mechanical elephant.

Kim had taken a shower. Or a bath. She opened the door in her dressing gown, with a towel wound in a turban around her head. Her cheeks were red, and beads of water or sweat stood out on her forehead.

She forked out the noodles and beanshoots on to two plates, and I followed her into the living room with the corkscrew and the bottle of wine.

'No meat in it, is there?' she said.

'Nope.'

After we'd eaten, she filled her glass again and tucked her legs underneath her on the settee.

'You know your trouble, Barney?'

'What's that?'

'You're spoilt.'

'Like how?'

'That money. The pay-out for Troy.'

'It was compensation. Negligence. Anyway, it wasn't much.'

'Well, it's kept you afloat for long enough. Why did they give it *you?*'

'Who?'

'Your mum and dad.'

'I don't know. They didn't need it, and . . . maybe they were watching out for me. Because they'd lost him.'

'That's what I mean. Spoilt.' She emptied her glass and leant forward to fill it again. Her bathrobe opened slightly at the top, then closed again as she sat back. 'Anyway, it's messed you up good and proper. Never had to work or worry. There it is in the bank every month, like magic. It's turned you into a total layabout. You're aimless.'

'I work. Odd jobs here and there.'

'Only because you're bored and you like nosing around in other people's business.'

'Well, it's pretty much gone now, the money. End of this summer, there won't be anything left.'

'A good thing if you ask me. Give you a kick up the backside.'

'Means I won't be able to pay you.'

'Yes, you will, you'll get a job like a normal person. Make a new start.'

'Maybe.'

'You know who you remind me of? One of those Japanese soldiers lost in the jungle who doesn't know the war's over.'

It was the wine talking. I stretched out towards the bottle but couldn't quite reach it without getting up. Kim put her leg on the coffee table and nudged it towards me with her big toe. 'I hear you've been seeing some of your old friends.'

'I hear you have, too.'

'How do you mean?'

'Stubbs. In the café.'

'I was having a coffee and he came in, that's all. I know what you're thinking, and you're wrong. It was a mistake, all right, but I've no reason to ignore him.'

'What did he say?'

'Just said you'd been hanging around together again. Playing football and stuff.'

'What else?'

'God, Barney, we were just chatting, all right? He was on some big nostalgia trip, telling me about school and things like that. He said he was surprised you'd got back in touch, because he thought you'd fallen out with him.'

'Why did he think that?'

'He didn't say. But I've got my own theory.'

'Go on.'

'Well, you're a year older than him and your other mates with their dozy nicknames, right?'

'Yep.'

197

'So you left school at the end of the fifth year. And you were waiting around for a year for Stubbs and the others, so you could carry on being mates together. But they stayed on to do their A levels – all apart from that fat boy. And then they went off to college, leaving you all on your lonesome.'

'And that's your theory, is it?'

'It is.'

'And what did you tell him?'

'Nothing. I said you never talked about it, which is true. Just kept it all to yourself. You've never been much of a one for letting it all out, have you, Barney?'

I shook my head. The wine was all gone so I went to the kitchen for another bottle. When I came back, Kim had put the video on.

'If it's *Top Cat* I'll kill you.'

I pulled the curtains and turned out the main light. I sat down next to her. She pulled the towel from her head, letting her wet hair tumble down around her neck and shoulders.

Kim watched the video without saying a word. The long, bumpy track across the Dales, filmed from inside the car. The steep hill and the lighthouse waiting on the other side. The red face and white beard of the retired captain in his captain's hat. The wooden, corkscrew stairs. The view. Zooming in to distant landmarks. Panning across valleys and hills. And the light, turning its slow circle, flooding the camera with brightness, the beam reaching out into the night, like the hand of a massive clock turning across hundreds of square miles of moorland and heather and grass. Under that spotlight the land had seemed unending, infinite, impossible to contain.

The video ended. Interference filled the screen. Kim got up from the settee and drained the wine in her glass.

'You can see yourself out, can't you?'

I nodded.

Then she turned away, and without looking at me said, 'Or you can come to bed with me.'

*

Some of the tulips had lost their petals. I swept them into my hand, opened the window and threw them into the yard, as if they were moths trapped on the wrong side of the glass. I made tea and took it upstairs on a tray. Kim had woken, and was sat up in bed with the pillow behind her head. Her hair was wild and all over the place.

'What time is it?'

'Half-seven. I should go.'

'Is Travis up?'

'No, he's still asleep.'

She put her face to the big mug of tea and drank from it, cupping it in both hands.

'Thanks.'

'For what?'

'The video.'

'Oh. Pleasure.'

I sat on the edge of the bed, then crossed the room and pulled back the curtains and looked out of the window.

'Is it a nice day?' she said.

'Yes. Not bad.'

'So how long have you had that tattoo?'

'What? Oh, that thing. A couple of months.'

'I would have said you'd be the last person in the world to have a tattoo.'

'I was bored.'

A dustbin wagon pulled up outside. A scrawny little man wearing a luminous-yellow bib and industrial rubber gloves carted the wheelie bin to the back of the truck, slid it on to the forks and pressed a button. Like somebody pouring a pint down his throat, the wagon downed the contents in one slow gulp, and the empty bin was deposited back on the pavement. A dead glass, they call it in the pub trade. Dead men.

'Do you think we should have done that?'

'I don't know. It *was* my birthday.'

'I mean, with the baby and everything.'

'There is no baby, Barney.'

'You told me you were pregnant.'

'No. I asked you what you'd say if I was. Do you really think I'd do something like that?'

'I don't know.'

I heard Travis stirring in his room. Singing or moaning.

'Are you on the Pill?'

'No. Why would I be?'

'So what if . . . you know.'

'I wouldn't mind. Would you?'

'No.'

'A little brother for Travis. Someone to watch out for him.'

'Or a sister.'

'With your sperm, I think that's pretty unlikely, don't you?'

I nodded my head and smiled.

'I don't love you, Barney,' she said.

I said, 'I don't love you, too.'

I saw myself out. Walked through the yard, past the black tulips in the window and the handful of black petals on the path.

30

It usually begins with matches. Swan Vesta. Bryant and May. Matches stolen from home. Cook's matches with the long wooden stems, for the lighting of ovens without the singeing of eyebrows. Books of matches from pubs and hotels. Any match, so long as it works. It's a kind of power. Firepower. It's a fascination as well, looking into that little bud of heat – beautiful, but not to be touched. Children are cavemen, basically. When they discover fire, it's science and magic, all in the same strike.

Cigarette lighters might be more expensive – especially ones with strippers bearing their bosoms and everything else – but they're less hassle and altogether higher status. No more trying to light a soggy match against a wet brick or, more dangerously, a zipper fly. No more trying to coax the flame into life behind a hand or under a coat in a howling wind. No more running to the shop every ten minutes for a new box. If children shouldn't play with matches, then cigarette lighters are out of the question, which made them an absolute must, especially the petrol models, which were the most fun on God's Earth. The refills came in the form of squashy, plastic capsules full of lighter fuel. They were cheap, plentiful, and could transform even the stupidest person into a lethal weapon. It was Pompus who discovered the trick, and Pompus who amazed us all at the bus stop one morning when he pricked one of the capsules with the pin of a badge, placed it carefully between his teeth, sparked up, lifted the naked flame to his lips and looked skywards. A five-foot flame shot out of his mouth in the direction of heaven. He spat the taste out of his mouth and laughed like a dragon, then lifted another capsule to his mouth. This time a plume of fire blazed horizontally, sending us all diving for cover, and missing the top of Winkie's head by inches. It became a game, a craze. Something to do in a morning before school. If a person pretended to yawn and lifted their hand to their mouth, you knew what to expect, and had to duck or run if you didn't want to go up in a puff of smoke. It came to an end when the tobacconist, despite the number of units he was shifting, decided that the sale of jet fuel to under-sixteens was not in his long-term interests. It was a case of closing the stable door after the horse had bolted, given that Tony Football had set fire to his nose the day before. Liquid fire dribbled down his chin and flames played on his skin until he snuffed his head in his jacket. Then Stubbs opened a fizzed-up can of Coke in his face, 'to make sure'. Tony stood there, smouldering and dripping and rubbing his eyes. For weeks after, his cheeks and his chin were dirty and black, like one of those half-shaven gangsters in the Ant Hill Mob. He told his mother he'd been looking up somebody's exhaust pipe when they drove off.

Fire was also the essential ingredient of Mischief Night. Knocking on doors and running away, pinning 'I stink' signs on people's backs, making kookaburra noises under the windows of the town's ornithologist – that's what the grown-ups meant by 'mischief'. That's what happened in their day. But we'd discovered fire. We'd discovered, for example, the art of bullroaring, the ancient practice of stuffing newspaper into the bottom of a drainpipe and setting fire to it. With a lighter. As the flames and smoke rose towards the gutter at the top of a house, the hot air sucked into the pipe made a terrible noise, like an Alpine horn played by a howler monkey. We'd hide in the rhododendrons or behind parked cars as terror-struck homeowners came tumbling out of their houses in pyjamas or dressing gowns to look for Godzilla or some other terrible beast caterwauling on the roof. That's if they could get out of the door. Most times we'd tied the handles of six or seven houses together with one rope, and set fires in each drainpipe, running along the street like pirates lighting the cannons of a fighting ship. Another trick was to tie the door handle to the rubbish bin, so baked-bean cans and chicken carcasses came spewing on to the street. On the bullroaring front, plastic drainpipes were to be avoided, although the number of warped and mangled fall-pipes in one area of town was evidence that we'd experimented a great deal before coming to that conclusion. The greatest bullroarer ever was in the eighty-foot cast-iron drainpipe at the side of Dyson's Mill, which we crammed with half a dozen copies of the *Sunday Times*, and a handful of kindling for good measure. The pipe glowed hot at the bottom, and the note it played at the top was so pure and loud it could have raised a whole population of weavers and carders from their graves, thinking they'd heard the morning hooter for work.

Arson was dangerous and illegal, obviously, but a fire in a skip was spectacular and reasonably safe. A pint of petrol tipped into one of those things, followed by a fizzing banger or a jumping jack, thrown from a safe distance – superb! And no one cares if their rubbish goes up in smoke, so long as it doesn't blister the paint-work on their new car. Sometimes we'd set fire to one of those things, and return to the scene of the crime half an hour later, only to find other residents in the street hauling boxes and old wardrobes out of their houses to throw on the flames. Fire brings people together, like striking miners around a brazier, like folk singers around a campfire. Winkie, of course, didn't have matches or a lighter. He turned up one night with one of those battery-operated, hand-held sparking devices for igniting gas fires and stoves. I can still picture him, clicking the trigger, trying to light the corner of the *Radio Times*. It would have been quicker to rub sticks together, or wait for lightning to strike. I've never read *Lord of the Flies*, but I remember Mr Shanks bumbling on about how a fire was started using a pair of glasses, and this was an error in the book, a physical impossibility, because the kid who wore the specs was long-sighted, or short-sighted – I don't know which. But if it had come to a race between the fat boy in the book with his prescription bifocals and Winkie with his sparking device, my money would have been on the specs, every time, physical impossibility or not.

I wouldn't try to excuse some of the things we did on Mischief Night, especially the smouldering skeleton of that decommissioned railway carriage in the station sidings, and the carbonated bus shelter. I won't even own up to the crispy remains of letters and packages inside the fire-blackened postbox on Wilton Road. Tampering with Royal Mail still carries a mandatory life sentence, the last I heard.

But I can explain it. It's tension. Excitement. Nerves. It's the fever pitch of thinking about the next day. Bonfire Night, which was the big one as far as I was concerned, and every boy I knew at the time would have said the same. I was an expert when it came to bonfires. Not Guy Fawkes and the Gunpowder Plot and all that historical stuff. I mean building them, chumping for wood, guarding them against looters and other gangs, building dens and crow's-nests and passageways into the growing pile, installing oil drums and bottles to go off like bombs and grenades on the night. Lighting bonfires, keeping them going for days on end, cooking spuds in the embers, galloping through the flames without getting burnt. I've forgotten more about bonfires than most people know. I once thought I might write a book on the subject, but that would be giving away secrets and ancient lore, things that should only be passed on by word of mouth.

The biggest bonfire we ever raised was in Seventy-five. It was eighty feet high if it was an inch. We played on it, worshipped it, talked about it non-stop, even slept in it one night. At half-seven on November fifth, somebody's Scoutmaster dad from over the road came striding across the park with his blowtorch and an oily rag. Like the mayor, turning up to open a supermarket or launch a ship. But he was too late. Deep inside we'd already doused a bale of paper with a can of paraffin and struck the flame. As he fiddled about in his leather gloves, telling the nippers to stand well back, smoke was already rising from the top and drifting over his head. It was the biggest blaze for miles around, a famous, legendary fire. It was the greatest thing I'd ever done – the most work, the best result – but it wasn't to be my night. Half an hour later, I stepped on a four-inch rusty nail, which entered my foot through the sole of my monkey boot and came out through the tongue. I didn't even feel it, but the nail was attached to a length of floorboard that was suddenly flopping around at the end of my leg like a wooden ski. As I bent down, I saw the point of the nail, glinting in the light of the fire, and fainted.

My father pulled the nail out before the doctor arrived. It had missed all the tendons and veins – I was lucky, he said. He gave me a tetanus jab in the behind, bound my foot with a mile of bandage, and sent me to bed. He made some gag about Christ on the cross, which I didn't get at the time. I watched the blaze from my bedroom, feeling the heat on the glass, watching the shadows of four boys as they fired Roman candles at each other, lobbed bangers on to the mill roof, and danced about at the edge of the flames. At the end of the night they sent four rockets my way, streaming through the dark, fizzing and flaring, then dying and dropping and falling short. I flicked the light switch on and off five times. Signalled back to them. Acknowledged the salute.

In early spring or late summer we'd cycle out of the town and set fire to the moors. The moors were either withered and pale after winter, like an old man's beard, or tinder-dry at the end of October. We called it tatching – collecting fire with a handful of dead grass, and setting a new fire a couple of yards away. That way it spread. A contour of flames could stretch for two or three miles, creeping forward, leaving a black and smoking landscape behind, like the surface of a planet too close to the sun. There was no real danger. The fire always came to a stop at the first road or the edge of a reservoir. But the fire brigade arrived all the same, to do battle with the advancing ranks of flames. I haven't seen the moors on fire for fifteen years. It isn't the climate, it's the kids. They can't go messing about on the hills because their backsides are welded to comfy chairs and their eyes are glued to computer screens and video games. Major tree surgery wouldn't shift them from their seats, they're grafted on for good. They say they're surfing the Web, that they're cruising the Information Superhighway. But they're not. They're garbage-pickers, stumbling around inside a cosmic dustbin.

It doesn't bother me. It keeps them out of my sight, stops them getting in my way.

And the hole in my foot isn't the only distinguishing feature on my body caused by fire, indirectly or otherwise. This blemish under my left knee came from a burn. We were melting lead with a candle, lead flashing stolen from windows and roofs. Long, pliable rolls of the stuff. The flame of a candle was more than enough to turn it to liquid. I was wearing shorts at the time and one drip splashed on my ankle. Amazing, how it's travelled across my skin as I've grown, how it's migrated halfway up my leg to its current resting place. It's not pretty – a glassy, marbled smear – and it hurt like hell at the time. But it couldn't have hurt as much as those burns on the arms and legs of my best friend, like a horrible tropical disease, like the black death. Astonishing, how much heat the tip of a cigarette can generate.

I should never have stolen those photographs. But through the serving hatch at home I'd heard mum whispering. About Stubbs. Just a regular check-up, she said, then something about a social worker being called, and then the police. Something about photographs, copies in his file, at the surgery. 'Shocking, absolutely shocking.'

'Poor little wretch,' I heard my father saying.

Waiting for mum the following week, after school, I should never have slid open the metal drawer, walked my fingers across the files until I came to his name. But that's how easy it was. Alphabetical. Not even locked.

At the dentist's I'd sit there reading the dog-eared magazines while my father tore into someone's molar with the drill. Howls came from the chair. Grown men passed through the waiting room, crying and holding a bloody tissue to their mouth. At the clinic, mum washed the lipstick from the doctors' cups, emptied the ashtrays, tidied the office, set the alarm and locked up, while I loitered in the office. It was the easiest thing in the world to roll open one of those filing cabinets and stuff a couple of photographs into my coat pocket. I shouldn't have. I almost wish I hadn't. But Stubbs was a mate of mine. My best friend. I needed to know.

And anyway hanging around after school made me a wiser person. All those back-copies of the *Reader's Digest* and *National Geographic* – they broadened my mind, made me a more rounded individual. If I'd have been one of those latchkey kids my parents were always talking about, I could have easily got into some sort of trouble.

Fire's a funny thing. It can start in the unlikeliest of places, sometimes of its own accord. A man I knew owned a chippy, and used to throw the scraps of batter and fat into a cardboard box at the end of the night, and stick it in the backyard. Some mornings when he opened the door to pick up the milk, there'd be nothing except a pile of warm ash where the box had been. Heat can go on living without a flame, can sink to the inside, intensify, until it reaches ignition point again, and combusts, and sometimes explodes. We once built a tree house in the woods. It was only a pallet wedged between branches, a platform with a rope swing for shinning up and sliding down, no walls or roof even. But there's something neat about being off the ground. The view, the air. The risk of falling and the excitement of throwing things down from a great height. There'd been a hut or shed under the tree at one time, belonging to an old man called Saggers. He'd been a Japanese prisoner of war, worked on the Burma Railway. Some said he'd been locked in a dog kennel for two years and had to eat beetles and slugs. Others said he'd been a collaborating grease-arse, and got himself a cushy job dusting and cleaning the commander's house. When he came home, he made an allotment out in the woods, and sat in the shed all day, and smoked his pipe and went round the twist till he snuffed it. They brought him down from the woods in a wheelbarrow. He'd been dead a couple of weeks, so I don't think he smelt too good.

The shed had gone, rotted away, but the concrete base was still intact, solid under a covering of moss and weeds. We'd haul stones up the tree, then throw them down. From twenty feet, they'd crash on to the concrete with a dull thud that made its way up the trunk and out along the branches, shaking the leaves. Sometimes sparks came flying out in all directions, as if they'd been trapped inside, waiting to be freed. Bigger and bigger stones were raised and dropped, boulders even, but the concrete base never cracked. The bottom of the tree was surrounded by broken fragments of rock. It looked like a fossil site, or a place where a chaingang did their hard labour, breaking the big stones of the world into smaller and smaller ones, for no reason. If we'd lived in a city we might have been taking drugs or stealing cars or wearing the latest clothes. But we lived on the edge of a small, northern town, with the moors up above. We made our own fun. We pulled rocks into a tree house, threw them out, and listened and watched.

Winkie was look-out up in the crown of the tree. When he saw a figure coming over the hill and through the fields one day, we pulled up the rope and huddled on the platform, watching through the cracks in the pallet.

'I know you're up there, so you can stop titting about.'

It was Troy. He was home on leave, prowling around with nothing to do. He stood at the base of the tree and looked up.

I peered over the edge. 'What do you want?'

'Let down the rope. I'll come up.'

'Don't,' whispered Stubbs, and Pompus and Tony Football agreed. 'He can't touch us up here. Ignore him, he'll go away.'

Troy had pulled out a knife and was cutting strips of bark from the trunk. 'Let down that rope, Barney, or I'll batter you when you get home.'

'Why don't you push off,' shouted Stubbs.

'Oh, do you want a leathering as well?'

Stubbs stood up on the platform with his hands on his hips and looked down at Troy. 'Just 'cos you've got no mates of your own, just 'cos you're all on your tod, Action Man.'

He broke off a small branch and arrowed it at Troy's head. I don't think Troy saw it coming through the tree, because it caught him right on the star of his forehead and knocked him over backwards. He went ballistic. For the next half an hour, we huddled on the pallet as he pelted us with stones. He'd gone absolutely crazy, strafing the platform with stone after stone, any one of which would have killed us had it connected. They thudded into the base of the pallet but it didn't split, and as long as we kept out of the line of fire, we were safe behind our wooden shield. Winkie, on the other hand, higher up in the tree, was a sitting duck, and took a few hits with smaller missiles. I guess Troy could have knocked him off his perch if he'd wanted. But it was Stubbs he was after, and then me.

The barrage died down. Troy sat on a stump and lit a cigarette. The smoke drifted upwards into the tree, and Winkie saw his chance to slither down the trunk and join us on the platform. The five of us on that wooden square – we were like shipwrecked sailors adrift on a makeshift raft. Me, Stubbs, Winkie, Tony Football and Pompus lying in a heap. It was a miracle it withstood our weight.

'I haven't finished with you bunch of queers yet,' shouted Troy, and disappeared into the woods. We should have legged it straightaway, but thought he might be waiting behind a tree. With his knife.

'He'll beat the crap out of us if he cops hold of us,' said Tony Football.

'He'll have to catch us first,' said Stubbs.

'You'd think he would have killed enough people in the army without coming after us. We're only kids. Jesus.'

Some time later, Troy reappeared, carrying a petrol can. He scavenged the area for branches and fallen wood, and we sat and watched as he stacked the kindling and timber around the base of the tree. He whistled as he went about his task, dragging the broken limbs of sycamore and mountain ash to pile on the bonfire, until the tree trunk was surrounded by dry, dead wood. I thought he was trying to scare us, that's all. But then he looked up, and I saw the bloody wound in the middle of his forehead, and knew he was going all the way. He walked the circumference of the tree, pouring petrol over the stacked wood. Then he screwed the cap back on and stuffed the can between the branches and twigs, into the heart of the bonfire, right under our feet.

He sat down about ten feet away, and lit a cigarette. 'So you can come down now, or you can do it the hard way. It's all the same to me.'

'He's bluffing,' said Tony Football, looking at me. 'Isn't he?'

I shrugged my shoulders.

Winkie said, 'If we all drop down together, then run for it, he can only catch one of us, right?'

'Cheers,' said Pompus.

'If we all go down together we could kick his head in. Probably,' said Stubbs.

But I pointed out there was only one rope, and that he'd pick us off one at a time as soon as we hit the ground. 'You shouldn't have thrown that branch. He's as mad as a bastard.'

'He won't light it,' said Stubbs. 'He hasn't got the balls.'

Troy looked calm. He looked easy. He swooshed a fly away from his face, and blew big, looping smoke rings, like lassoes. 'When the flames get going, that pallet will last about ten seconds. So you'll fry, or choke. And if you're still alive, there's a petrol can in the middle that'll go off like a shell, and blow you all to flying fuck. So, anyone coming down?'

Nobody moved. A magpie bounced along one of the branches in a nearby tree, flashing its wings in the sun and laughing its stupid laugh.

'Suit yourselves.'

He took one last puff on the cigarette and flicked it into the pile of wood. There was a noise, a sort of wafting noise with a whiplash sound within it, like shaking out a blanket or sheet. Whap! Then the whole base of the tree was alight, and heat and sparks and petrol fumes came racing up the trunk, through the slats of the pallet. Pompus just jumped. He ran to the edge of the platform and bloody well jumped, twenty feet or so, and seeing his chance,

Winkie jumped on top of him, and the two of them went rolling down the hill towards the stream. Tony Football threw out the rope, slithered towards the flames, then managed to kick himself clear of the fire. He bolted for the woods, hurdling the broken-down wall of the old allotment, and disappeared into the trees. I started to haul up the rope, but the frayed end was already alight, like a fuse. So I edged out along the bottom bough until it started to bend and dip with my weight, and inched further and further, holding on to the branch above, until it lowered me halfway to the ground. At the point where I thought it might crack, I dropped to the floor, twisting my ankle as I landed. I picked myself up and tried to run, but my weight on the sprain was nauseating. I hobbled and limped and scrambled my way to the top of the hill, then turned, expecting Troy to be standing over me with a big stick or half a brick. But he was still waiting at the base of the burning tree. Looking up, I could just make out Stubbs through the smoke, perched in the crown with his head between his knees and his jumper pulled up over his nose and mouth. Then Troy was walking backwards, away from the blaze. Then he was running, and then came the biggest bang I'd ever heard as the petrol can exploded, and bits of wood and leaves and stones shot out every which way. I didn't hang around to see the damage. I clawed my way over the banking and dropped on to the road at the top. It was about half a mile to the house – more with a twisted ankle – and before I went in through the door I looked back towards the top of the hill, where a line of smoke was still rising straight into the sky from over the other side.

I was sitting with my foot in a bowl of warm water when Troy came into the house an hour or so later. I thought he was going to give me a thick ear as he walked past the back of the settee, but he flopped into the armchair and turned the telly over with his big toe.

'*Blue Peter*? It's for kids and queers.'

I didn't answer back. BBC was normality in our house. Switching to ITV was a kind of minor rebellion. *Magpie*, the tall, thin bloke with the microphone hairdo. Troy was obviously still in a bit of a strop.

After a while I said, 'I thought you were going to batter me, then.' I had to speak. Violence is like a blister sometimes. Better to pop it and get it over with, even if it hurts to slide the needle in.

'Don't think I've ruled it out,' he said.

The adverts came on, and that public information film – the grim-reaper character in a black sheet telling children not to play by water. *I'll be back, back, back* . . .

Troy turned and looked at me. The cut on his forehead had dried into a dirty red circle, more like a love-bite than a war-wound. There was something comical about it, as if he'd been hit with one of those toy arrows with a sucker on the end.

'And you can tell your friend Stubbs that if I ever catch hold of him, I'll kick his teeth so far down his throat he'll have to clean them through his arse. All right?'

He pulled himself out of the chair, slammed the door behind him and went stamping upstairs. The smell of smoke from his clothes stayed in the room.

After tea, I said I was going down the youth club, but limped back up the road and looked into the fields. The tree was amazing. Like one of those British space attempts, where the rocket blows up on the ground. It stood in a circle of embers and ash. The trunk was carbon black, right the way to the lower branches, and all that remained of the pallet were a few wooden spars wedged in the main fork. Every leaf was crozzled and charred to at least halfway up. Only the crown was green and untouched by the flames. There was no sign of Stubbs.

Poking around in the rubble, I could feel the concrete base of the old hut was still warm from the fire. And when I kicked the dirt away, I saw it had splintered into a jigsaw of shapes. All those rocks we dropped from the tree, and the slab never cracked or chipped. Now either the heat had caused it to shatter, or the exploding petrol can had done the trick. As I looked down at my feet, I thought I saw something move. When I looked again, rocking from foot to foot on the loose concrete, a puff of dust came up from the ground as a seam of ash disappeared through one of the cracks, like sand through fingers. With a stick, I levered up one of the smaller chunks. The concrete was seven or eight inches thick, but set on some kind of wood-and-chicken-wire frame that had rotted away. I levered another hefty segment out of the base. It was dark underneath, a darkness like the universe, not solid and dense, but full of emptiness and depth. More ash slipped over the edge of the hole.

I've never been one for sticking my hand into a dark place. I'll never grope about under a floorboard trying to find an electric flex, or clean out a drain without a glove. I even think twice about fishing down the back of the settee for the remote control. But there was something about this particular hole I couldn't resist. On my knees, I pushed my arm as far as my elbow until I felt rubble and soil. It wasn't that deep. I leant further in, up to my shoulder, and sent my hand on a big, clockwise sweep of the earth.

To be honest, I was disappointed. When you're thirteen and find a dirty canvas purse under a slab of concrete somewhere out in the woods, anything less than a bar of gold or a million in used fivers is a let down. What was I going to do with a boring old statue of some Chinky-looking bloke with a ball in his hand? I cleaned him up with a bit of spit and polish, put the concrete chunks back in place, then wandered home. I threw the little green man in the bottom of the wardrobe and forgot about him. For two years. It wasn't until the day after the funeral that I found him again. I was putting some of Troy's clothes away in plastic bags, saving his jumpers and jeans and shirts. One day they'd fit me.

I'd no idea he was worth anything at the time. If I had, there's no way I would have planted him in the gravel the next morning, then dragged the others up to the shunting yard for a game of cricket. But when you're introducing people to a little piece of magic, they've got to be in it from the start, they've got to witness the moment. This little green man was the god almighty of good luck from now on. I couldn't just pull him out of my pocket like a new catapult or a quarter of sherbet lemons. It was the summer.

There was nothing else to do for the next two months, especially for those four dingbats without one creative spark between them, without one good idea to their name. They should have showered me with praise, gone down on bended knee and kissed my brother's black leather boots, all shining and bright, even if they were three sizes too big.

Fire. It was ritual. Religion. It was the same impulse that made all school-leavers set light to their blazers outside the school gates on the final day. My brother did it when he left and so did I. I swiped a clothes prop from a neighbouring garden, hung the jacket on the end, held my lighter against both the cuffs and the hem, then hoisted it into the air. It flared. Like the golden fleece. Like a boy, burning alive. Buses went past – it shone in the glass, and kids shouted and cheered through the windows – and the deputy head paced up and down on the other side of the fence. There was nothing he could do. It meant I was never going back.

It was the start of the summer. I was sixteen. I got a job in a cardboard-box factory, worked eight till seven every day and Saturday mornings as well. It was a shit job with shit pay, but there was nothing else to do, and anyway I was saving up for America. Stubbs and the others, they'd still got a year to do. It was the holidays but I only saw them at night, a game of soccer in the schoolyard before it went dark or a bottle of cider in the bandstand. Then it was winter – they'd got their homework, I'd got my cardboard boxes. I was wishing my life away, waiting for my friends. Twelve months went by, until the day arrived. At three-thirty I turned up at the school gates with the same lighter. The summer stretched out in front. A summer like the year before last, the five of us going wild all over again. Then America, me and Stubbs and the rest if they wanted to come. Thumbing it from state to state. Occasional jobs. Getting into situations, getting out of scrapes. That was the plan, and today was the first day. I waited, but Stubbs didn't show. He'd sloped off across the playing fields. Like a traitor. And Tony Football went by on the top deck of a school bus, looking the other way.

Like a thief. And Winkie was ill. I clenched the little green man in my fist, dug my nails into the jade. Only Pompus turned up, his blazer torn to shreds by the rest of the morons in his remedial set.

'Barney. Throw me the lighter.'

'Where are the others?'

'No idea.'

'Where's Stubbs? I told him I'd meet him here to do the business.'

'I don't know, all right? But he's not going to want his jacket tatching, is he?'

'Why not?'

'Not if he's staying on next year. What's he going to come to school in – his vest?'

31

Friday night.

He came in without knocking. I was expecting him. I looked in his face for some kind of sign, an indication of which way things were going to go. He wasn't calm. He wasn't boiling over, but he wasn't calm. I could see that. Some people can hide their feelings behind their face, but only up to a point. A bricked-up window is always a bricked-up window – never a wall. I looked further into his face. Controlled rage? I stared at the floor. He pulled a letter out of his pocket and waved it at me.

'I took this valuation certificate into a jeweller's. It's a fake.'

He tore the paper to pieces, and showered them in the air. He screwed the envelope into a ball and threw it in my face. I let it bounce off my nose on to the floor. I didn't fight back or even flinch. It was nothing less than I expected. What I had coming, you might say.

'I took this little green man into an auctioneer's in Sheffield. It's a fake. It's not worth a shit. It's one big scam, and you're one sad little lying cunt.'

'It isn't a scam, it's the truth.'

'You're so confused you don't know what the truth is. You need help.'

'It's real.'

He let out an astonished cry. 'I don't know what happened to that little piece of green junk we used to play with, but this isn't it. You're a conman, Barney. Nothing more, nothing less.'

He could have been a lawyer on his feet, exasperated by the bare-faced lies and downright deceit of the man in the dock.

'You swore on your boy's life.'

'I know I did.'

He shook his head and turned away. I thought about standing

up at that point, but I've read articles about body language in dangerous situations. You should stay put, keep still, and stay low. To rise could be interpreted as an aggressive move, and to meet the other person at eye level is a challenge or even a threat. You just have to be cool. You don't have to play dead, though. That's bears. Or maybe sharks, when they smell blood.

'Can I ask a question?' I said.

'Oh, be my guest.'

'How did you get the other three to play along with taking Travis last Friday? What was in it for them?'

'You mean you still haven't figured it out?'

'Well, I can see you wanted me out of the way while you ransacked the house. It was a good plan. It worked.'

'I was just keeping my word. Turning up, like you asked.'

'Yes. Brilliant. I'll give you that. Killing two birds with one stone.'

'Playing one little man off against another. That's how I'd put it myself.'

'Whatever. But Winkie and Pompus and Tony – did you pay them, or what?'

His face changed. With his mouth closed, he poked his tongue into the wall of his cheek. And he actually grinned. I got the feeling I was in for a big speech. I'd only asked him the question to give him the power, to let him feel in control. To humour him. It didn't matter to me if he'd threatened the other three with a cattle prod, or called in a few bets, or paid them all in used tenners out of his own wad. I was complimenting him, in a back-handed sort of way, on his small moment of triumph, the little scam he'd managed to pull off. I didn't care what the answer was.

Except, when it came, it was hard to believe. I have to admit that. It was a gobstopper all right.

'Something you should know, Barney. We all got sick of playing this stupid game a long time ago. But we wanted the money, and you had the statue.'

He pulled out a cigarette and lit up. He was enjoying this. Still edgy, but enjoying it. Milking it, even. I wanted to tell him to stop pulling his pudding and get to the point. I wanted to sigh and pretend I couldn't care less, but it was too late. Way, way too late. He'd been looking forward to this for a long time. Everything about him said so. His jet-black eyebrows, the wedding ring flashing on his left hand, his perfect white teeth.

'After that night with Winkie and the sperm test, I felt sick to the stomach. Disgusted. What the hell was I doing creeping about, leaving condoms in garden ponds, humiliating old friends.'

The soft spot. The bleeding heart. I should have made a note of that.

'Well, we had a little meeting of our own, and worked out a plan. What we needed was to get things to this point, just me and you, with this piece of rock in my possession. Then we could split the money – if there was any money. And if there wasn't we wouldn't be spending every Friday night like performing seals, jumping through hoops for your entertainment. *Can you see what it is yet?*' he said, in his Rolf Harris voice.

I shook my head.

'We've been having you on.'

'What do you mean?'

'I mean, you've been shafted, Barney.'

'I know you opened the tunnel gates. I know Pompus isn't scared of the dark.'

He sniggered. No, it was more of a whinny, like a horse laughing at a donkey. 'Correct. But I'm not just talking about a key and a padlock. I'm talking about the last three or four tricks. Don't you get it – it's all been a fix.'

'Rubbish.'

'A set-up. A sting. A put-up job. What do you think of that, Barnaby?'

'I don't believe you. You're not that smart.'

'They're not, but I am. Credit where credit's due, and this was genius, even if I say so myself. Some good acting, though, don't you think? Pompus in the tunnel – outstanding effort, as he'd say. That was Tony Football's idea. He's a clever lad with a camera.

And what about Winkie with the blood – that was worth an Oscar, don't you think? Mind you, it's taken it out of him a bit, poor lamb. He's had to have some time off work.'

'Rubbish. What about the shit?'

'Veggie sausage he brought with him in a bag. Linda McCartney. A bit dry on its own, but the ketchup was a nice touch.'

And he wasn't lying. His face was covered with the truth. Like a fox with chicken feathers around its stupid mush. *Great jeopardy.*

'Very clever.'

'Yes. I thought so. We all did. I'm meeting them down the pub later on, we've got quite close recently. You're not invited, obviously.'

He raised his eyebrows and nodded. What do you think about that, then? Put that in your pipe and smoke it. Read 'em and weep. Touché.

'It's still real,' I said.

'What is? What's real?'

'The little green man.'

Stubbs shook his head, and his mouth tightened and closed.

'OK, let's do it your way, you completely fucked-up person. It's my dare, yeah?'

'Yes.'

He produced the little green man from his pocket and held him in his hand. His bald, green head poked out above Stubbs's fist.

'So throw this piece of junk as hard as you can against the wall.'

He lobbed the statue at me and I caught it.

'Throw it, Barney. Or I'll take it off you and do it myself.'

The statue was warm, a nice thing to hold, a smart piece of work. It could have been a hand grenade, or a worry-egg. I pictured the little green man riding around in Stubbs's pocket for the past week, being poked and prodded and scratched by some sweaty South Yorkshire auctioneer more used to house clearances and second-hand cars. Some fat, hairy-arsed gavel-banger, mauling and pawing this piece of art. And why Sheffield, for God's sake? Hardly the jade capital of the Western world. Was that Stubbs's idea of taking it to the very top – driving over the hills to the big city in his big, black Volvo? Pathetic. He might as well have gone into Ratner's or Samuel's in the precinct, bought himself a pair of stainless-steel cufflinks and a Mickey Mouse watch at the same time.

The force of his hand against my ear is more of a shock than anything else. Not painful, but loud. Not really a punch but more of a hard slap.
  'Throw it, I said.'
  My right eye begins to water, he must have caught me with his wedding ring. The next slap is even harder, and this time it hurts. Bang, like a thunder-clap. I imagine the mark on the side of my head, the shape of his fingers tigering my cheek. Then a third time, vicious, this time, with his fist, a real knuckle-sandwich on my temple. If this was a comic strip I'd be seeing stars, out for the count. Bluebirds would be circling and twittering. But it's real, skin to skin, a close encounter. Stubbs pulls back his arm, reloading his punch. I don't want a broken nose. I don't want a split lip, a chipped tooth. When hatred spills over into violence, it goes for the face. Drunken men fighting in pubs or on the terraces – they go for the face, especially the mouth. Not because that's where it hurts the most. But because that's where it feels best, landing the full force of a blow where the talk comes out. I don't want to give him that particular pleasure. So I get to my feet, and he pulls back, thinking I'm going to take a swing. My eye is closing, clamming up. I squeeze the little green man in my hand, take aim at Stubbs's head and watch him duck. Then I swivel on my heel, turn to the big blank space of wall above the mantelpiece, and let it go.
  It should be a starburst. A million green fragments pinging through the air, like the moment the spaceship accelerates beyond the speed of light and stars go whizzing past in the blink of an eye. But it hits the wall almost without noise, and half a dozen chunks of green clay fall in the hearth and on the carpet. Not exactly a special effect. Not much of an impact at all.

32

I'm a resourceful sort of person.

So said my father the time he'd lost his keys, and I lowered myself into the dental surgery through a skylight over the storeroom, and opened the door. But every now and again I don't mind asking for advice. If you look hard enough, there are literally thousands of people all lined up, ready to help. And dozens of places in every town where a person can play dumb. Take the Community College at the bottom of the road. There's a drop-in centre in the afternoon and a whole timetable of adult-education classes every night, and it's all for free if you're out of work. They've got computers, a recording studio, a workshop full of lathes and circular saws and the like. They've even got a kiln.

Take Leonard. Leonard had taken a bit of a shine to me right from day one. I told him I'd like to do something with my life, channel my energy in one direction for a change, make something I could be really proud of. His face went all big and happy, like a birthday cake.

'What about pottery?' I said. 'Don't suppose I could do much damage with a lump of clay.'

'It just so happens you're talking to exactly the right man,' he beamed. 'When would you like to start?'

I showed Len my little green man, told him how me and a bunch of friends used to play with him when we were kids.

'I'd like to make a replica, as a gift. You know, for old times' sake.'

His eyes grew wide as he handled the jade, like two soup dishes full to the brim with poacher's broth.

'Well, Barney, that's quite a task you've set yourself, young man. Quite a task.'

'But can it be done?'

'Well, no harm in finding out?' he said, and held out his hand.
We shook on it. It was a done deal.

What Len didn't know about clay you could write in capital letters
on your thumb nail. He'd learnt his trade in Stoke-on-Trent, 'the
Potteries', and watching him work was like watching someone
cooking a meal. On our first session, we modelled the piece.

'I thought stoneware at first. Then I thought, no, a porcelain
body. It'll shrink, mind, but it's not like we're trying to put one
over on Christie's, right?'

'Right.'

'In the Eighties, you know, General Electric figured out how to
duplicate the chemical composition and crystalline structure of
jade. So, technically speaking, we could simulate this piece to within
a whisker of the original, but we'd probably need two or three
hundred thousand pounds and access to their scientific archives. I
don't suppose you're one of those computer hackers, are you?'

'I'm not.'

'No. So we're back to clay, then. Amazing stuff, clay. What
people don't realize is how many of the great works of art of this
world are made from nothing more than the ground beneath their
feet. There's plenty of it around here, of course, all those shale
banks above the streams.'

'Yes, they're very argillaceous. And fissile, as well,' I said.

He looked funny at me over the top of his specs.

'Yes. Also, it'll be very light, in comparison.'

'Hollow, you mean?'

'Yes. It's a ceramic. It's not like we're baking a brick. There's a
lot of water trapped in a lump of clay. Leave it solid and it might
explode, and we wouldn't want that, would we, Barney boy?'

No, Leonard, we wouldn't want that.

Len did the donkey work, built the thing up from little sausages
and balls of clay, then set about it with a modelling knife.

'Fancy a go?' he said, dropping a blob in my hand. 'Go on, have
a bash at the head while I'm brewing up.'

He was gone for over an hour, answering phone calls in the little glass office, dealing with a day-release student who wanted to swap to business studies, filing a great pile of papers. When he put the steaming mug of tea down in front of me I offered him the head on the palm of my hand. The big, bulging skull, the slitty eyes, the drooping moustache and beard. Len slurped his tea and gulped. He was impressed.

On week two we fired the clay. I pictured the replica little green man in the bright orange blaze of the kiln. Seeing him there in a thousand degrees of fire, I thought he might crumble or split, even melt. But he stood his ground, resolute and strong, the peach in his hands like a miniature sun. He didn't even break sweat – quite the reverse, in fact. He was taking it all in his stride, absorbing every degree of that fantastic heat, soaking it up. He was basking in the glow.

On week three I got a lecture about glazes.

'Here's the recipe. Feldspar, China clay, flint, dolomite, zinc and whiting. But feldspar's the main ingredient. The Orientals used it on its own – dug up the rock, crushed it, mixed it with water – lovely stuff. Of course, these days it comes ready-mixed.'

'What about the colour?' I said.

'Yes, I've been thinking about that. A sort of cabbage green. One per cent iron oxide should do the trick. Then we'll need to crank it up to Cone 11 at least. Maybe Cone 12.'

I didn't ask.

Week four I turned up ready to watch the glaze being fired, but it wasn't to be.

'This kiln's no good to us any more,' announced Len. 'No combustion in an electric kiln, therefore an abundance of oxygen. Result – the glaze will go brown or black. Not green.'

'So we're stuffed?'

'Not so fast, Barney boy. What we need is a wood-burner. Starve out the air.' He clenched his fist, like he was wringing the neck of a turkey. 'Reduce the iron oxide to its base state.'

'And where do we get one of those?'

'Like I said at the beginning – you've come to the right man.'

Basically, he had one in his garden. He invited me round to watch, but there was something about Len. Working with him at the college was one thing, but I didn't fancy visiting his house, bumping hips with him in the potting shed or wherever. Anyway, I'm amazed that ordinary people are allowed to generate that kind of heat in a residential area. Very dangerous, I would have thought. Must look odd from those spy-satellites up there in space, 1,300 degrees of charcoal suddenly glowing on the infra-red map at 24 Acacia Avenue. You might think a licence would be needed, or some kind of permit from the Council, but apparently not.

Week five was the big one, the moment of truth. Len was wearing a tie, and had carried the statue from home in its own sarcophagus – a wooden domino box, stuffed with bubble wrap. He slid back the top and poked about in the packaging. Using his finger as a hook, he raised the statue out of its tomb, pulled it upright, then lifted and placed it on its feet, with the upturned box as a plinth. It was really something. Stunning, in fact. I stood the original next to it, side by side. The replica was darker, perhaps, and smaller overall by an eighth of an inch, and lacked that certain texture only age can bring. But, seen on its own, it was certainly up to the job, and to anyone who hadn't clapped eyes on the little green man for two decades or so, it could only be real.

'Amazing,' I said.

'Thank you.'

Thank you. Like it was his idea in the first place. So before he got all self-congratulatory and me, me, me about it, I picked up the two pieces and shoved them in my bag.

Then I held out my hand. 'Len, it's been great.'

'Er, are you . . . I thought we might . . .'

'I've got to run. I'm taking my kid to the circus.'

'Oh, you're a dad. How nice.'

'Yes. Travis. He's seven.'

'Won't we see you again? There's a life-drawing class beginning in two weeks. I even wondered about the foundation course? I'll send you the brochure.'

'That's not such a bad idea,' I said to him, over my shoulder. 'I'll be in touch.'

Perspective. Scale. Light and shade. You have to work in the cracks and chips, the flaws and defects, every little blemish. That's what deflects the eye, stops people seeing the join. Of course, it also helps if you can take the original out of circulation for a short while. That way you don't get people looking too close, eyeing things up, comparing like with like. And when I got it home I had to apply the finishing touches myself. Stuff it with Polyfilla to make up the weight, and glue a small patch of felt on the base, like a protective cover, to mask the truth. But I've always been good with my hands. I've always been good with my brain as well. Just because I don't have a degree in astrophysics or biochemistry or clinical psychology hanging on the toilet wall doesn't mean I don't know how to boil an egg. And the thing is, I couldn't have that bunch of apes messing around with the real thing. Sooner or later someone was going to get all underhand and force the lock of the bureau, or lose their cool and smash him to pieces against a wall. De Beers might put the world's biggest diamond on public display from time to time, but don't you believe it, the thing you're getting all frothed up about is nothing more than a lump of glass. The real stone is tucked away in a vault somewhere. Like my little green man, stashed in the pencil-case all warm and snug. I couldn't have those philistines spilling beer over him, tossing him across the room like he was something that fell out of a Christmas cracker. Put it this way: you don't need a proper rabbit at the greyhound track. Stupid mutts, running round in a circle. If they don't know the difference between a common-or-garden *Oryctolagus cuniculus* and a motorized fur hat, whose problem is that?

With modern technology, there's very little you can't do, even though I see myself as a bit of a traditionalist at heart. A craftsman. Take that valuation certificate. I thought at first if four grown men don't know a photocopy when they see one, then it's their own look-out. But putting the two together, I had to concede they were pretty similar. A perfect match, in many respects, except for the extra nought I'd thrown in at the end. I couldn't resist. Then the other one I'd added, just to be sure. Because I'm a bit out of touch with money and wages and all that palaver. To me, 7,500 pounds is not to be sniffed at, but maybe that's nothing these days. Maybe a traffic warden can earn that sort of dosh in a few months and wouldn't get out of bed for less. I haven't kept up with financial trends. Just to be certain, I raised the stakes, upped the ante, rounded it off to a cool three-quarters of a big one. Ironic, I suppose, making something greater by adding a couple of noughts. Like my father's favourite joke. Question: what gets bigger the more you take from it? Answer: a hole. And I sculpted those zeros with love and care. Sketched them in pencil, traced the outlines in black ink, blotted them off, dusted them down. Even under a magnifying glass, you'd have to be Sherlock Holmes to say that certificate wasn't for real. Handicraft. Ancient skills. I felt like a monk in his cell, illuminating the word of God.

As for the shining emerald in the stone head of the little green man – that was a downright lie. Whoever heard of a precious stone implanted in a jade statue – you'd have to be a moron. If they'd have sussed it there and then, those boys with their qualifications and wives and houses and jobs – I'd have held up my hands, told them it was all for the sake of having a good laugh one night after a game of five-a-side. But they were hungry for it. You could even say they brought it on themselves.

33

'Is it still real?' said Stubbs, crushing one of the chunks of clay under his foot. I didn't say a word. 'You're deluded, Barney. OK, we had some fun when we were kids, mucking around with a green statue we found in the dirt. But that was all in the past. It's long gone, all that.'

I said nothing.

'Go on, tell me how you did this. I'm sure you're dying to.' He was holding the X-ray.

I rubbed the side of my face, which was stinging, and noticed blood on my hand, from my nose.

'Took a photograph of the carving and had the negative enlarged. Then stuck a sequin on to it, for the emerald, then photographed the negative.'

Stubbs crumpled it in his hands and tossed it into the bin, where it crackled and rustled like something alive in a plastic bag. 'Very arty. Very crafty.'

'Thank you.'

'Had us all going at first. But it backfired, big time, didn't it? We've beaten you at your own game. You need help.'

The door banged and he was gone. I sat on the floor, among the fragments and the litter of paper squares. In the hearth, the head of the little green man was still in one piece. His face was calm and collected.

How many times can you cut a worm in half before it stops wriggling? Is it true what they say about headless chickens? When people die, do their hair and nails really keep growing for several days? Sometimes dead bodies sigh, or fart, or twitch a little, even moan or raise an arm. That's a fact. But it's nothing to be worried about, just science doing its stuff. Take the key out of the ignition on a hot day, and the fan kicks in under the bonnet, cooling the engine, even though you've come to a dead stop.

I didn't know an eye could close up so tightly and so quickly, like disturbing a limpet on a rock. I fingered it in the mirror, felt a puffiness under the skin and a soreness above the cheekbone. I've never had a shiner in my life and this probably wasn't the genuine article either, but it was near enough. I thought about laying a lump of sirloin steak across my face, but didn't know if that was a proper medical practice or something I'd seen in a comic. Anyhow, the fridge was empty, apart from a couple of Scotch eggs and a few slices of roast ham. I didn't want to end up looking like a piece of modern art. Never try and tackle a job without the right tools.

My father used to tell the same story over and over again – he'd heard it on *Thought for the Day* – about a king who wanted his portrait painted. Painting the king's picture was a privilege, but this was a tricky job, because the king had a hunchback, a wonky eye, and one leg shorter than the other. And the penalty for falling foul of the king was death. The first artist came along, and glossed over the king's deformities. He looked a picture of health and happiness, perfectly normal in fact, but this annoyed the king, because it was cheating, which was wrong. So the artist got the chop. One down, two to go. The second artist made sure the king's disfigurements were properly illustrated. In fact, he made such a feature of them, the king looked like the ugliest creature ever born – like something that crawled out of a swamp. The artist was executed, and his head stuck on a pole. The third artist asked the king about his favourite hobby. 'I like to hunt,' said the king. So he painted him crouched over his gun, with one leg on the stump of a tree, and one eye closed, taking aim. The king was as pleased as punch, and so was my father, whenever he got to the end of the tale. 'Which made the king a very happy man, and the artist a happy man, and a rich one at that.'

My brother would yawn. Personally, I thought it was a good story, but wondered about the moral. Was it about finding the right way of telling the truth, or a smart way of telling a lie? Was it about disabled people being beautiful in some way? Or necessity being the mother of invention? Or the vanity of royalty, or the cunning of artists? Maybe it was a story about kindness and charity, but coming from my father, that made me suspicious. For instance, whenever we went on holiday to the sea, he'd put his loose change into those little plastic lifeboats on the counters of cafés and shops. But that was because, one day, he wanted to own a yacht.

The door came flying back open.

'I forgot to give you these.'

Stubbs kicked me three times, twice in the ribs and once in the balls.

'One from Tony, one from Pompus, one from Winkie. We're even now. So why don't you crawl back in your hole, and leave us alone.'

34

It hurt.

And so did the bruises and sore bones.

I'm a cunning little sod. At least, that's what Winkie's mother said the time she barged into the bathroom and caught me applying a few drops of Super Glue to the toilet seat. But Stubbs and the rest of them, taking the piss all those weeks, putting one over on me like that. It really hurt. And so did the thick ear, and the swollen cheek.

Then again, you've got to lose the odd battle to win the war – isn't that what they say? You've got to accept the embarrassment of one or two spectacular own goals on the way to winning the cup. It's all part of the game. A learning experience. Get rid of the colour but keep the swelling – that's what they say you should do, after a kick in the balls.

When my father calls, I know it's him, even before I pick up the phone. Don't ask me how – I just do. A cynic might say it's all to do with the time of day, or the number of times he lets it ring before hanging up, or the fact that he hasn't called for a couple of weeks. Statistical significance – that kind of thing. But I'm not so sure. Because if I'm in the shower, or just going out of the door, or settling down in front of the box with a curry on my knee, the remote in one hand and a stubby of beer in the other, and the phone rings – it's him. Like you can tell when someone's reading the paper over your shoulder. Like you know when someone's laughing behind your back.

We had the usual conversation. The crap weather in England compared to the efficacious climate of the Algarve. The favourable rate of the pound against the escudo. I told him about the flooding in Dorset and the latest rise in the cost of unleaded fuel, and even from several hundred miles away I could see the smile on his face.

'Speaking of petrol . . .' he said.

'Go on.'

'We've got a huge favour to ask you, Barnaby.'

'Go on.'

'We'd like the car driving out here. Now, before you say anything, I know it's a long way, and of course we'll meet all the expenses and so on, but, well, we've got this huge four-wheel drive and we only use it for tootling into town and down to the coast now and again, so we'd like you to bring the hatchback out, and take this brute of a thing home. What do you say?'

It meant they were out there for good. It meant they were staying there for ever, growing older, getting slower and smaller until they ground to a halt and disappeared altogether. They were never coming home.

'OK,' I said.

'Good lad. Thank you, Barnaby. You'll be doing us a favour.'

He started talking me through the route, which ferry crossing to take, which toll roads to avoid, about one particularly complicated junction somewhere in the Pyrenees.

'Pity you're not coming on the train. Are you writing this down?'

'Yes.'

'Excellent, excellent. And once you're here, why don't you stay for a couple of weeks, or even a month? It would do you good.'

Like I was ill. Like I needed a break. From what? 'Maybe.'

Then his voice changed, dropped a few megahertz, as if he'd switched from an FM traffic report to something deep and meaningful on long wave.

'Er, tell me, son, how are you off for money – there can't be much left now? I'm sorry we can't help you any more.'

'No, it's fine. I mean, you've helped enough already.'

'I've been talking it through with your mother. We could re-mortgage the house if you want, free up some cash . . .'

'Honestly. I don't want it. I need to . . .'

'What about that place at Art College? Have you decided yet?'

'No. The offer's there. I haven't made my mind up. Maybe.'

'Oh, well. It will be good to see you. Have a word with your mother before we go. We're using one of those phonecards. It charges it back to the bill at home. Bye for now.'

I heard them fumbling and jostling, imagined the two of them squashed against the glass wall of some stifling call-box near the beach, my father pointing at his watch, telling her not to be too long. In the background, in a stage whisper, he was telling her I was coming out to see them, with the car.

'Your father says you'll come and see us. That's lovely.'

'Yes.'

'When will you come, do you know?'

'I don't know. Next week?'

'As soon as that? Lovely. Oh, do you know, you sound as clear as day on this line, you could be stood here next to me. Now, how's that grandson of mine?'

35

On Monday I re-wired a telephone point for the Polish woman along the road. She wanted to answer it from the armchair in front of the telly, rather than plodding out to the hall every time it rang and standing in a draft for half an hour talking to her cousin in Krakow.

'Have you thought about getting a cordless? You could go anywhere you want with one of those, even the garden.'

'No. Ven I hold on to de vire, I know if dey iz lying.'

I found myself telling her about Internet cam-phones, seeing the other person on a computer screen while you're yapping with them. She shook her head.

'Dey iz not my proper cuzin.'

It's detailed work, work on a fine scale. The thin coloured wires, the teeny screws. You need a good eye and a steady hand. When I crack open the socket cover, I see myself as a heart surgeon performing a life-saving operation, teasing the threads, uncoupling and reconnecting each vital cord, cleaning out the wound, then stitching it all together. The operator phones me back, and it rings. It works. I haven't had one die on me yet. I left Mrs Szlachcic sitting in the armchair, phoning the speaking clock. It's always a bit of a gamble, doing work for a neighbour or a friend of the family, in case they think it's a favour, out of the goodness of your heart. And when I opened the envelope outside, I didn't even try to catch the dog-eared fiver that fell out and blew off down the street. Think of it as a lesson, I told myself. Make it mean something. Let it go.

On Tuesday I serviced a heating system for a friend of Kim's. It's not really my thing, wrestling with something as mundane and time-consuming as a dodgy radiator or a dickey water pump, but I felt obliged.

'Kim said you wouldn't mind, and I'd be really grateful.'

In the end, it was more fun than I'd expected, being a question of brainpower rather than brute force. After switching on, the whole house began to rattle and shake. Some of the pipework visibly moved, as if there were an earthquake brewing up down below, or a train coming through.

'It's an airlock,' I said.

'Is that serious?' she wanted to know.

It was half-ten in the morning and she still wasn't dressed. She stood above me in a housecoat and slippers, sipping a huge mug of tea. I prefer to work on my own. I prefer to be given the run of the house, rather than making small talk or explaining every thought in my head. I don't like being on show and I don't like being watched.

'It's just a question of tracking it down and coaxing it out.'

'Coaxing? That's a nice way of putting it,' she said. 'How are you and Kim getting on these days?'

Fortunately a neighbour called round, and she went out into the backyard with the biscuit tin and a packet of fags. I don't know why she was at home during the day, I didn't ask. I couldn't care less if people don't work for a living – I'm not exactly a career person myself. But you'd never catch me in my pyjamas at lunchtime, unless I was ill, and even then I wouldn't go swanning around outside. There's always work to do, something to fix or mend. I made myself a coffee, and got on with the task in hand. Whenever I bleed a radiator, I think of that bit in *Far From the Madding Crowd*, when the sheep in the field are exploding with gas or wind, and Gabriel Oak pops them all with his knife, and saves the flock. We did it for O level. I never read the book but the film was pretty good. I suppose the air from a radiator is less smelly on the whole, which was a good thing in this case, because each one let out a long, hissing breath before brown, rusty water bubbled from the valve. I drained the system, topped it up in the loft and poured a measure of inhibitor into the tank. When I fired up the boiler again, everything coughed and spluttered for a couple of seconds, then settled down. Ten minutes later it was purring like a cat.

'You're a treasure. How much do I owe you?'

I've never found it easy to talk about money face to face, especially with someone only half-dressed.

'I'll give you a ring, when I've totted it up.'

She wanted me to come back. 'I've got some other bits and bobs I wouldn't mind you having a look at.' A garden fence was mentioned, and a gas oven. I didn't say anything, but to be perfectly honest I can live without those kind of jobs. Digging holes – that's hard labour. Navvy work. And I've never been keen on messing around with gas. Highly inflammable and totally invisible – not exactly a combination to fill you with confidence. You could say the same thing about electricity, but at least there are fuses and switches and meters and insulation and screwdrivers with bulbs in the handle to tell you if you're about to get zapped. Gas seeps, spreads, creeps through the air. You've got to trust your nose, then you've got to strike a match. It's not worth the risk. I stopped to eat a sandwich on the towpath on the way home, and left my set of socket spanners there, propped against the wall of the iron bridge. But I didn't go back. I imagined some kid lobbing them one at a time into the thick black water of the canal. Imagined the silver tools bedding down for ever in mud and filth. And a stream of tiny white bubbles, like pearls, rising from the murky depths.

On Wednesday I went up to the new hotel on the ring road again. The duty manager told me they were getting rid of their normal supplier, and wanted to know if I'd take on more work. He was talking about signs, cards, stationery, guest directories, photographs, brochures – the whole lot, if I wanted it. He didn't know I was just one man sat in a bedroom with a few coloured pens and a stencil set. He thought I was the genuine article.

'I'll give you some costings, let you know.'

'Sound,' he said.

In the car, I worked out I could do all the artwork in my spare time, bung it all off to a printer's or copy shop, and still make a tidy sum. It felt odd to be contemplating a proper job, the kind that other people have. Might even mean buying a computer, if the worst came to the worst, going down to the PC superstore and having some specky fourteen-year-old whine on about megabytes and graphics cards. It also felt strange to be thinking about the future, long-term. I think that's a part of my brain I don't use very often, which is my excuse for clipping the wing mirror of a Ford Mondeo as I pulled out of the car park. I would have just buggered off, normally, let some rep come back after a liquid lunch to a pile of glass on the floor, let some company pick up the tab. But I must be going soft. I wrote out my name and address on a slip of paper and stuck it under his wiper.

On Thursday, a woman had lost her cat, and thought it was locked in next-door's house. They were away on holiday, so she'd been spooning cat food through the letterbox for a week. I've no idea where she'd got my number, and I felt a little bit uneasy, breaking into someone's property without their permission. But the lady was desperate, saying she could hear the cat crying behind the door, saying she'd take the blame and smooth it all out with the neighbours as soon as they came home. So I chiselled out the latch and opened up. There was a pile of stinking meat going mouldy on the floor with several letters sticking out of the brown goo, but no cat. I fitted a new lock and left her crying on the doorstep. My parents had a dog before I was born, but I've never had a pet myself. More trouble than they're worth.

I won't do this stuff any more, I said to myself, leaving the chisel set next to the dustbin for old man Everill to throw on his cart. I won't stand ankle-deep in Kitekat for a few measly quid, won't lurch from one labour to the next. Who am I anyway? I'm not the *Yellow Pages*, for Christ's sake. I'm not Hercules.

On the way home I stopped off at Troy's grave. I call it a grave – it's just a small stone at the side of the drive leading to the crematorium. When I die, I want to be buried. I don't mind the spiders and the worms. I once saw a programme about a place in Italy where they dig up dead bodies after a couple of years, and the family get to weep and slobber over their dead relatives all over again, and generally get pretty hysterical about the whole thing. The corpses are dusty and dry and still in one piece, so it isn't so bad. Not putrid or crawling with maggots. I once left my fishing bait in the greenhouse all summer, then prised open the tin. Blow-flies and bluebottles everywhere. Like Pandora's box. Amazing. I wouldn't mind that, erupting out of the grave into everyone's face. I wouldn't mind being opened up again after a year or so, but who by? My parents won't be around, unless something's gone badly wrong. Kim will be glad to see the back of me. And Travis? What would he do? Poke me with a stick? Ask me for a biscuit?

I sat down, breathed on the brass plaque and buffed it with the elbow of my jumper. There wasn't much left of Troy by the time they'd winkled the bullets out of his head and finished slicing him up for evidence and facts. He'd been dead six months when they gave us his body back. Cremation was the only sensible thing to do. Couldn't be laid out in a funeral parlour looking like he'd been hit by a train. But when I go, I want to be planted in the earth, body and soul. I want to stick around for a while. I want to be bones and remains, like the man they found in the ice after 5,000 years, all leathery and knotted and gnarled. I don't want to be burned.

36

It took the whole of Friday to sort everything out. Booking the ferry, buying a road atlas, queuing in Thomas Cook's for three-quarters of an hour for foreign currency.

'I'll need money for France, Spain and Portugal.'

The woman behind the glass screen said, 'Why don't you just take euros instead?'

'Does everybody accept them now?'

She disappeared into a side room to ask her supervisor, then came back to her chair. 'Let's start with the francs.'

On the same theme, my father wanted me to put GB stickers on the car. 'And not one of those new European ones with the circle of yellow stars on a blue background.' In his mind, he probably imagined the Union Jack would guarantee me an unhindered passage through foreign fields and preferential treatment at border controls. In *my* mind, I thought it might get me rammed by French lorry drivers or pulled over by Spanish police, grumbling about Gibraltar.

'We don't sell many of these,' said the bloke in the Auto Discount Centre. He was a cockney, when he spoke. 'I think people are embarrassed to say they're British these days. I don't know why. You go to America and everyone's got a flag over the door or in the garden. They've got the right idea, those Yanks. Wouldn't you say?'

'Maybe.'

He rubbed his stubble and leant forward. 'I've got some under the counter with the skull and crossbones over the flag of St George, if you're interested?'

'No, thanks.'

'OK, no harm in asking.'

Before I went, I said, 'So did you find your dog?'

But by the time he recognized me I was out of the shop and away.

My passport, when I found it, was almost out of date. In the picture, I was wearing a combat jacket and a length of webbing around my neck. I could have been some young German doing his year of national service. I looked serious. Mean.

It was lunchtime by now, but I still had a list of jobs as long as a snake's neck. Lots of tying up loose ends, lots of closing everything down and putting things to rest. Paperwork, mainly. I laid the three envelopes and a shoebox on the table in front of me, then labelled them with the correct names and addresses. Kelvin Macker. Christopher Cunningham. Anthony Elliss-Ward. Joseph Stott. I slipped Pompus's birth certificate into the first. In Winkie's envelope, I put the A4 print-out of an on-line pharmacy: their Web page, complete with a glossy, colour image of a bottle of blue, diamond-shaped tablets, and a description of their proven, medical effects. With a pea-green marker pen, I'd highlighted the e-mail address, and underlined details of how to go about buying the product on the Internet. Personally, it will be a long time before I think of the World Wide Web as anything other than a chat-line for mutes. But, after peering over someone's shoulder at the Community College, watching which buttons to press, I've got to admit it could be of benefit to some people, especially those with empty lives. And for anyone with a complete lack of imagination, patience or artistic ability of their own, there's definitely something in it.

Into the box I lowered the scabby old leather football – deflated, like a shrunken head – and sealed it with masking tape. Then into the last envelope I pushed the old police photographs. Black-and-white pictures, six by eight. A full-length shot of a twelve-year-old boy in his underpants, his eyes looking away from the lens. Then a close-up of two, weeping blisters above the elbow, and another close-up of three, circular scabs below the knee. *I, Joseph, having five spots . . .* I

239

didn't look. I didn't need to see them again. I licked the end of my thumb and smeared it along the gummed edge, then banged it down, hard, with my fist.

From the writing drawer of the bureau I took a smaller, blue envelope, and wrote Kim's name in capital letters on the front. My father once told me never to write in capital letters, 'unless you're a kidnapper, that is'. But I didn't want any cock-ups. I wanted to make things as simple and clear as possible. The valuation note was still crisp and clean: Sprake and Co. Estimated value for insurance purposes: £7,500. I folded it once, twice, a third time, and pushed it into the envelope, then lifted the razor-sharp edge of the paper up towards my tongue and licked, then ran my finger, slowly, along the flap, until it was properly and perfectly sealed. The kitchen clock was just starting to gear up for its big, midday strike. I looked at it out of the corner of my eye.

Loading the car took for ever. Then I made a tour of the house, closing the curtains, setting the timer switches on various lamps, turning off the water and gas.

I know exactly where he is.

I stand at the top of the stairs, the darkest, innermost place in the house. I pull the stepladders down from the loft with the long-handled hook. They slide into my hands, cold to the touch, creaking and rickety as I climb.

I reach for the light cord, somewhere to the left. A low-energy bulb comes on, brightens softly and slowly like an old valve, and the attic falls into place. My breath steams in front of my face.

I haul myself up and tread carefully over the joists. Suitcases are piled on top of wooden crates. I slide between old banana boxes crammed with books and magazines, duck beneath the bike hung from the six-inch nail banged into the main beam. How did we get that in here? Some of the slates have slipped or cracked. Hard to believe the outside is just inches away, that these thin sheets of stone tacked on to the spars keep out the weather and the sky.

I know exactly where he is. I click open the two locks of the big trunk and lift its giant lid. A smell drifts up from the past. Memory. More books and magazines, the bag of golf balls, the dartboard with stubble sprouting through the wire frame, rolled-up papers slotted in a cardboard tube. Tins of pencils and crayons like rounds of ammunition. The modelling knife. Drawings and doodles, sketches, tracings, prints. I pile them all to one side.

In the bottom-left-hand corner there's the shoebox. I take out the objects one by one, unzip the pencil-case, which is stuffed with a piece of cloth, folded and rolled into a neat parcel and tied with a length of wool. I let it unravel towards the floor, and feel the weight within it shift and slide and fall. Its possession spills into the air . . . I snatch it cleanly with my right hand. When I open my grip, the little green man is snug in my palm.

On the way through town I slowed up outside the post office, parked on a double-yellow with the engine ticking over and the hazard-warning lights on, like the car was radioactive or about to explode. I looked at the three envelopes and the box on the passenger seat, and clicked my thumb against the end of the handbrake. Then, suddenly, without indicating, I reached for the gear-stick, knocked it into first and pulled out into the traffic. The car behind had to brake and almost slid into the back of me. It was a near miss. A close-run thing. On the other side of the ring road, I went bumping across a piece of waste ground where an old cinema was being reduced to rubble by bulldozers and stone-crushers, to make way for a DIY superstore. I lifted the envelopes and the box and posted them into a battered orange skip full of slurry and twisted iron. Kelvin Macker. Christopher Cunningham. Anthony Elliss-Ward. Joseph Stott. They slithered down the metal wall into rainwater and rust-coloured mud. That's how easy it was. I didn't even get out of the car.

It was about half-two when I got to the school, but the door was locked. I had to walk into the playground and bang on a window.

One of the teachers eventually came to the hallway and spoke to me through the letterbox.

'I'm Travis's father.'

'Do you know the password?'

'No. My wife usually picks him up.'

'Didn't she tell you the password?'

'No. We don't live together.'

Ten minutes later, after quizzing me on just about every aspect of my private life and my intimate knowledge of Travis and his habits, she finally conceded that I probably was his father, and snapped open the latch.

'Can't be too careful these days. Some of the parents have insisted we step up the security arrangements.'

'So what is the password?'

'"Open Sesame",' she said.

'Right. I think I can remember that.'

Through a glass panel in the classroom door I could see him. He was standing in the corner with his head back, blowing at an animal mobile hanging from the ceiling. For a while I watched him puffing up his cheeks, clenching his fists and aiming a slow stream of breath towards the blue cows and red donkeys suspended from a coat-hanger by lengths of fishing line. They dithered and twisted in the breeze, and he watched them until they slowed and stopped, before launching another burst of air in their direction. In the cloakroom I found his gabardine coat on a peg under his name. Beneath the coat was his school bag, and his yellow report book. 'Friday's activities: singing, counting, jumping, heuristic play. Notes: Travis has had a good day and continues to make slow but steady progress with literacy and numeracy. Today he counted the number of fish in the fish-tank and wrote the answer in his work-book. Travis is still wary about sharing his possessions and his time with other pupils. Work will continue in this area.' His tiny rubber gym shoes were still warm inside as I slid the little green man into the left and the rolled-up blue envelope into the right.

In the classroom, he was still gazing up at the mobile. Momentarily, he glanced towards the door, and I waved, but he seemed to look straight past me or through me, then turned again to stare at the coloured animals floating in the air. The afternoon sun was reflecting on the glass, so he couldn't really see me standing there on the other side, waving. Otherwise he would have waved back.

It's always a good idea to try and get to the other side of Leeds before rush hour. Not being a regular member of the workforce it's rash of me to comment, but people do seem to be sneaking off earlier and earlier these days, especially on Friday. Leave it any later than half-three in Leeds and you're going to find yourself sucking on someone's exhaust fumes for a couple of hours, gazing at the hills on the horizon. My father tells me that, when I was eleven or twelve, I wanted to be a bus driver. I don't remember myself, but he swears it's true. And not just some common-or-garden double-decker, but a coach, National Express, pulling out of the depot in the early hours of the morning, cruising down the M1, looking down on the cars and vans. Seeing the world through the big window at the front.

'Then one day I told you, trust me, Barnaby, you'll spend 90 per cent of your time crawling along in first, and the other 10 per cent with the handbrake on, and that is God's honest truth.'

I think his own father had said something similar to him when he'd expressed a boyhood interest in becoming the driver of a train, so he knew very well how to choke the life out of a dream with one carefully worded sentence. Apparently I never mentioned bus-driving again.

After Leeds, though, it all goes quiet. No one goes to the East Coast any more unless they've gone wrong in York. Suddenly you're on your own. Trucks pull in to lay-bys and cafés, cars turn into side roads and streets, caravans sway and wobble then swing north for the moors, tankers head for the pilot lights and coloured fumes to the south. The land flattens. You're alone. Even the radio fizzles out after a few more miles.

To get to Dover from the Pennines via England's glum and

crumbling East Coast isn't exactly the route recommended by the Automobile Association of Great Britain, but the sailing wasn't until next morning.

And, anyway, like the final sweet in the bag, I'm making this one last.

I'm driving past farms and churches and hills I remember from childhood holidays. I'm driving from memory, without a map. The spherical compass stuck to the dashboard, like a robot's eyeball in its glass socket, says East, but that's all. Eventually the sea comes round a corner, comes over the top of the hill, grey and everywhere and inevitable. How can anything live in that flat, dead-looking drink?

'The first person to see the sea wins a pound,' says my father.

'There it is, I see it,' says Troy, lying, pocketing the money.

Mum's hand appears over the back of her seat with a paper bag full of humbugs or barley sugars or butterscotch.

'No, thanks. Not for me.'

Finally the road runs out. I remember this place. Somewhere further up the coast a whole street fell into the sea. The people who live here are holding on by their toes as the sea comes to plunder the cliffs every day. You only have to look at the beach down below to see that this part of England is nothing more than brown, chocolatey sludge. Not land at all but mud. You can't build a life on mud. Greenhouses and garages disappear overnight. What the ocean doesn't devour, the rain turns to paste and mulch, or the wind flattens in its path. This was a picnic area once, with seashells marking parking bays and the perimeter lined with railway sleepers and painted tyres. Now there's a warning sign at forty-five degrees, a red triangle, rocks tumbling down a crumbling slope. There's a five-bar gate across the road, but it isn't locked, and I drive through, steering round potholes and cracks in the surface, heading down the hill, dipping between second and first, using the engine as a brake. Pulling up about ten yards short of the drop, I push open the door against the barging wind, and walk to the end. One day the sea must have taken a running jump at this part of the coast and torn the road like a strip of liquorice, left it aiming into mid-air. The tarmac even overshoots the cliff-face by a foot and a half, jutting out over a drop of, what, forty, fifty feet on to a beach of dirt and soil. And I've read this stretch of the coast is littered with unexploded shells and mines from the war. If the sea doesn't get you, the Ministry of Defence will.

After opening the back of the car, I swing round and reverse, a foot at a time, then inch by inch, as far as I dare. The rear-view mirror is full of boxes and crates. The wing mirrors are full of leaden, colourless sky and lifeless grey sea. Cut the whiskers off a cat and it can't tell a mouse hole from the Grand Canyon – that's what they say. The rear wheels can only be a foot or so from the brink when I anchor on and pull the handbrake up. Climbing between the front seats, I crouch in a tiny space, my knees up by my ears, facing east. Then I push. At first, the luggage doesn't want to budge, all that junk jammed in the car. Then something gives. I push until my legs are straight, push with my arms against the headrests until I'm flat on my back and every last carton and carrier bag has spewed out over the cliff, and up ahead there's nothing but one dull horizontal line where the sky rests on the sea. Emptiness. I flip over, crawl to the very back of the car and peer down over the bumper towards the beach. It's quite a sight.

Picture it from the other side, somewhere out on the waves. A car pulls up at the edge with its hatch-door open, spewing its load. Cardboard boxes tumble and fall, explode on the cliff face. Balls, toy cars, comics, soldiers, badges, plastic guns fly out in all directions. Carrier bags burst like balloons, showering the beach with tiddlywinks, gonks, pens. A metal Slinky uncoils and flexes, then comes to a dead stop, buckled and sprained and lifeless on a ledge. Drawings, paintings, certificates, documents are creamed from the top of a stack of papers by a strong wind and whipped up into the air, riding the therms. Board games shake out their counters and dice like crumbs. Chessmen are strewn in the aftermath of battle. A big trunk lands like a depth charge on the rocks below, atomizing its contents. Scalextric track and railway lines are everywhere – Toy Town after a nuclear war. Then the final crate – a large apple box that ruptures and unfolds, disgorges itself on the muddy slope. Hibernating miniature men, and floodlights and goalposts and grandstands and shining, golden trophies are suddenly pitched into broad daylight, scattered to the wind, cast out of pristine boxes and neat packages and delivered into the big, wide world.

Lying flat on my belly, I looked down to where the litter of broken toys and games were scattered among stones and sludge, or floating loose in the swell of the sea, picked up by the tide. A dozen or so seabirds dangled and bounced on imaginary wires, scavengers, waiting to cut loose and spiral out of the empty sky, swoop on the spreading mess of rubbish and scraps.